unleashed

a highland historical
trilogy

Kerrigan Byrne

Cover Art © 2012 Kelli Ann Morgan / Inspire Creative Services

Interior book design by Bob Houston eBook Formatting

Table of Contents

Dedication

To those who have taught me what the word "family" really means.

Acknowledgements

I have my own clan of people to thank for making this book possible...

First of all, to my fellow musketeers – Aramis and Athos, aka bestselling authors Cindy Stark and Tiffinie Helmer. I feel like I get to stroll down a path that you've cleared by hacking down many obstacles. But don't worry; I've always got your back.

To the Writers of Imminent Death – Heather Wallace, Mikki Kells, Heidi Turner, and Tiffinie Helmer. In memoriam of all those we've ruthlessly slaughtered through the years.
And then laughed about it.

To Cynthia St. Aubin – Thanks for the inspiration, empathy, validation, and tireless encouragement. But I still hate you most of the time.

To Kerrigan's Celts – You guys give me great reasons to drag myself out of bed on Mondays.

To Jessica Menasian – Who taught me that self expression isn't confined to the use of words.

To Lynne Harter at Word Nerdy Editing – I apologize for a certain word you'll never escape and all the descriptive "ing" verbs that go before it.

To Kelli Ann Morgan at Inspire Creative Services – Your vision and creativity know no bounds.

To Dawn Winter – For letting me read what you wrote fifteen years ago. This is all your fault.

To my darling husband – For all the heavy lifting you do, physical and otherwise.

unspoken

a highland historical novella

Chapter One

Aberdeen, Scotland: July 23rd, 1411

Death shrouded everything. Not even the horses were spared. Blue tabards, stained crimson, adorned hundreds of scattered, broken bodies.

She frantically searched the carnage. His body was not among the fallen. She must find him. Must warn him! So much blood. Had one man shed all this blood?

Evelyn Woodhouse shivered despite the close, heavy air. Still unable to shake the residuals of last night's violent dream, she did her best to block the visions and images barraging her mind's eye.

Beware the Blue.

Her brow wrinkled again at the divination that had whispered through her thoughts all day, leaving shadows of dread in its wake. The dead men in her dream, they *all* wore blue. What did it mean? Oh, why did she never know until it was too late?

Dropping her forehead against the common room window, Evelyn welcomed the chill of the glass against her feverish skin as she stared out into the night. Occasionally, the shadow of a man or gleam of a weapon crossed the flames of distant fires that winked like fallen stars across the mist-shrouded fields of Aberdeen. Foreboding wound through her along with the certainty of the poor fellow's fate. She possessed "the sight." At least, that's what people called it before she learned to keep it to herself.

Before she'd been abducted by those who would call themselves righteous.

Closing her eyes against the sting caused by stale peat smoke and utter exhaustion, she hissed in a fortifying breath and hefted the supper tray to her aching shoulders. A reference to Atlas came to mind as she picked her way through the crowded kitchen. She didn't carry the world on her shoulders, only a soldier's supper, but the load compounded the tension of the inner burdens she stored there.

She shouldn't be focused on such heavy thoughts now, not when there was work to be done. Scotland had become her refuge and managed to keep her relatively safe if one didn't count the constant barrage of clan wars... like the imminent one brewing just outside the city.

Stealing among the crowd as a wary thief might, a whispered word rose above the muted rumble of terse male conversation.

Berserker...

Evelyn glanced to the doorway where a dark mass filled the space to overflowing. In the dim shadows of the common room she couldn't make out any features, just the suggestion of a man swathed in black and the size of a small mountain. The tension hovering like a sword over Moorland's Inn and Tavern spiked palpably higher at the curious arrival, but Evelyn wisely retreated to the kitchens.

"What's a Berserker?" she asked aloud, and instantly berated herself for not thinking the better of it.

"A breed wot's killed plenty of ye bloody English, that's *who*," growled Robert Moorland, the proprietor. He plunked a tankard and pitcher of ale onto her tray hard enough to make her flinch.

Evelyn swallowed a defensive retort. Back in London, she'd arduously learned to bite her unruly tongue courtesy of the rod wielded by Sister Mary Ida in the convent where she'd spent her tender years.

"I 'eard the black-hearted warrior was commissioned from the great MacLauchlan clan to help the Stewart defeat the Donald. Only the blood of a Gael or Northman can hold the Berserker, so the likes of *ye've* no' seen such a lethal creature." Despite his cantankerous words he lowered his voice to a confiding tone. "It's said that Roderick MacLauchlan is the fiercest warrior wot's ever been seen on the battlefield."

Creature?

"It's good that he's here then, I suppose." She offered him a smile, encouraged by his rare dialog.

"Ye, suppose..." Moorland sneered at her as he thrust another bowl her way. "I'm no' payin' ye to *suppose* ye daft woman, I'm payin' ye to *work!*" He punctuated with a shove to the shoulder, nearly upsetting the balance of her tray. "Get yer lazy English arse out there and doona let them see the bottoms of their tankards."

"Yes sir," she mumbled.

Steeling herself for the long and miserable night ahead, she made her way into the common room with shuffling steps to avoid the tangle of chair legs and male feet. Adept at deciphering importance from the various plaids and bejeweled adornments on their tartans, she was careful to set fare before nobles and clan leaders first.

As she approached the table, the smile she attempted felt brittle and tight, the muscles in her face heavy with apprehension. Stewart nobles were deep in speculative conversation, ignoring her as she squeezed through their hunched shoulders to place dishes in front of them. Praise be for small blessings. Snippets of their whispered conversation burned her ears.

"I 'eard he killed more than a hundred men by himself when the McHughes battled the Brayden last spring."

"It is said that he has to drink the blood of wee babes to maintain his strength."

"He's a servant of the devil and ought to be burned!"

"Bah! Doona be ridiculous, he's blessed by the old North Gods, and we're lucky he's here! I'll no' be having ye anger him with yer talk! No' with the Donald's bearing down upon us with his ten thousand men."

Clutching the now empty tray to her chest, she scanned the torch lit room, her gaze skipping past woven kilts of many colors. Men from clans Burgess, MacKintosh, Stewart and a few others unfamiliar to her, assembled to Aberdeen from surrounding lowlands to protect the bustling seaside town from the advancing clan Donald of Islay. The Donald's determination to lay claim to the Earldom of Ross meant tearing it from the hands of Robert Stewart, the Duke of

Albany and Regent of Scotland. Tomorrow, the outskirts of their home would become a battleground.

Following the furtive glances stolen by the surrounding crowd, Evelyn peered into the nook where *he* sprawled comfortably, farthest from the glow of the fire. Flickering light rimmed his silhouette, yet it seemed he conjured the darkness to cloak himself.

Evelyn caught her breath. If she lived a hundred years she would likely never see a man so large again. Shadows obscured his visage. She could see naught but impossibly thick, long legs which splayed at the knees, encased within heavy, tall black boots.

Involuntarily swallowing her surprise, she knew his relaxed posture was utterly deceptive.

She also knew the Berserker, Roderick MacLauchlan, would die tomorrow.

Chapter Two

"Make 'Evy do it, Moorland, I'm no' goin' near the man!" Abby McFayden made a rude gesture to the innkeeper, and then crossed herself against evil.

Evelyn bristled at Abby's insolence, knowing that Moorland's acquiescence followed. If she'd never stumbled upon them in the kitchen that day, her life would be much easier now. Evelyn suppressed a shudder at the vision of Abby's legs braced against the counter of the island and Moorland's pants around his ankles.

"There ye are!" Abby's dirty hazel eyes glittered with malevolence. "Be a dear, and take this to the black knight in the corner, would ye?" She yanked away Evelyn's empty tray and shoved a large bowl of stew into her hands.

Moorland jerked a finger in her direction. "And doona be bothering him with yer senseless chatter. I've been told that the man is mute and I doona want you to be angering 'im. You hear me girl?"

"Yes, sir." She nodded and turned back to the din of the common room. Unable to keep her shoulders from sagging, she moved whisper-quiet, avoiding contact with the rowdy crowd.

The atmosphere felt as grim as the faces circling the wooden tables. Clan Donald outnumbered the Stewart's strength of three thousand more than three fold. As they scowled and talked, men knocked back ale with single-minded determination as though fortifying themselves against the inevitable. Amidst such pessimism, Robert Stewart and his son, Alexander, did their best to recruit whom they could to hold Ross land that spread from Skye all the way to Inverness.

Creeping along the back wall, Evelyn made her way towards the large leather chair in which *he* sat. Quelling the shiver of apprehension that coursed down her spine, she squinted at him through the dimness. Perhaps, if she looked hard enough, the intangible element of unnatural darkness that seemed to emanate from him would reveal its secrets.

She instinctively knew the moment he noticed her. He became more still, if possible. His muscles rigid with a tension that instantly vibrated in the air between them. Feeling like a rabbit exposed to a hungry predator, Evelyn froze as unfamiliar awareness washed over her. It pinned her where she stood, and stunned her with its intensity.

Vibrant green eyes momentarily glowed with an unnatural light as they regarded her from the shadows.

She swallowed and quickly averted her gaze. *'Tis only a trick of firelight'*, she told herself.

Attempting a casual approach, she couldn't bring herself to lift her eyes above the table before him. "I've brought you supper, milord, if you're inclined to dine," she told his knees.

Silence.

She tightened her grip on the bowl to still the tremor that threatened to slosh its contents into his lap.

"I—its Moorland's specialty of mutton and potato stew." Why couldn't her eyes seem to find a place to rest? Table. Large hands. Sword. Thighs the size of boulders. Fireplace! Stew. Yes, the stew.

"It's quite good, and... important for building your strength for the morrow." She winced, cursing her need to fill the deafening silence. Heaven help her if Moorland was watching.

Evelyn couldn't stop a startled glance as his upper torso and face slowly emerged from the shadow of the wall.

He was terrifying.

He was beautiful.

The loose-fitting black tunic did nothing to diminish his shoulders, which were easily twice as broad as hers. Evelyn wondered if his skin struggled to contain the sheer mass of him.

Long ebony hair spilled to the middle of his chest, the forward locks pulled away from his face and secured at the back of his head.

The glittering green eyes held her captive from features so powerfully masculine it almost hurt to look at him. A broad forehead and thick, even brows offset a roman nose. The skin of his face and hands tanned to a gleaming bronze, his stark jaw made darker by the threatening shadow of a beard.

Don't be a fool, she admonished herself, unable to swallow around a dry tongue. *Nothing about him is blue. You should be safe.*

Evelyn's eyes dropped to his mouth out of habit, waiting for his response in the loud din of the room.

In all of her life she'd never seen such perfection, such sensual beauty on the face of a man. Tan and lush, his lips twitched with the slight movement of his jaw.

He gently took the bowl from her hand instead; startling her so much that the stew would have sloshed all over him had he not a firm grip.

"I'm sorry," she whispered, horrified. How could she have so quickly forgotten the innkeeper's warning? Of *course* he wouldn't reply.

One ebony brow lifted.

Dangerous. This man was dangerous. He had killed many and would do so again before his death on the morrow.

Those compelling green eyes held her prisoner.

"Would you like me to bring you some ale?" she asked, desperate to shake the yawning darkness that unexpectedly accompanied the idea of his inevitable demise. The least she could do was offer the man a drink. "'Tis a lovely summer brew, light and malty and it goes well with the stew. Uh, I don't drink it much, only because I'm not allowed without it being taken from my pay, oh, and because I can't be inebriated while I serve, besides. But, I snuck a tip from the cask once, and I thought it quite refreshing." She flinched and bit her tongue to halt any further inane speech from leaving her fool mouth. He must think her dull witted and awkward indeed, which apparently, wasn't a stone's throw from the truth.

His jaw dipped in a nearly imperceptible nod.

"Right then." Flashing him a nervous smile, she adjusted her itchy cap and escaped back to the kitchen.

If only she could catch her breath! All but throwing her tray to the counter, she rushed to the pantry, flinging herself against the door, heedless of the darkness. Bending at the waist, she clutched at her apron and panted as though she'd run a league.

What was happening to her? It had ceased to be this difficult so long ago. Not since London had she so battled with her conscience. Instead, she'd struggled to accept what knowledge she had, to do what she must to *survive*. Nothing should be asked of her beyond that. She didn't choose this curse, this *sight*; it'd beset her at birth. And, unfortunately for the wicked and beautiful Berserker, she'd never been able to alter the fate of another, no matter how urgently she desired it.

Chapter Three

"See, I told ye he was an eerie bastard." Abby nodded to Nellie, another serving maid with copper hair and a mass of freckles. "Nearly scared the slippers off Evy, here."

Evelyn grimaced at the nickname that Abby had coined for her. They didn't call her 'Evie' or 'Eve' but 'Evy' as it rhymed with 'heavy'. Painfully aware of her rounded figure, she couldn't stop herself from smoothing her apron self-consciously.

"He would like some ale, sir," she mumbled to Moorland, ignoring the women.

"While you're at it, take this pitcher to the Mackay table. Those lads be needin' a drink after their nasty battle wi' the Donald a se'nnight ago." He clucked in sympathy

She hoisted the tray onto her shoulder and left, dreading the Mackay table. They'd had much to drink already and were becoming over-loud and bawdy.

"Here you are, Milord," she carefully placed the fullest tankard on the table at the Berserker's elbow, "and I brought you linen to protect your thighs—trews!"

Christ's Bones! To mention a body part was impropriety of the highest nature. But she'd been staring at his sinuous legs while she'd been talking and noticing the cords and ropes of muscles visible beneath the shamefully tight leggings.

Cheeks burning, she risked an upward glance.

He reached his big hand out and removed the linen from her fingertips, draping it carefully across his lap and looked back to her, a twinkle of amusement glinted in his devilish eyes.

The brackets around his hard mouth seemed carved into a

frown. Had he not much reason to smile? She stomped on her curiosity. It was of no consequence, besides, tomorrow he would be—

"Well, if you'll excuse me, enjoy your supper." She turned around and grimaced once more, closing her eyes and shaking her head at her stupidity.

Making her way to the Mackay table, she swore she could feel his dark and potent regard caress her spine.

Alarming, that.

Don't look at him. Do not look back. As she made her way through the throng, speculation regarding the mysterious stranger drifted to her on the heavy air.

"I heard that when they berserk, they flash lightning from their eyes."

"It's true he's mute, the gods took a price before blessing him with the Berserker rage!"

"He has the strength of ten men, he does, just look at that sword!"

"Makes one wonder about his *other* sword." Evelyn narrowed her eyes at Abby's annoyingly feminine purr as she swished passed with a full tray.

Unable to stop herself, her gaze strayed back to the quiet man consuming his dinner in thoughtful bites. Sighing, she couldn't help but notice the occasional play of torchlight over the strong lines of his face, the flex of his temple as he savored each slow bite of stew. For a man reputed with such violence and brutality, whose very presence emanated lethal menace, he commanded himself with almost gentle self-constraint. His manners compared with that of any noble present.

Better, in most cases.

'Do their careless words sting you?' She wondered, distracted and enthralled by the silent and lonely figure as she noted the manner in which every person in the room gave him a wide and fearful berth. How like people. To enlist his help in a time of crisis, but shun and exclude him from their ranks. They ought to be ashamed.

"About time ye fill our tankards lass, I can nearly see the bottom."

She needed to concentrate on the task at hand.

"Well, that won't do," she responded quickly. Awareness

of a dark and vital energy shimmered through her very blood.

"Speaking of *bottoms*, isna' that the finest English arse ye've seen, Angus?" Even through her skirts the sharp swat stung her backside.

She whirled on them. "How dare you!" Both men laughed uproariously at her outraged expression.

"Come now, lass, we're just enjoyin' yer charms a little." His hand snaked out and tweaked her nipple.

"You keep your hands off me!" She brandished her tray like a shield. "This is a reputable establishment and I am a respectable maid." Blushing as she noted the curious glances from patrons about the nearby tables, she prayed she wouldn't be dismissed for creating a disturbance. She squared her shoulders. No matter, her dignity was her only possession and she refused to relinquish it to the likes of him.

Angus' dirty brown eyes narrowed as a perverse smile touched his lips, "Ye can be *just* as respectable perched upon here, my lady!" he crowed, while snaring her in a painful grip and yanking her down upon his lap. Evelyn gasped as his erection ground into her backside. Gagging as his foul breath hit her face, she froze like a rabbit caught in a snare. "Show a downhearted warrior some warmth before he goes inta battle on the morn."

"No." The whispered plea sounded feeble to her own ears. The jeers of his clansmen dashed her hopes for assistance.

"You doona mean '*no*'. Give us a kiss."

"Take your hands off me *traitor*." She hissed, then reared back and slapped him, putting all of her anger and humiliation into the blow. Pain shot up her arm. Disgusted, she realized she'd hurt herself more than she'd hurt him. "We wouldn't even be going into battle on the morrow if the MacKay had held their ground as they'd sworn to do!" She surged against his painful grip.

Pushed to the ground by vicious hands, her eyes flared as Angus loomed over her.

"I *know* of your treachery Angus Mackay." Her tone lowered to just above a whisper, the voice of prophecy spilling from her lips before she could stop it. "The shadow of death resists *every* man at this table, even though they go to battle in the morning. Why do you bargain with the enemy?"

Angus' eyes widened in stunned disbelief, as did those of his clan who were within earshot. "I'll cut out your tongue, you English witch!" His fist rose above his head, closed and ready to strike.

Protect your face, cover your eyes. Evelyn braced herself for the blow. She knew what came next: blood, swelling, explosive pain.

The smell of leather, horses, and fields of heather wafted by on a sultry breeze followed by a sickening crunch and a bellow... yet she felt nothing.

The room fell utterly silent.

Chapter Four

Cracking an eyelid open, Evelyn drew in a shocked breath as she looked up, and up.

Roderick stood between her and the Mackay with Angus' wrist caught in a crippling hold.

"Ye've broken me arm!" the man cried. Shock and pain etched in his dirty features as he squirmed in the unyielding grip.

Roderick's lips pulled back into a silent snarl, murderous rage etched into his savage features as he held the other man effortlessly immobile. Angus' arm bent at an unnatural angle.

A Mackay kinsman bravely stepped forward. "All right! All right, man, we'll leave the wench alone! Doona be crippling another sword arm when they're sorely needed."

The berserker remained motionless.

The room seemed to hold its collective breath. Expectant fascination and unease permeated the moment. Would he berserk in the middle of Moorland's common room?

Tentatively, Evelyn reached out and touched his leg. "Really, milord," she murmured. "'Tis finished now. No harm done." A dark part of her wanted to see him break each Mackay finger that touched her. She squelched the vindictive feeling, somehow knowing if she voiced the hideous request, it would be immediately carried out.

Through the buttery leather trews, she felt a quiver of solid muscle beneath her fingertips. She could sense his reluctance to liberate his quarry, and the self-control it took to do her bidding.

With infinite slowness, he released the squirming Mackay.

The fluid grace of his movements was astonishing for

someone his size.   He turned and lifted her to her feet as though she weighed nothing.

After performing a cursory inspection which, despite its brevity, left her feeling naked and vulnerable, he met her gaze.

She whispered, "Your eyes, milord." The pupils swallowed the irises completely and the ebony bled into the whites of his eyes, creating a cold and eerie contrast.   Disbelief snaked through her.

Impossible!

She watched dumbly, her blood roaring in her ears, as he stooped to retrieve her tray.   He straightened and held it out to her.   Irises the color of Irish moss glimmered at her.

Had she imagined the change?   Evelyn always prided herself on being of a practical nature, not prone to fanciful imaginings even through the acceptance of her own anomaly.

He took her limp hand in his enormous one and with gentle care, wrapped her fingers around the tray. Once she had steady hold of it, he released her and cut a pathway back to his seat, leaving Evelyn feeling oddly bereft.

"Thank you," she whispered, unable to speak until he was out of earshot.

A pause in his step caused her to wonder if he had, in fact, heard her.

Hastily she mumbled "Pardon me," to the assembly at large before cutting a retreat to the kitchens.

"Well if that don't tickle me stones." Moorland roared with laughter, "Ye've a Berserker champion, and ye doona even know what that means!"

She refused to ask and give Moorland the satisfaction of berating her ignorance.   Instead, she lifted her chin, grabbed a fresh rag to clean the tables, and headed about her duties, her heart lighter than it had been in months.

Lud, the day had been long.   Evelyn tried to squeeze the tautness from her lower back for a stolen moment and warm the icy fingers of stiff pain that spread through fatigued muscles.   The witching hour hastily drew to a close when she bent to pick up the final basket of clean bed and pallet linens for the morrow.   She grunted.   This particular load must weigh ten stone and the distance to the back door was a mile if it was one more step.

Evelyn felt the tiniest bit rejuvenated by the quick and cold scrubbing she'd just given herself from frigid water she'd pulled from the washhouse. She thanked the heavens to be clean and also for her small mattress of straw that awaited her on the attic floor. A shiver of yearning ran through her as she pulled her grey cloak tighter against the sudden chill.

The extremes of the Scottish climes never ceased to amaze her. Just this afternoon, excessive warmth had streamed through the meandering summer clouds. Tonight, however, a moist chill blew in from an approaching ocean storm.

Small price to pay, she supposed, for the safety of anonymity. Escaping as she had from the convent after the final disastrous "calling" she'd been set to by Bishop Grimstead, no corner of her home country felt safe.

She huddled beneath her cloak. Had the temperature dropped another ten degrees? Looking up from her basket, she squinted at the back door of the inn.

Black spots immediately danced before her eyes as the building began to blur in her vision. Frigid and foreign fingers grasped at her legs beneath her skirts, pinning her in place. After a moment of extreme disorientation, her vision cleared. She found herself staring through the trees at the *front* of the building; a completely different position than before.

What is happening? Her mind was suddenly interrupted by the thoughts of another in a frenzy of quick and foreign calculations.

The inn doors are thick and the ceilings high. Too high to jump. Clever innkeeper doesn't want unwelcome visitors in the night.

The voice permeating Evelyn's thoughts was arctic, sinister. And *Male.*

A dark chuckle choked her, filling her throat with malevolence and bitter envy. *No matter, the soldiers camping in the fields tonight will be crushed on the morrow.*

Cold hatred reached out toward the structure, emanating from this body she inhabited. If she'd been capable, Evelyn would have cried out with the chilling force of it.

Yes...He's here, the triumphant voice hissed.

Whose thoughts were these?

As if lured by the evil stirring the air, the traitorous McKay and his clan ambled on unsteady legs in the direction of the front guest entrance. Evelyn was startled to feel amusement and recognition in this foreign conscious she somehow inhabited.

Angus, favored a splinted arm. "Once we find her, I'm going to enjoy plundering an English cunny as her countrymen have plundered our lands for centuries." A drunken, riotous chorus of agreement sounded from his five or so kin. "Then, I'll let ye all have a turn wi' her."

"We'll ugly her up, after, so no one will stand to look at her face, the haughty witch!" Evelyn recognized him as the man who'd reasoned with Roderick in the tavern.

They're after me! She panicked. Desperate to return to her body from... whatever was happening, she struggled with all her will.

Unfortunate little witch. The whispered laughter followed her as she somehow ripped from his presence and slammed back into her own being. Her eyes flew open to behold the rear of the inn again and the small kitchen door. Plucking up the basket from where she'd unwittingly dropped it, Evelyn scrambled for refuge as though demon hounds bit at her heels.

Chapter Five

She sped across the empty dining room and plucked a candle from its perch, intent upon using its wan light to wind her way to the hidden linen closet beneath the stairs. There she might make her bed. Grimacing, she turned down the back guest hallway, which was only a short few doors on the way to the stairs. Evelyn had never been fond of small spaces. They terrified her, in fact. Her stomach twisted uneasily at the idea of spiders that surely made their nocturnal homes in the dank recesses of the cupboard.

Better to spend her night with them than the MacKay. Spurred on by the terrifying thought, she hastened her steps toward the foot of the stairs. She intended to ponder on the strange and frightening phenomenon she'd just experienced once safely locked away.

She jumped at the unexpected sound of heavy boots making their way towards the hall. Within seconds, the man would cut her off from her intended hiding place.

Panicking, she snuffed her candle and shoved it in the linen basket, hoping to dispel the fresh smoke. Then, she ducked into the closest guest room doorway alcove and balefully eyed the closet and its comparative safety, now steps out of reach.

Holding her breath, she flattened herself against the doorjamb, certain the darkness veiled her completely.

The weighty footsteps paused before rounding the corner where Evelyn hid. Tremors weakened her legs, and a throbbing pain pulsed in her jaw where she clenched it tightly. After a moment's hesitation, the footsteps resumed and a large, dark shadow passed her hiding spot trailing the clean smell of leather, earth, and heather.

Roderick MacLauchlan.

What was *he* doing out so late? And how was it possible for him to make his way in the darkness without the aid of a candle? Even with eyes adjusted to the dimness, Evelyn had difficulty distinguishing his hulking form.

He stopped ten paces beyond her and turned the key in its lock. The lamplight of his room spilled from the open doorway and onto the burnished skin of his bare torso. Fortunately, the illumination didn't reach her alcove.

Her breath caught again as she drank in the sight of his unclothed back. He momentarily filled the expanse of the entry, and then disappeared into the room.

As his door latched, cloaking her in darkness once more, Evelyn sagged against the wall. A whispered prayer of relief escaped her lips. But before she was able to form a coherent thought, the door burst open and Roderick stepped out into the hallway pinning her where she stood with his unrelenting glare.

Alarm spiked her heartbeat, and his nostrils flared; as did a banked fire in his fathomless glittering eyes.

At that moment, Evelyn began to understand the nature of a Berserker. A man possessing the speed to leap across an entire dining room faster than the eyes could track. That could easily break a brawny man's thick bone with one hand. Someone who had acute hearing and night vision akin to that of a bird of prey and who could easily identify the scent of fear.

Evelyn couldn't slow her breathing as they stared at each other. The way his eyes insolently traveled the length of her body, even with half of it covered by a heavy linen basket, caused peculiar warmth to spawn low in her belly, and tendrils of it to curl upwards toward her heart and spread out through her fingertips.

Embarrassed and confused, she lowered her gaze to the expanse of his smooth, hairless chest. The rounded muscles flared into immense shoulders, which ebbed and crested into the thickest biceps she'd ever seen. Long, thick and veined, his arms remained hairless until below his elbows where a light dusting of black hair gleamed in the lamplight and crawled toward his wrists. As he stepped out of the doorway, more hair caught her eye, this trailed between the obdurate ripples of muscle that made up his torso and disappeared into his dark trews. The glossy strings of his damp ebony hair confirmed a recent bath.

The niggling warmth became a pervading flood and hot bewildering moisture pooled between her thighs, which she was suddenly aware she'd been clenching together.

Roderick's nostrils flared wider and he tightened his jaw, an unholy knowledge lurking in his otherworldly eyes.

After a tense moment, he broke their mesmerizing connection to slowly gesture with his eyes toward the light of his room and then looked back at her. He jerked his head toward the doorway a few times. An unmistakable invitation.

He was asking her into his bed.

Roderick remained patiently immobile as she battled her uncertainty. What if bedding a berserker was dangerous? Could he control his formidable strength? What if, in her ignorance, she did something to make him angry? Evelyn knew a little of what happened when a man took a woman. She'd come frighteningly close to understanding it in the convent where she'd spent her childhood. In any case, her entire limited experience lent her to believe that she was better off a virgin for the rest of her life.

Yet, a knowledge that lay dormant all of her twenty years whispered that she unequivocally desired to see the rest of this magnificent man.

Shifting her eyes to the cupboard, images of being stashed in other closets and nooks danced before her. Listening to conversations no innocent child should be privy too and saving or damning people with her *sight* at the point of a bishop's dirk. Crying in the night as the blood of the innocent dead called out against her in her dreams.

The sound of irate masculine conversation carried down from the stairwell. Moorland's Inn stood only three stories high and she knew without a doubt who descended from the attic in search of her.

Hastily making her reckless decision, she ducked past the half-naked warrior into his room, laundry basket and all.

Chapter Six

Evelyn couldn't decide where to rest her jumpy gaze. So, she examined the room she'd prepared earlier that afternoon. It wasn't one of the biggest accommodations the inn boasted, but agreeable nonetheless. A basin with a pitcher of fresh water perched on a stand next to the window, and an oil lamp glowed golden atop a rough hewn chest next to the sturdy bed.

The clean rushes on the floor rustled beneath her footsteps as she set the basket down against an unoccupied space of the wall and turned uncertainly to look at Roderick.

He cast a curious glance towards the stairs and she worried that his exemplary hearing would hone in on the MacKay's intent toward her. If she caused an altercation, she'd be dismissed. The streets of Scotland were full of men like the MacKays.

"Ah, I'm Evelyn."

He cocked his head toward the door as he studied her, narrowing his eyes in displeasure at something he heard in the hall.

"Evelyn Woodhouse of Kent." A note of desperation crept into her voice and she took a step toward him. She didn't want any more trouble with the Mackays, nor the malevolent presence lurking in the forest outside. She just wanted him to shut them away from all that. At least for the night. "And you are Master Roderick MacLauchlan."

He turned to study her. After a tense moment, he cast a hard glare down the hallway, but stepped all the way into the room and latched the door.

Relief caused her to smile.

"Um, we haven't been properly introduced and I figured

that you should at least know my name if..." She gestured towards the bed, abruptly feeling bashful.

Wrapping her arms about her waist within her itchy cloak, she chewed on the inside of her cheek wondering what a worldly, experienced woman would do next when locked in a bedchamber with such a man.

How did one go about seducing a Berserker?

Roderick held his large hand out to her, gesturing for her to hand him her cloak.

He was being a gentleman. Well, good.

After hanging it on a wall hook, he turned back to regard her, a sensual tilt to half of his sinful mouth. Bending forward in a fluid motion, he lifted his leg to unfasten his boot.

Oh! He was undressing. Whirling to face the bed did little to slow her racing heartbeat, but Evelyn couldn't bring herself to watch.

Of course he is getting undressed, you twit, she berated herself. With trembling fingers, she grappled with the ties of her bonnet while she stared at the clean green coverlet in front of her.

There would be no marriage bed for her, no tender husband to give her babes. She remained a spinster at twenty and two, with no prospects, no money, no dowry, no past, and no family. But tonight the Berserker would keep her safe from the MacKays and the unknown evil lurking in the woods. It would only cost her virginity. Perhaps, in some small way, she would be an adequate companion to the warrior on his last night alive—

No, she couldn't think of that now. Squeezing her eyes shut against a pang of deep regret, she somehow managed to finally pull the bonnet off the tightly braided knot of hair at the nape of her neck and drape it across the bed frame. She reached behind her to start on the laces of her kirtle, her usually nimble fingers picked and yanked with no success.

Large, strong hands surrounded hers and she jumped at the contact. Roderick kept her hands captive as he pulled her back against his chest and wrapped her arms around her own waist, covering them with his. His warmth soothed the tremors coursing through her.

For a moment, she stood encased in a coffer of muscle and

flesh. The foreign intimacy of the embrace was startling as much as comforting. She detected a trace of dominance in the gesture along with gentle restraint. The contradiction comforted her somehow. Allowing herself to sag against him, her eyes fluttered closed, her head pillowed between the deep groove of his pectorals.

This was how it felt to be held. To be protected.

It felt *marvelous*.

Unbidden tears sprang to her eyes, and she quickly blinked them away.

She stood passively as he took his time undressing her, not letting their skin come into contact as he slid her kirtle off first, then her under shift.

The kiss of the chilly evening air on her skin caused gooseflesh to blossom everywhere, and her nipples to constrict into aching beads.

Her chest heaved with wild breath. She'd never bared herself to a lover. Were her hips too wide? Her arms too plump? Her breasts too heavy?

Surprised to hear his breathing quicken along with hers, she waited with vibrating anticipation to see what Roderick would do next. She couldn't have been more shocked if he'd dragged her to the rushes and taken her like a stallion.

He started at the very end of her braid and methodically unbound the silken locks, running his fingers though it until thick golden waves fanned about her shoulders and tickled the small of her back. It seemed like he might be torturing himself, and her in the process, by denying the contact of their exposed skin.

Aware of a dull, moist ache between her legs, Evelyn fought the persistent need to squirm. She leaned back a little, searching again for the comforting warmth of his hard chest. Instead, she encountered blunt, hot velvet as it stabbed the cleft of her back and angled upwards.

Oh dear lord.

Delicious curiosity snaked though her. That warm steely hardness pulsed against her lower back. It flexed against her, tangling with the feathery ends of her hair.

She squeezed her eyes shut. What was she doing?

Hot breath stirred against her ear as he closed his large

hands around both of her shoulders.   Calloused fingers abraded her skin lightly.   Sensation reverberated through her bones as he caressed the thin sensitive skin of her clavicles and angled south to follow the line of her figure.   Both hands spanned her ribcage before moving back up to run a fingertip along the sensitive undersides of her full breasts.   A deep rumble, almost a purr, vibrated against her, the sound unlike anything she'd ever heard before.

Absorbed and over-stimulated, Evelyn let out the breath she'd been holding in one great *whoosh*, on which a tiny groan escaped without permission.

She felt his smile as he pressed his mouth to her temple.

Finally cupping the mounds in both of his warm hands, he lifted them gently, testing their weight in his palms. Massaging the pliable skin in tandem, his lips found her sensitive ear lobe, her jaw, and then her neck. He burrowed there, moistening it with his tongue. When he nipped her lightly with his teeth, a flare of crippling desire and surprise caused her knees to buckle and give.

Collapsing against him with a gasp, she trembled with the force of sensation coursing through her.

Roderick took in a slow breath and exhaled for an eternity before gently setting her away from him.

Evelyn was unable to name the emotions surging through her. Awe, incredulity, power, emptiness, need, and uncertainty clamored for attention inside her desire muddled brain.

Unable to stand it any longer, she spun to face him.

Roderick stared at her with such intensity, such naked desire. He seemed larger now that she could plainly see the dramatic taper into lean hips, the ropes of his stomach muscles spilled all the way down to...

Oh my. She felt her throat work over an audible swallow.

Even that wasn't dwarfed by the size of his corded thighs. Could it possibly fit?

Judging from the fierce look on his savagely handsome face, he intended to try.   Roderick bent toward her, a dark intent in his gaze.

Chapter Seven

The bed caught her when Evelyn's knees refused to hold any longer.

Eyes glowing and jaw clenched, Roderick seemed to be waging an intense battle with his lungs. Dragging his gaze from her, he reached for her bootlaces.

Funny, she'd forgotten she still wore them. Considering how much they'd pained her over the course of the long night, it spoke to his powers of seduction.

He tugged one boot off, then the other, dropping them haphazardly onto the floor with a *thunk*. Rough hands slid up either side of her coarse woolen stockings until they reached the twine corded tightly around her upper knee. Immense relief washed over her when he released the knots and the sensation turned to bliss when he tucked tender fingers inside and stripped them slowly off. His mouth returned to kiss each irritated indentation left by a long day of wearing them. She'd given just about anything to afford a proper ribbon to hold them in place.

His unexpected tenderness touched her as a direct dichotomy of his brutal visage and reputation. She'd half expected him to toss her skirt over her head and have a quick go at her. He couldn't know how much his gentle seduction pleased her. She reached a tentative hand and captured a damp ebony lock as it trailed across the flesh of her thigh.

Silk.

He tracked her movement, hunger sharpening the harsh lines of his face. Joining her on the bed, his muscles bunched and rolled as he crawled up her legs bringing their faces flush.

Would he kiss her?

Evelyn warmed with anticipation and moistened her lips, drawing his notice. Instead of accepting her unspoken invitation, he brought a hand to the curve of her neck and plunged it into her hair until he lightly supported the back of her head. Easing himself farther forward, he pressed her down until she stared up at him, prone and completely covered by his sleek body.

Such a large hand tenderly cradling her head seemed a contradiction the possessive heat threatening to singe her from his regard.

Air hissed between his clenched teeth as her fingertips explored his ribs. She could feel the flex of his cock against her thigh. Emboldened, she drew her fingers up, discovering the hardness of his smooth chest and then his shoulders and arms. Beneath her questing hands, every taut muscle jumped and flexed.

His eyes demanded that she continue.

Tracing a more direct path, she traveled down his chest, past trembling stomach muscles, to the narrow curve of his hipbones. She hesitated, blushing to her hairline.

"Is this all right?" she whispered, feeling the warmth of her own breath with his face so close to hers.

Of course, Roderick didn't answer her, but he parted his lips and hot, rapid bursts of air hit her skin in wordless demand. To punctuate, he arched his back slightly giving her hands more room to explore.

She didn't expect the pure heat of his throbbing sex when she delicately wrapped it in her fingers. The outer skin was a silk glove around pure molten steel. She gently tested its mobility, squeezing as she slid one way and then the other.

His hand fisted, pulling lightly on her hair as he ground his jaws together. Again his hips surged, pushing his need farther into her hand as a harsh gasp tore from him.

A heady sensation washed over her as she realized that for all this dominant man's dangerous command, *she* wielded the power. Desire spiked as a world of possibility unfurled before her. What else could she do to his body that would render him defenseless?

Catching her lower lip in her teeth, she explored the rimmed tip of his cock with her fingers. Finding a curious bead of moisture, she spread it around what skin it would cover.

His low growl warned her milliseconds before she found both of her wrists bound by an iron grip above her head. If his muscles corded any tighter, they would surely rip through his straining skin.

Would he kiss her now? She tilted her head to run her burning lips against his neck. His pulse jumped beneath her mouth, its rhythm strong and hard. She rubbed shy, lingering kisses across his jaw line. The stubble of his shadow beard abraded her sensitive skin.

He drew back, shaking his head. A flicker of something like regret passed through his eyes before he blinked it away. He took a breath, allowing his free hand to roam the curve of her waist. His mouth lowered to pay her attention, but the moist exploration began at the hollow of her neck.

Distracted, she twisted beneath him, a slave to the fingers warming her skin, and then to his hot mouth branding it. When he reached her breast he lingered there, taking her nipple into his mouth, causing her back to arch off the bed in helpless accord.

A strangled cry burst from her as his teeth lightly grazed the untried bud, causing the pressure in her abdomen and core to become a wild, unmanageable thing.

As if heeding her undeclared need, his hand languidly trailed the curve of her waist and the flare of her hip until it brushed against the downy nest between her legs.

"Oh!" She gasped, seized by sudden uncertainty.

What if she were too innocent to understand what he required of her? Would he be revolted by the abundant slick moisture he would find when he touched her? She knew nothing about pleasing a man, and he couldn't verbally command her. What if he found her inadequate in some way? Did he expect her to do anything other than lie beneath him? Such insecurities threatened to choke her for a moment, and she found herself wishing he would press his mouth to hers. She felt the wordless comfort of a kiss would allay her fears.

Instead, a single fingertip traced the seam of her nether lips, and all coherent thought fled.

Her hips surged toward him of their own volition.

Triumph shone on his face as he raised a knee and worked

it in between hers, gently forcing her legs to part. Running the same finger along the identical path, his low growl washed over her again as he encountered the pool of wetness. Her fears swiftly dissipated as his eyes rolled shut in apparent delight, and he drew his fingers one by one through the silky dampness.

Evelyn's cheeks warmed in a furious blush. Still trapped by the strong hand capturing her wrists above her head, she lay helpless to do anything but let out a thin, shocked cry as his slick fingers brushed against the engorged flesh at the apex of her core. Foreign pleasure snaked through her like the lightning from a violent sea storm, and she bucked against the unfamiliar sensation.

A slow, sensual smile spreading across his chiseled face, Roderick traced soft, glossy circles around her clitoris stopping to dip his fingers and retrieve more of her nectar, which sprung from a never-ending well. His other hand released her and traced its way through her hair to her neck and shoulders, caressing down to cup and knead her breasts.

Once released, Evelyn wound her arms around his brawny neck and tried to draw his mouth to hers. She needed to be doing something other than lying in a puddle of mystified pleasure.

His eyes locked on her lips. A prolonged blink and the most insignificant pause of his fingers caused her concern before he ducked his head and dragged his warm lips against the sensitive skin of her neck.

Feeling oddly denied, Evelyn only had a moment to wonder before his hot tongue stroked the beaded tip of her nipple, and his fingers began a wondrous plucking rhythm against her tender flesh.

Her blood ebbed and flowed with the expert movements of his fingers as they harmonized with the strokes and swirls of his sinful tongue. Elusive building tension caused her limbs to writhe helplessly as it rapidly converged into her core before exploding outwards using her body's intrinsic currents to course pleasure from the epicenter of his ministrations to the outermost recesses of her fingers and toes.

Crying out in astonishment, Evelyn was helpless to do anything but allow the spasms to break over her like the roll of the tides. Wave after wave of sensation carried her deeper and deeper into the fathomless emerald sea that stormed in Roderick's expressive eyes.

When the pleasure became too much to bear, and his strokes burned the previously untouched nerves, Evelyn whimpered and trembled, arching her hips away from the incessant pressure of his fingers.

Roderick seemed to understand instantly and his warm, magical hand left her.

Within the space of a few stolen moments, her tedious, dismal existence had been utterly altered. Enthralled, scandalized, and thoroughly pleasured, Evelyn watched as Roderick palmed himself with slick fingers and spread what little moisture he could on his thick shaft. His skin stretched tighter over high cheekbones, and his breath came in short rasps, heaving from his lungs as if he were carrying a heavy load.

Evelyn instinctively knew what he wanted, what he needed from her. Feeling shy, she widened her knees, spreading herself before him, offering her body for the taking.

The heat in his eyes threatened to consume her as he positioned the hot blunt head of his manhood at her aperture, moistening the tip as he settled his bulk atop her, creating a silken curtain with his dark hair. Their chests heaved together as they each silently struggled for breath.

As his hips nudged forward, he breached the opening of her body. At the first searing hint of pain, her muscles seized and bore down, clamping shut against his entry.

Evelyn winced and caught her lip between her teeth as she watched a fine sheen of sweat break out on his brow. Roderick trembled with visible effort now, yet he stroked her hair and whispered a tender 'shhhh' between his teeth in an obvious attempt to relax her enough to grant him entry.

Oh God, what if he were too big to fit?

At a loss for what to do, she remained locked with him in a sexual battle for a few tense moments, him gaining a few inches before her offended muscles tensed against him.

Pulling back, worried questions wrinkled his brow, Roderick started to push up away from her.

"*Wait,*" she pleaded softly, grasping him in an attempt to

stop his retreat, "I know I can do this." Her voice trembled. Shame heated her face. "Would you...kiss me?"

From the hard, stunned look he gave her, she was certain of his denial and her heart seized. Cupping his clenched, unyielding jaw in her hand, Evelyn brushed a thumb across his full lips testing their texture and tracing their flawless contours. She whispered again, "Please?"

He blinked at her. That rough, foreign rumble emanated from his chest again as he seemed to seriously deliberate the appeal.

Was it such an arduous request? How she wished he could express his thoughts to her.

He held his tremendous weight on one arm, lifting a hand to cover hers on his cheek. Turning his head, he pressed his lips to her palm before closing his eyes and nodding, as if to himself.

Resolute surrender flashed across his features a moment before he descended to claim her mouth. The contact exalted her soul and seared her lips. The damp heat created by his kiss spread through her, warming her rigid muscles, slowly soothing her until they unraveled beneath him, becoming pliant and replete.

Massaging her lips with his, Roderick groaned with pleasure and ran his tongue along the seam much in the same way he'd run his finger along her womanhood earlier. She opened to grant him entrance.

He took her then. With a powerful surge of his hips, he buried himself to the hilt, entering her with his tongue simultaneously.

Tears pricked her eyes, and for a moment, Evelyn felt as though his manhood would rip her asunder. There had been a tearing sensation, and she wondered if he'd damaged her.

But his mouth still pressed against hers, his wet tongue exploring the recesses of her lips, laving, stroking, cajoling and singularly focused upon her ravishment. Deep, moaning pleasure rumbled from the back of his throat, and vibrated pleasantly against her lips. Lost in the consuming passion of their kiss, Evelyn relaxed and allowed her body to accept his. Muscles yielded instead of fighting against his intrusion. They fit against his velvet length like a glove, pulling him deeper.

Then he moved. And the world ceased to exist.

Exquisite pleasure pierced through the dull discomfort that persisted as he slid out slowly, and impaled her again. Gone was her tender seducer, replaced by a primal beast rhythmically torturing her with his slow, methodical strokes.

He didn't stop kissing her, devouring her relentlessly as he introduced her to the carnal nature of a man. He kissed as though he was a man dying of thirst introduced to a mountain spring.

An urgent pressure, familiar now, unfurled in her core where he currently resided, making demands of its own. Shifting slightly to alleviate it, she found, only made it worse.

Or stronger.

Tendrils of thrilling heat reached into her womb, stabbing her with each deep thrust, begging her to meet them with thrusts of her own. It was nothing at all to raise her hips to meet his sex with hers, drawing him so deep, their hips met.

Gasping out a harsh breath, Roderick seized her hips and pinned them to the bed, violently shaking his head as he reared back and accelerated his rhythm.

Entranced, Evelyn's conscious separated from her body as she marveled at the savage beauty of what she was experiencing. Her eyes hungrily devoured him, following the path from his passion-glazed irises to glistening, freshly kissed lips. His muscles strained and bunched with the controlled frenzy of his movements within her, the ropes of his abdomen corded with each gratifying thrust creating slick and delicious friction were their bodies joined.

Her mind and body slammed back into the moment as a throbbing pressure caused her feminine muscles to clench around him. Once. Twice. And then her existence shattered into thousands shards each with prismatic spectrums that burst behind her closed eyelids.

Tossing her head back against the bed, she arched so powerfully against the all-consuming sensation that his arm came around her, pulling her body against him. His guttural roar drowned out her own cries as he followed her into oblivion.

For what seemed like minutes after, Roderick stroked her back and shoulders as she trembled and convulsed, still held tightly against him. They remained intimately joined as she felt him shrinking from his formative girth and slipping from inside her. Evelyn focused on the feeling, letting his tender fingers soothe her. The immensely powerful impact of their orgasm overwhelmed her, and she fought tears of intense emotion while her body recovered.

After a silent while, he laid her back and withdrew from her. A look of sated incredulity relaxed the brutal planes of his face. Leaning in to kiss her, looking as though he thoroughly enjoyed the act, he left the bed to retrieve the towel that hung next to his wash basin. He yawned expansively as he washed himself without looking.

Evelyn took the opportunity to shamelessly ogle his godly backside.

He rinsed the cloth and wrung it out before he turned around with it still in his hand. Roderick abruptly froze, his eyes locked between her legs.

Looking down, Evelyn was mortified to see the tell tale pink of her virgin's blood mixing with the aftermath of their joining, staining the sheets and her thighs. Gasping, she seized the top sheet to cover her nakedness, hiding the evidence from him.

It was too late.

Chapter Eight

Evelyn watched as swirling black swiftly overtook pools of green, and then infringed on the whites of his eyes. His protruding veins rushed with blood as muscles heaved upon each other until he grew even larger. She hadn't thought it possible.

Even his flagging erection pulsed with blood and became gloriously full again.

Witnessing the evidence of a power more tangible and elemental then she could imagine culminate into the perfect masculine form before her struck her dumb with wonderment.

This was the Berserker.

With a bestial snarl, he advanced upon her, hands clenched and chest heaving with deep, growling breaths. His teeth gleamed sharper, more predatory.

Evelyn wondered if she was destined to become a blood sacrifice to his Gods.

He ripped the covers from her, exposing her naked body. His eyes zeroed in on the blood, and he growled. It wasn't the rumbling purr she'd heard before. This sound was filled with lethal menace. Deep and hungry.

"Don't be angry." She kept her plea level and soft, swallowing a surge of dread as he stalked closer. "I – I'm sorry I didn't tell you that... I'd never..."

He paused, cocking his head to the side in a now familiar gesture. Bristling like a great cat, his nostrils flared and he examined her with his cold, black eyes like a curious specimen.

Dear God. The thrill of her first orgasms still pulsing in her veins spiked even higher as she imagined all kinds of terrible ends for her in the clutches of this monster. Why did excitement tangle with her panic? She'd always feared death and avoided danger. Feared there was nothing after for her but bitter judgment and possible damnation for the things she'd done.

For whom she was.

Yet this creature had nothing to do with all that. He was a creation of a different deity. He existed as a holy cleric of some other, more ancient order. He wasn't bishop, templar, monk, or confessor.

He was an executioner.

His presence forged the outcomes of war and established the conqueror from the conquered. Though he subjugated no one, his sword drew the lines of possession in the soil, and then cut down the opposition. A berserker didn't discriminate. He killed everyone.

He won't kill me. Like all her knowledge, Evelyn didn't understand where this came from. She just—knew.

"I'm not afraid of you," she murmured, rising to her knees on the bed.

He tracked her every move.

Her trembling hand made her a liar as she reached out to him, resting her palm against his heart. The muscle twitched beneath her touch, his flesh hot and feverish.

That strange ticking rumble, somewhere between a growl and a purr reverberated from deep in his chest and vibrated against her hand. Then she was falling into the air where he'd been standing.

A strong arm clenched beneath her breasts, saving her from toppling head first off the bed. Evelyn let out a small squeak as she was pulled back against his strong body and set between his open legs.

She hadn't even seen him move. One moment, he'd been standing in front of her, the next, crouched behind her on the bed. They were leaning against the headboard, her backside pressed against his arousal.

Instead of taking her, or hurting her, he settled her back against his rumbling chest and leaned against her. Evelyn gasped as a rough hand wound in her hair a moment before his face buried in it.

He was scenting her?

All right. She let out a breath of relief. *This is... strange, but not altogether unpleasant.*

He released her hair and heavy arms created walls on either side of her as he reached forward. She'd completely forgotten about the damp cloth he'd been holding until he used it to gently cleanse her thighs.

Blushing, she hid her face against his arm, and he made an animalistic noise of amusement. She smiled against his skin.

"I was planning to sleep in the cupboard tonight with the spiders. At least until the MacKay were gone. But I'm quite glad I didn't." She hated her propensity to babble that whenever discomfited or embarrassed. Biting her tongue, she admonished herself to be quiet.

Roderick grunted when she said 'MacKay' and it wasn't a happy sound. Folding the cloth the opposite way, he parted her folds and washed her intimately as well, the cloth wiping away any evidence of her virginity.

She cleared her throat and squeezed her eyes shut, trying not to focus on the unfamiliar intimacy of his actions. "I, uh, used to be locked in a lot of cupboards and such when I was a girl." She couldn't seem to help herself. The words tumbled out of her in reckless succession. "The London convent where I was raised sometimes held prisoners as well as orphans. I dare say we weren't treated much differently. When we misbehaved or— when they wanted something, we'd be locked away. Sometimes for hours... or overnight." She didn't dare tell him that she'd been locked away more than any other child. That the bishop had used her gift for knowing truths and forced her to listen in on countless tortured confessions. She'd rarely been able to save any of his victims, though. Even the innocent ones.

Roderick discarded the cloth and pulled her closer against him, nuzzling the curve of her neck. It felt good. Warm. In a short time, this had become her favorite place, this haven of his solid body wrapped around her. Perhaps the Berserker wasn't as dangerous in this form as she'd originally thought.

"Anyway, I'm not fond of small spaces, to say the least. I suppose I'm thanking you for, well, inviting me in here. For protecting me from the MacKays—and the cupboard."

He nodded against her skin, capturing her earlobe in his

lips and scraping his teeth against the sensitive flesh there.

Goose pimples erupted all over and she shivered.

Searching for her knowledge, she was paralyzed by the desperate hope that perhaps his fate had changed, as they sometimes did through no fault of one's own, but of others or circumstance.

Nay. His life ended on the morrow. She closed her eyes against hot tears as grief snaked through her.

What could she do? Should she warn him? Should she tell him of her ability and risk his lethal censure? Did one night of love-making addle her wits so much that she forgot about self preservation? They turned to each other for pleasure, yes. He might be using her body for distraction before a battle. And, in turn, she used him for protection against a fate worse than death at the hands of the MacKay. Yet, she *refused* to let anyone use her ability against her again. In the hands of the church, using it in the name of one God, it had been a nightmare. She shuddered to think of what it would become in the hands of an entire Norse pantheon. She'd risked her life to escape to Scotland, and she didn't have enough money saved to take herself any farther.

No, she couldn't tell him. It wouldn't change anything. She'd tried before to save people from their destiny. It wasn't to be done.

Though, how she wished things were different.

She tried to focus on something, *anything*, else. His chest felt unerringly solid as she rested her head against him, noting his grunt of appreciation.

So, the man and the Berserker could create sound... Evelyn blushed a bit, recalling the ecstatic noises he'd made earlier. Burning to know why he was capable but unable to speak, she ultimately decided against questioning. *It didn't matter now*, she thought miserably.

Yawning greatly, Evelyn felt a weighty fatigue settle upon her, as if honey flowed through her veins rather than blood.

"Roderick?" she murmured sleepily, "I-I don't wish to return to my bed, may I sleep here with you tonight?" Tilting her head up and to the side, she wasn't surprised to see that his green gaze had returned, though he did seem affronted.

Tightening his arms around her, he rolled them so she lay

down and faced the wall on her side. Settling in behind her, his back to the door, he drew her bottom close against his erection, but didn't press it into her.

Resting her head on his curled bicep, she relished in the feeling of the front of his tremendous body pressed flush against the back of hers. His arm, still tucked beneath her breasts, secured her to him.

The only sound in the softly glowing room was his breath stirring the top of her head. Languor stole all reason and Evelyn only distantly registered the room plunging into darkness.

Magic. She thought dreamily before drifting into velvet oblivion. *If only she could break this curse...*

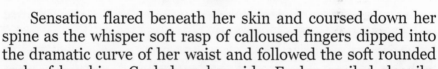

Sensation flared beneath her skin and coursed down her spine as the whisper soft rasp of calloused fingers dipped into the dramatic curve of her waist and followed the soft rounded arch of her hip. Curled on her side, Evelyn smiled sleepily, refusing to open her eyes lest the subtle, unfettered exploration cease. Instead of dropping to the front of her, the caress paused and then retraced its journey back toward her ribcage as if indulging in the softness of her skin there.

Warm breath caressed her face and a nose nudged hers before probing lips settled across her mouth in a languid kiss. This had to be the most pleasant way she'd ever awakened, Evelyn decided, as heat seeped through her sluggish veins.

Silvery tinged darkness barely outlined the form of the naked Berserker facing her when she resolved to lift her heavy lids.

As dark as the night, his jet hair and bronzed skin melded with the shadows. Only his eyes gleamed as he pulled his lips from hers.

"Roderick," she whispered, feeling shamed and sinful, every nerve ending alive and vibrant.

His great body stiffened, fingers clamping on her hips, digging into the sensitive flesh and pulling her forward, thrusting his hard sex against her thighs.

"*I want...*"

Without warning, he seized her other hip in an iron grip

and lifted her, full bodied, as though she weighed no more than an infant.

She gasped as he rolled onto his back and held her entirely above him, demonstrating his preternatural strength. Before Evelyn completely registered what he was doing, he balanced her on her knees encompassing either side of his head, his eerie eyes burning up at her from between her legs.

No! He couldn't mean to—

"Oh... my." She breathed as the flat of his tongue split her apart. Aghast, entranced, Evelyn was thankful for the darkness or she wouldn't have been able to bear the depraved act. Arousal flooding her womanhood, she shuddered when his unrelenting tongue dipped into the resulting wetness, and he swallowed, an appreciative moan vibrating against her clitoris.

Trembling thighs gave out and she belatedly realized that his strong hands at her hips not only supported her entire weight, but imprisoned her there.

Another unhurried lick stole her breath. He cleaved her with his tongue, stopping right before he reached the most sensitive peak. Circling it, nipping at it with his lips, teasing the moist flesh surrounding it, Roderick tormented her with his mouth, chasing away all reason with searing pleasure.

Evelyn bit back moan after moan, throwing her head back, reveling in the feel of her long hair brushing naked skin. She shamelessly surged against his mouth.

"Roderick... please." Her hands desperately grasped at his. "I need..." She grit her teeth and hissed, kneading his strong arms and wordlessly demanding release.

Shoulders shaking in a silent male chuckle, eyes glittering with purely masculine delight, he latched onto the engorged peak of her sex and centered all movement just below it, creating an overwhelming burning sensation.

A hot ache built beneath it until she squirmed to escape what she knew would be next. Throbbing pleasure engulfed her core as wave after wave of gripping ecstasy flowed from his tongue into her body. Wracked with tremors, Evelyn bucked against the strong hands gripping her hips. Frustration at her inability to move heightened each pulsing sensation of her climax.

When the last tendril of pleasure wrung from her body, her

berserker still allowed no quarter. Kissing her playfully on her sex, he lifted her from his drenched mouth much the same as he had before, and deposited her upon his torso, finally letting go to wipe her juices from his lips.

Drunk with pleasure, and feeling rather bold, Evelyn's hand slyly traced the contours of his lean abdomen behind her until she found his pulsating erection twitching against his belly.

Wrapping her fingers around it, she wondered if her lips would have the same magnificent effect on *his* body.

His hands rested on her thighs, his fingers curling as Evelyn stroked the skin of his velvety shaft, her touch feather-light.

Sliding her down his body, he positioned her against lean hips, the slightest tremor in his hands indicating of the intensity of his need.

Nudging her slick entrance for a moment was all the warning he gave before pulling her hips down, impaling her on his thick cock.

They both gasped at the impact of the joining. Evelyn stilled in his hands, letting her sore muscles again adjust to his intrusion. This time, only the slightest twinge of pain permeated the haze of her passion. A sense of fullness, of heady command spurred her to act on every primal urge that danced along her senses.

Clenching her intimate muscles, she enjoyed the jerking of his body, the short intake of breath, so she did it again, eliciting the same response. Grasping him with her insides, she slowly rose and slid down upon him again feeling every glorious inch of his breadth inside of her.

"Ohhhhh..." The moan escaped her as she rode him with delicious languor. "Oh that feels so..."

A familiar growl warned her before strong hands again seized her hips and held her immobile. Roderick set a furious rhythm plunging deeply into her, angling her forward to heighten her pleasure. Ceaselessly thrusting upwards, the pad of his thumb found the sensitive little nub his tongue had so expertly toyed with moments before. Softly swirling it in time to his thrusts, he brought her to peak so hard and fast she couldn't hold the desperate cry that tore from her throat.

Roderick waited until the storm passed before pounding into her with abandon. Evelyn knew when his release was upon him because she could feel him swell within her before hot spurts of seed shot against her womb, his entire body taut and trembling beneath her.

After her breathing slowed sufficiently and she became fairly certain she could walk, Evelyn reluctantly withdrew and padded blindly to her linen basket, selecting something to clean herself and ministering to him as well.

"It's still a while until dawn," she observed, a heaviness settling upon her shoulders. Did the morrow have to come? Couldn't they stay here forever?

A hand caught hers, pulling her down over him until she was splayed across his body and engulfed by his arms.

"No." She giggled in spite of herself, "I'm too heavy."

Grunting softly, Roderick tightened his hold and pressed a tender kiss into her hair.

Exhausted, Evelyn counted the decelerating beats of his heart. She felt as though time, itself, sped toward an inexorable meridian while she lay in the darkness. What if, just this once, things could end differently? What if, she could save him, as he saved her this night?

'Dangerous thoughts.' She told herself, squeezing her eyes against futile desperate frustration. *'Dangerous desires.'*

Chapter Nine

Instead of shivering awake in the arid, dusty attic as she did every day, Evelyn drifted into awareness on a sumptuous shaft of silver light, which gained strength as the morning began to peak over the crests of the sea.

The creak of leather and the click of metal armor dumped her into full consciousness and to the comprehension that she lay naked in the bed of a Berserker.

Roderick mysteriously remained cloaked in shadows, his ebony hair pulled into a tight queue at his nape. He fastened a fearsome spiked bracer about a wide wrist, his brutish features set in a grim mask.

"Don't fight near the Mackay." The whisper escaped her, knowing that his exceptional hearing would pick up the trembling uncertainty in her voice. "Please, be careful. There's... someone out there. Someone dangerous."

His eyes lit upon her and softened, yet a dark brow lifted almost scornfully. No doubt, he assumed she feared for his safety after his insult on her behalf the night before. Even heavier now, dressed in his black armor, he sank to the bed, causing her to lean towards him. An armored hand reached for her, then hesitated when he glanced at the stained glove and scarred bracer dangerously close to her skin. Instead, he dropped his arm and worried the leather at his cuff.

"Just..." Should she tell him? Would it change the outcome or be the cause of it? "Angus and his clan have already betrayed the lot of you. I- I overheard them speaking of it last night." Squeezing her eyes shut, she called herself every form of coward. "Hundreds more horsemen are even now hidden to the north and west waiting to flank you if the battle turns in favor of the Stewart."

Roderick kissed her, hard. Not the gentle brushes or passionate tending of lips from last night, but a possessive branding of flesh. As he plundered the depths of her mouth with his tongue, heat bloomed between them, heedless of the battle gear that separated their flesh.

He didn't touch her, not once allowing his armor to come into contact with her skin as he thoroughly devoured her. Slick moisture pooled between Evelyn's aching thighs in understanding that, no matter how sore she was, he would be welcome inside her.

Abruptly ending the kiss, he glanced at the grey light of dawn turning more golden with each passing moment.

Stunning her with sudden movement, he leapt from the bed and swiped his sword from where it leaned against the wall next to the headboard. Strapping it to his lean hips faster than she thought possible, a look of dangerous anticipation played across his features.

The sounds of other men preparing for battle permeated the silence between them. Horses whinnied and stamped the ground, carts of weaponry clamored up the rough hewn roads and camp fires sizzled as they were doused.

Roderick paused at the door. Their eyes locked.

Thousands of questions burned behind her lips, holding her tongue heavy with fear. She dare not open her mouth for fear they would come tumbling out, humiliating them both.

What was he going to do? Would he heed her request? Would he live through the day? Would he come back for her if he did? Would she ever see him again?

Did she mean anything to him now?

A torturous agony coursed through her with a strength she'd never before encountered. This must be the crippling horror every woman experienced when she sent her warrior off to battle.

Her heart in her throat, she watched, paralyzed, as he bowed to her, his right hand grasped over his heart. Still, she kept quiet as he turned on his boot and quit the room. The door closed with a click that reverberated through her bones.

Trembling with the force of it, she allowed the tears she'd

been holding with an iron will to flow freely down her cheeks. *What had she done?*

Chapter Ten

Roderick adjusted the grip on his weapon as he waited in the shadows of the forest.

The lovely lass had been right.

The Stewart army boasted more mounted knights, but the sheer number advantage belonged to the enemy. And here, three acres of forest away from the battlefield, maybe two hundred and fifty horsemen awaited their signal to attack in the unlikely case that the battle turned against the Donald. Their colors and language branded them Northern mercenaries, paid per battle to fight for the highest bidder.

He bared his teeth in half a wicked smile, half derisive sneer. They wouldn't get the chance. Not today.

Watching them mill about their crude camp, preparing their horses as stealthily as possible, he knew it would be easier to start taking them out before they mounted and stood at the ready.

Her name floated to him on the breeze that noisily disturbed the heavy leaves of the oak in which he perched. Looking toward the city of Aberdeen he breathed deeply as if he could find her scent on the wind and take it inside of him.

Evelyn... The most beautiful woman he'd ever encountered with her thick, honeyed hair and shy, whiskey colored eyes.

And that arse.

He'd meant to possess her for a night, to shelter her from the cruel MacKay and give and take pleasure from her body. It did him good to spend his seed before a battle. For then the rage did not take him as entirely. He was less likely to slaughter his allies.

But she'd been a virgin. A bloody *virgin*!

He should have known. He should have read the signs; her trembling, her shyness, her unpracticed guileless passion. It wasn't unusual for him to encounter difficulty with a woman who was unaccustomed to a man of his size and girth. He'd thought her tense and nervous, maybe in need of coaxing.

Kiss me... Please. Closing his eyes, he relished the sweet memory of his own surrender. Och, but she'd been tighter, *sweeter* than any woman before and now that she'd tamed his beast, there could *never* be another woman after. 'Twas the way of his Berserker bloodline. Once sworn and mated to a lass, the bond was eternal.

Roderick cringed at the danger he'd inadvertently put her in. What if his berserker had rejected her as his mate? She would have been killed! But, nay, magic lay behind the lass' warm eyes and an innate knowledge and acceptance of the truth of things. Any man or beast would have to be insane not to want her, to do anything to possess her, to protect her.

To *love* her.

He would return to Aberdeen and claim her. Take her to his family home in the highlands. Just as soon as he dispensed with his contracted charge.

Taking in another deep breath of briny ocean air tinged with heather, he silently drew his blade from the scabbard, taking care not to let the sun glint off the weapon and alert his prey.

Slicing the blade across his left palm he embraced the familiar white-hot rage that surged at the sight of blood.

Yes...

This caused the Beast to rise within him, filling him with the power of Freya, passed down to some clans through a Northern ancestor.

His vision honed to shades of grey, but sharp as that of a predatory bird. Colors would not distract him, only movement. And the beast, once unleashed, indiscriminately destroyed *anything* that moved.

Painful breaths exploded from her chest as Evelyn raced through the forest, hands fisted in skirts to hold them above her knees.

The blue berserker. He would kill Roderick. He lurked, waiting to strike, to kill.

Could she warn Roderick in time? She'd been in *his* thoughts the night before! Why hadn't she known who his quarry had been then? Clenching her teeth and calling herself nine kinds of idiot, she crashed through the brush, ignoring the burning in her lungs.

The wind held a metallic trace, all her senses alert to the deadly stillness of the forest permeated only by the sound of the leaves.

Breaking from a line of trees, she couldn't hold back a cry of dismay at the staggering carnage that lay before her. Panting frantically, she cringed at the scent of blood invading her nostrils and mouth.

She *knew* what had happened here. Not because of any ability of hers, but because of what she'd told the man with whom she'd shared a bed the previous night. Hundreds of slaughtered knights lay strewn about the clearing; their limbs sprawled at incomprehensible angles, if they even remained attached.

Not even the horses were spared. Just like in her dream.

Frantically searching for black armor among the blood-stained tunics, she skirted the clearing, swallowing convulsively against the bile crawling up the back of her throat. She let out a trembling breath. He wasn't there.

Horrific sounds of violence filtered through the morning. He would be at the battlefield, but it seemed foolhardy to follow there.

It didn't matter, did it? She had to find Roderick. Warn him. *Save* him.

Her legs threatened to buckle as she forged on toward the battlefield. Uncertain of what she could do to reach him, but desperate to change his fate.

Sometimes *berserkergang* made him mindless, and he barely registered the destruction he wrought. Today Roderick was pleased to perceive the pained astonishment on the faces of the Mackay as they turned on their kinsman and signaled for mercenary reinforcements which never appeared. As he plunged into the fray, already streaked in the blood of his enemies, Roderick cut a gruesome path through Donald clansmen, a singular focus causing his peripheral to haze.

The beast and the man, in union, wanted at the bastard who dare threaten his mate. Typically, the foes that fell before his sword remained a part of the faceless masses, but today he roared with pleasure as he severed the head of Angus Mackay from his body.

Roderick and the ferocious Stewart not only held the Donald at bay, but systematically drove them back. As afternoon settled upon the valley, the victorious sounds of triumph rippled through the Stewart clans and kin.

Even after the worst of the berserkergang passed, soldiers still gave Roderick a wide berth as they knew he might sever a limb for a congratulatory pat on the back.

"Wait until his eyes return to normal," the old ones murmured while some younger men made signs of the cross against him and regarded him with both awe and antagonism.

Growling with unspent aggression, Roderick paced the battlefield.

He felt danger lurking nearby. Something lethal, familiar, tinged with—

His heightened senses perked as honey and vanilla notes caressed him over the repugnant odors of battle.

Evelyn. His mate. She drew near.

Someone would have been dispatched to the town to tell of their victory. *'The lands of Ross are safe.' 'Come and collect your dead and wounded.'* She'd come for him.

He knew it.

Feeling like an expectant boy, he wiped his bloodied sword on the grass and sheathed it. Her scent drifted from the safety of the woods, beckoning him. Feeling encouraged that she'd come out to meet him, he looked down at his blood-streaked armor and frowned. How would seeing him like this affect her? For once a Berserker chose his mate, he still had to wait for her to accept him. Often, he was called upon to deal death in the name of Freya and the fates. It would take a rare and exceptional lass to understand his role in the world. Could she?

Roderick long ago accepted that his inability to communicate with women, in addition to his menacing appearance and pagan reputation, would prevent him from being accepted by a mate.

How am I going to get her to understand what she is to me?

He faltered in his path, gripped by sheer indecision. It hadn't been easy to get a woman into his bed in the last years he'd spent without a voice. How could he possibly get a woman to share his life with him?

Perhaps he should write her a letter. He wondered if she could read. More scholars littered his bloodlines than berserkers. If it weren't for his beast, he'd be content deciphering a scroll from ancient Rome or Greece. If she couldn't, he'd teach her to love the written word as much as he did. The irony didn't escape him; a man who loved language whose voice had been stolen from him.

Once they married, she would have the responsibilities of a Baroness and unofficial stewardess of the MacLauchlan clan until his brother Connor, also a berserker and the laird of the MacLauchlans, took a wife.

So, likely always. He rolled his eyes. That man was infinitely more hopeless than he. And Connor had no speech impediment.

Roderick crested the hill and plunged into the tree line. He should probably just abscond with the lass no matter her objections and lay siege to her body, spending his every night fulfilling her wildest fantasies. And creating a few that she'd never thought of.

Of course, he would spend his days satisfying her every other corporeal need whilst introducing her to the many wonders of his homeland. Her life would become so full that she couldn't *consider* needing aught else.

Breaking into a jog, he tallied a list of plausible enjoyments for her: tending the extensive herb and spice garden, riding horses together from his family stables, archery, mayhap even the stag hunt if she were the out-of-door sort. Surely, other more genteel pastimes might interest her; perhaps needlework or musical instruments, or um... beading hairnets and the like.

He mentally shrugged, if she wished it, he would gather

threads of the richest colors and finest silks for her. He would take her to exotic markets and let her have her pick of the loveliest shells, pearls, beads, and gems. His clan was prosperous, and he'd been handsomely paid as a mercenary for many years. She would want for nothing.

His blood quickened at the thought of planting babes inside of her, as many as she wanted, a half dozen at least! Another Berserker to carry the line, of course, and many doe-eyed cherubs with honey-colored hair to fill his family's silent castle with happy chaos. Mayhap she was already—.

"Roderick!" He pivoted at her breathless cry.

Color instantly vanished from the forest, all but for the cast of blue, which meant—

Berserker.

No gradual welling of hot rage, not this time, no thrill of power coursing through his veins.

Only Icy wrath. Bleak fear. Certain and lethal retribution.

Chapter Eleven

Evelyn struggled for breath as the golden-haired Norseman squeezed her throat, cutting off her warning. Drawing his sword, he pinned her against his armor, creating a shield with her trembling body. She had no choice but to watch helplessly as her lover lunged toward them from across the small clearing, the promise of swift and brutal death etched in his unnatural black eyes.

She couldn't bear to watch. Squeezing her eyes shut, she searched for her knowledge.

Nothing. Blackness. She'd never been able to see her own fate.

This was all her fault. She was going to be the cause of Roderick's death.

Despairing, Evelyn fought back tears as her captor unexpectedly shifted her position, jerking her eyes open.

As if blocked by an invisible barricade, Roderick paced in front of them, panting and raging, his movements wild, threatening and predatory.

Evelyn took in the blood splattered across his armor and face. He was filled with the killing rage. Why, then, was he not coming for her?

"See that?" The malevolent, foreign accent chilled her. "He can't do anything that might put you in danger. *You* are his mate."

"I- I don't know what you mean," she stammered, unable to look away from her growling berserker.

"Did he claim you, woman? Did he kiss you on the mouth?" His fingers tightened painfully. "Have you already seen him like this?"

Unable to speak, she nodded her head.

"His berserker has chosen you as its mate. Had he not, you would have been instantly killed." His dark chuckle repulsed her, "I can smell his *stench* all over you..."

Dumbfounded, she stared into Roderick's onyx eyes and saw the stark anguish of the man inside.

Her...mate?

Oh God! She hadn't known what she was asking when she'd begged for his kiss, hadn't understood the significance of his tenderness when controlled by his berserker. How perfect. This extraordinary man *would* have embraced her own unnatural ability, would have allowed her to be herself and never exploited her. This she *knew*. Tears welled as the knowledge that she could love him overwhelmed her. She'd never known anything like that before. Not about her own future.

"I want you to understand, the name of your mate is now Alrik the Blue, should my berserker accept you, of course." His sword flashed as he nicked her arm, drawing a tiny bit of blood. She whimpered before she could stop herself.

Roaring, Roderick drew his own blade. Desperate sounds burst from him now. He stalked them, seeking access to Alrik who kept her firmly between them no matter how she struggled.

"I possess his voice. I never thought he would be able to find a mate without it. Look at him. Roderick the Black," he spat the title as if it tasted sour on his tongue. "Too young to even control the blood-rage. Wields only fledgling magic. Pathetic!"

Evelyn remembered the night before, the candles extinguishing by themselves. A cry burst from her as he punctuated with another slash of his sword across her skin, this time a deep gash opened on her thigh, drawing an alarming well of blood.

Roderick's unholy scream terrified her. He lashed out. The older berserker dodged and thrust her in front of the blow, pulling Roderick up short.

"He is favored by Freya, even after I cursed him! And now, the first among what remains of us to find a mate, which will increase his power tenfold."

Evelyn's teeth clattered together as he shook her for emphasis.

"I am the oldest and most potent of Freya's Warriors. *I* wear the color of the Goddess. There is no way that a *Celt*, the latest born of the Berserkers is going to rival *me!* I challenge you, Gael, for your chosen mate and don't think for a *second* that she won't accept me."

"*Never.*" she vowed. "And you're a coward for holding a woman as a shield. You *shame* your warrior Goddess!"

He didn't strike her as she feared. His lips drew sickeningly close to her ear. Serpentine fingers of evil caused her blood to run cold as his breath brushed her neck. "There are things I could do to you that would ensure your acceptance and, mark me, I would enjoy *every* moment."

She shuddered, forcing her mind away from the frightening images he conjured. "What does my acceptance have to do with any of this?"

After a shocked pause, Roderick moaned and Alrik burst into laughter. "You haven't *accepted* him? Of course! How could he have told you?" He vibrated with mirth. "You simple tavern slut. I'm going to enjoy making you—"

"Yes, I do!" She cut him off, unwilling to hear his threats. "I accept Roderick MacLauchlan as my...uh... mate." There. That ought to accomplish something.

Both men gaped.

"It doesn't matter." Alrik recovered first. "I can still challenge for you."

Evelyn's breath slowed as she met the swirling eyes of her mate and witnessed the power flow through him. Her energy fused with his and a bond of celestial weaving clasped into place. "No," she whispered. "You cannot if you're dead."

With a barely perceptible nod to her mate, she went perfectly slack in Alrik's arms, dropping her head below his chest before Roderick's sword arced toward his neck.

With unnatural force, she was thrown to the ground, Alrik needing both arms free to deflect the lethal blow.

Evelyn winced. Her leg bled heavily now as she scrambled out of the way of the dueling warriors. Weakness crept through her, and she knew she didn't have much time.

Alrik's blue eyes had been overtaken by familiar onyx as

his beast burst forth to meet his foe. Moving at speeds she could barely detect with her mortal eye, she could only watch helplessly as every so often, they slowed with a particularly powerful collision of their swords.

Locked in epic battle, they didn't see her tremble, didn't feel the chill that stole through her emptying veins. "Roderick," she whispered. "Please hurry..." She gaped at the puddle of blood forming beneath her. Pressing on the wound with her soiled skirt, she moaned.

Her berserker was truly something to behold. The speed and grace with which he moved was a stark contrast to the raw power in his blows. The older, faster Alrik thought to be the aggressor, but was thwarted at every attempt. An elemental command spurred Roderick forward, as he hacked at the blue knight with such ferocity that his enemy stumbled backward.

With one last enraged cry, Roderick delivered the final blow that sent Alrik's head sailing through the air. His body crumpled to the ground, twitching with the last impulses of life.

Dropping his sword, Roderick was at her side in a moment, lifting her to his lap. Panting moans of denial exploded from his chest as she squinted up at him, hot tears tracking to her hair from the corners of her eyes.

"*E, Eh, Ev, Evelyn!*" He ground out, his voice returned by the death of its possessor.

The darkness took her while she listened to the foreign sounds of his beautiful voice muttering desperate words against her forehead.

Chapter Twelve

Where am I? Warmth cocooned her nude body in between the sumptuous sheets of the massive bed upon which she lay.

"Kilrock Keep." The thick brogue startled her. She'd been unaware that she'd spoken aloud, or that she was not alone. "Yer new home."

"Roderick." She breathed. Bolting upright, she greedily took in the man standing before her clad in nothing but a heavy blue, green, and black kilt.

Eyes glittering with pleasure, desire, and possession, he slid the kilt down his lean hips and joined her on the bed.

"I can't. My leg…"

What about yer leg?" He rumbled in her ear, sliding his very large, very *naked* frame against her skin.

"What?" No gashes, no pain, only healthy pink skin streaked with fine veins.

"Magic," he whispered with hot lick at her lobe. "Ye've made me quite powerful, my lady. My Mate."

Shivers wracked her as his hot breath touched her skin at his words, causing liquid warmth to pool between her thighs.

He breathed deeply and pressed his throbbing length against her hip. "I'm afraid ye've accepted me, Evelyn. I canna let ye go now. But I can love ye, 'til the end of my days if ye'll let me."

She silently regarded him for a moment, turning to face him, resting her head on her palm. He looked arrogant, aroused, vital and… vulnerable.

"Which will be a long time, I'll have ye know."

Winding her fingers through his loose and silken hair, she cupped the back of his head and drew him to her for a heady kiss. "I suppose I'll just have to love you in return." She whispered and tightened the hand in his hair, pulling it sharply.

With a pleasured growl his head snapped back and his eyes closed. When next they opened, the burning darkness of the beast peered out at her.

Rising to his knees and roughly rolling her to her stomach that strange, preternatural ticking purr permeated the room.

Yes, a sensual thrill coursed down her spine. *Now* she would acquaint herself with her Berserker.

UNWILLING

A highland historical novella

Chapter One

The Scottish Highlands, Autumn 1411

"I want his death to be quick and painless. He's my brother, after all." Rory MacKay didn't meet Connor's eyes as he said this. Instead, he tracked the armored coach trundling along the river Tay where the water ran into the loch, which boasted the same name.

Connor knew it was around noon, though storm clouds hid the sun. From their vantage point in the trees above, he counted twenty mounted highlanders in the coach's vanguard. Twenty he could kill on his own, but it would be a blood bath. "I take pleasure in the death, but no' in the killing. It willna take long once I start."

Rory winced, but nodded. His doe-brown eyes closed as he took a bracing breath.

Connor MacLauchlan studied the second born twin of the MacKay nobles. Rory's bronze hair matted to his handsome face where fat rivulets of rain had plastered it. He was a strapping lad, but even in his heavy hide cloak he didn't compete with Connor's own bulk. This was a good man doing evil for the sake of his clan. Yet the blood would stain his hands, just like it would saturate Connor come sunset.

"If yer having doubts, now would be the time to voice them," Connor prompted. "We can ride away from here and never speak of this again."

Rory's shoulders slumped. "Nay. Since yer brother, Roderick, defeated our father at Aberdeen, Angus has been raiding all over Argyll. He's split our clan and made us weak. Anyone who doesna swear fealty to him is terrorized. He's pillaged and burned farms and houses... wi' people still inside. I didna want to believe what I was hearing, but a woman begged refuge for her and a bairn at the Keep. She said he ran her husband through the belly with his sword, then made the dying man watch as he...took her." Rory's throat visibly worked over a swallow. "Angus is my twin. We used to protect each other from our brutal father. We used to play together in the fields and ride our horses along the coast until we could see the end of the world..." His eyes hardened. "He canna return to the Keep, MacLauchlan. I willna let him be the ruin of my clan. No more innocents can bear his tyranny." A tear escaped the corner of the young man's eye and he swiped it away with his bracer.

Connor's saddle creaked as he reached out to clap Rory on the shoulder. "I have a brother of my own," he said. "I'd die for him."

Rory nodded his head in appreciation, his jaw working back strong emotion. "Actually, I thought it would be Roderick who answered my missive, what with you being Laird and all. Oh, and a Baron now, besides."

"My brother is newly married. He promised his bride he'd build her an apothecary in Strathlachlan. There's no tearing him away from her side for the time being." Connor huffed out a chuckle at the memory of his brother following his wee curvy mate about the Keep like an addled puppy, a load of planks on his broad back. God save him from the same fate. Roderick was patient and steady as the day was long. Connor didn't have the temperament to deal with a wife.

Besides, courting a Berserker could be deadly. And he had enough blood on his hands already. Better not to risk it.

"I see," Rory let his mouth relax into a faint smile that didn't reach his eyes. "There's another conundrum of mine. The next Laird of our clan is betrothed to Lindsay Stewart."

"The Regent's niece?"

"Aye. I'd not see her in the arms of my brother, royal beauty that she is."

"I heard she's also a royal pain in the arse."

Rory shrugged. "I've never met her. But I wouldn't give an animal I liked to Angus, let alone a noble lassie."

"Right." Connor turned his attention back to the road.

The Mackay had almost reached the foot of the loch. They would angle southwest, then, following the road along the river.

"They mustn't reach Loch Lomond." Rory pulled a heavy purse out of his saddlebag and handed it to Connor, who nodded.

"I'll get them at Benmore. There's forest for ambush and caves where I can camp for the night. Besides, Lomond's too close to MacLauchlan land for my comfort. I'll no' let him get close to my clan."

Pulling his hood up against the rain, Rory turned his horse.

"Go to a busy tavern tonight," Connor ordered. "Buy everyone there a pint and maybe tumble a lass or two. Make sure you're seen."

"All right," Rory nodded. "And... Godspeed Connor MacLauchlan."

"I doona need yer God's blessing," the berserker murmured as the other man rode off into the mist. "I have a Goddess to keep me."

When the berserker rage took him, he became lost in it. It was as though another beast lived dormant inside of him and burst free at the sight of blood. Only, Connor never disappeared into the grey oblivion. Nor was he merely a spectator. He became a mass of rage and wrath and indiscriminate destruction. Every man possessed some part of the spirit of the berserker. For some it was a whisper. For others a roar. But the nature of humanity tempered the beast with reason, logic, fear, love, and ambition. For a few ancient blood lines, Freya, the Norse Goddess of war, unchained the beast within chosen warriors of the line and gifted them with unnatural strength and speed. The part of the mind that processed logic, consequence, and emotion became chained but never completely dormant.

Connor turned and watched the heavy coach make its unhurried pace through the late afternoon. Closing his eyes he waited to feel the requisite thrill before a good battle. God help the marauding tyrant within. For once his Berserker beheld the first hint of blood, there would be no survivors.

Endless hours in the stuffy coach made Lindsay Stewart squirm with restlessness. She couldn't read to pass the time, for within minutes of bouncing through the mud-rutted roads she'd be green as Irish moss and her afternoon meal would make an unwelcome reappearance. She'd rather have ridden out in the fresh autumn air with her vanguard, but her uncle forbade it. In fact, he'd been *quite* forbidding since taking her father's place as Regent of Scotland. Every time their last discussion ran through her head, she could feel the embers of her temper ignite all over again.

"There's nothing I can do to help ye, Lindsay," he'd said with a dismissive wave. "The betrothal contract was signed between yer father and the senior Angus MacKay in agreement for a trade of MacKay lands and their swords against the Donald. Both men who signed the contract are dead now. I canna go against yer departed father's wishes. Ye're Laird has sent for ye. Ye'll go to Angus the Younger and be an obedient wife."

"But the late Laird Angus was a traitor and ended up fighting for the Donald. Surely that negates the contract." Lindsay had argued.

"There's still the land. The agreement stands." Robert Stewart had folded portly arms over his belly and jutted the foremost of his chins out at her. The movement reminded her of the Neapolitan Mastiffs he kept as hunting dogs. There were many jests about the Scottish court as to how much dogs and master resembled each other.

"You would trade your niece for a few paltry acres of peat moss and heather?" she'd asked, aghast that her uncle could care so little for her. She'd been a good companion to his ailing wife for some time. That, at least, deserved some deference. "I've heard that Angus is a brute. Would you have me treated unkindly?"

"I'd have ye do yer duty to clan and country. If yer father hadna waited so long to marry you off, he wouldna have had to settle on the MacKays. But because ye were a raven-haired beauty like yer mother, he couldna bear part with ye and die alone." His eyes had narrowed into red-rimmed slits of cruelty. "Yer no' the first noble girl who had to lie beneath a husband she didna like, and you willna be the last. Show a little gratitude. There are several lassies who'd slit yer throat to take your place."

"Then let them," she'd spat.

"Doona tempt me!" He'd thrown her out of his richly appointed study, then. Ultimately, she'd ended up stuffed with a fraction of her belongings into what the MacKays had dubbed a "gilded coach" and surrounded by dozens of reeking highlanders.

Lindsay looked around the cracked and peeling interior of the conveyance. Perhaps it had been grand once. Last century. At least she'd been allowed her privacy. And, her betrothed hadn't come to collect her, himself. He'd sent this sinister looking band of brutes to conduct her from Inverness to Dun Keep, the MacKays' highland castle on the other side of the bloody isle. She parted the dingy curtain of indeterminable color and tried to let some fresh air into the close interior.

A nebulous and sinister mist had abruptly rolled off one of the many nearby lochs and blocked out the autumn afternoon. Lindsay could taste the moisture of it on her tongue and breathe it into her lungs. It smelled of ripe berries and freshly fallen leaves. Squinting through the soupy swirls of silver and gray, she assumed she was looking north, as they'd endlessly been traveling east to reach Dun Keep. It was hard to tell though, as the trees, rock formations, and the river all lay hidden in the fog.

The sounds of anxious horses and the low murmurs of her guard caused the fine hairs on her body to rise with awareness. She could see the forms of the three closest men to the coach. The flashes of their green kilts and drawn swords would sometimes come into view before disappearing back into the thick cloud.

"Is everything all right?" she asked the closest highlander. A scrawny man whose age remained indeterminable beneath his shaggy locks and what had to have been a summer's worth of grime.

He shifted his horse closer and leered at her, revealing that he'd lost most of his teeth and all of them on left side. Whether from rot or battle, she couldn't be sure, but the effect was most unsettling. "Nothin' ta fash yerself with, lass. Just a bit o' fog makes the horses jumpy. Ye never know if there be a wolf or what not in the woods."

"Oh." His words didn't relieve her worry. Something about *this* particular mist was unsettling. Maybe a bit unnatural. It slithered around them, its silver fingers reaching through her clothing to leave a cool sheen on her flesh.

She shivered.

If yer in need of diversion. I can come in there, teach ye a few things." His tongue made an alarming appearance though he kept his teeth clenched.

The burly warrior next to him smacked the back of his head. "Ye canna be saying those things to the lass!" he chided. "She's wedding the Laird. Angus'll cut off yer sacs and feed them to his dogs while ye watch... and that's just fer lookin' at her sideways."

The scrawny lad had the decency to look stricken. "Ye'll no' be mentioning it to 'im, will ye lass? Ye know I meant nothing by it."

"Your secret is safe with me," she shrugged. Best not to antagonize the fellow. Who know what a desperate man would do?

"Yer lucky she's a sweet wench." The other burly man cackled. "Or ye'd likely not live to see yer next—"

An axe imbedded in his skull, effectively cutting off the rest of his sentence.

Chapter Two

A dark demon stalked the mist. As soon as the axe had appeared, it was retrieved by a monstrosity who moved too swiftly for her eyes to track. The panicked sounds of dying men, muffled by the heavy vapor, rose like the crescendo of a macabre dance.

Lindsay froze at the window. Her mouth formed a silent scream as she watched the man with the head wound slump from his horse and disappear into the haze. She'd never seen a man die before. Not violently. She'd never known what the matter inside a skull looked like.

She knew now.

The grimy man waved his sword about, calling for various compatriots. "How many are there?" he bellowed. "What colors are they wearing?"

Only the crunch of bone and the screams of the dying answered him.

The blurred form she'd briefly seen didn't wear a tartan or clan colors. Only black. Lindsay could feel tears of fear burning in her eyes, but she couldn't bring herself to blink. If she did, perhaps the demons would find her in the darkness behind her eyelids.

A handful of men rallied to duck behind her side of the coach. Their backs to the heavy cart and their shoulders together, they frantically traded what little information they had. They kept their swords at the ready.

"There has to be at least ten of them."

"Fecking swift bastards. They killed five at once!"

"They're even killing the horses."

"How can they see through the mists?"

"They canna! Just run them through!"

Lindsay clung to the windowsill and frantically scanned the vapor. She could maybe see three spans in front of the men's heads crouched beneath her window. The sounds death abated, and an eerie silence hung as thick as the mist. No birds sang in the trees. No insects hummed in the meadows. No horses moved or whinnied in the distance. It was a though the earth held her breath. It took a grave burn in her lungs to realize she did the same.

A soft gasp escaped her. It sounded as loud as a scream in the permeating silence. Lindsay couldn't tell if the sudden rushing in her ears was the nearby river or her own blood. Were they gone? Had they allowed a few survivors? Maybe they were horse thieves, and they only killed the ponies they could not keep or take with them.

A knife sailed through the air and found purchase in the ledge of the window. Lindsay stared dumbly at it vibrating in the wood not three inches from her eyes. A choked sound escaped her, but in a flash of inspiration she wrapped her fingers around the handle and pulled.

It wouldn't budge. Throwing a panicked glance into the swirling mist, she tried with both hands to no avail.

The axe came out of the mist next. A stream of blood and gore slung from its honed blade before it claimed yet another victim. A MacKay head rolled to the earth, and the axe rested atop its former post. That left five men alive.

Lindsay dove into the coach. If only this wretched contraption had another exit on the other side! Not even a window to create a crosswind. She would have made a frantic dash to the west. That is, if they didn't have the entire conveyance surrounded. She frantically looked around for something, *anything* she could use as a weapon. Faded cushions on the sparse and uncomfortable benches, her blanket and cloak were her only companions.

Maybe she could use the cushions to block out the gruesome and horrific sounds from outside. She grabbed for one, but something stopped her. The thundering roar of a raging beast. The gurgling cries ripped from throats filled with blood. Metal slicing the air. Bones crunching beneath heavy weapons.

As soon as those warriors finished dying, she would be next.

If those villains murdered her today, they would not find her body cowering beneath ugly cushions. Not Lindsay Stewart. They would say that she died bravely. Fighting like a hellion for her life and her virtue.

She hoped it wouldn't come to that.

With grim resolve and trembling limbs, she forced herself to sit back on the bench. The moment she settled in, the latch burst and the door exploded open. To her utter surprise, the scrawny soldier lunged in. His wild eyes bulged from a face drenched in blood. His horrific mouth opened in a primal scream of terror.

"It's the very reaper come for our souls!" he wailed, gripping at her skirts with his dirty hands. "We're damned for our crimes!"

"What do you mea—" Lindsay's very breath abandoned her when she saw *him* framed in the door.

When priests read the bible at Mass, they would tell that Lucifer was once the fairest and most beautiful of all the angels. They would say not all his minions looked like satyrs and fiends. Some of them, the most dangerous of them, bore the visage of pure temptation. They were fallen Seraphim and Incubus. You would worship them and beg for pleasure as they dragged you to hell. You would writhe in ecstasy as they damned your soul.

He was surely such a creature.

Though he had the body of a man, it was like no man she'd ever seen. A veritable leviathan, he had to turn his immense shoulders to fit through the door. He'd been the monstrous black shadow she'd seen in the fog. Everything about the man was black. His armor, his shorn hair.

His eyes.

Lindsay cringed from him with a horrified grasp. Where his eyes were supposed to be, an abysmal miasma of darkness swirled about like the fog. The mist followed him in, and she absolutely believed he'd been the one to conjure it.

In one silent and fluid motion, he raised his broadsword and brought it down upon the scrawny highlander at the very place where his neck met his shoulder. The sword didn't embed in the man. It cleaved him in two, covering Lindsay in a warm spray of blood. Then, he grabbed the pieces of the dead man and hurled them out of the cabin.

She screamed then—dignity be damned—but regretted it instantly. She'd drawn the creature's notice.

Once, she'd watched a man on his death march to the gallows. His feet planted and his eyes had pleaded into everyone's they met. It was as though he couldn't believe there was no mercy left in anyone's heart for him. No compassion. That his life meant so little and everyone would just go about their business after he was gone. The moment he accepted this, realized his insignificance in the wide world, had been painfully apparent. His shoulders had slumped, his eyes dulled, and he'd merely trembled as the soldiers dragged him to his fate.

Lindsay had never forgotten that man. And in this moment, she understood exactly how he'd felt. *She'd* remembered him always. Perhaps because maybe no one else would. And she thought of him now as the beautiful monstrosity before her let a primal roar as his sword arced toward her trembling body.

Chapter Three

The slice through the front of her didn't cause any pain. The terrible sound of her kirtle and shift flaying open reached her ears and she wondered if flesh didn't sound the same. Perhaps shock delayed the pain? Or, if your organs were spilling out of you, you didn't feel them anymore?

That would be a mercy, at least.

Lindsay couldn't bring herself to look down at the damage. So, she glared at the demon, feeling her chest still rise and fall in rapid succession. It *was* getting harder to breathe. A band encircled her lungs, threatening to stop their movement altogether. This could be the end.

He blinked those soulless, onyx eyes at her and cocked his head to the side. Funny, he resembled a bewildered dog when he did that. More like a hell hound. A half-hearted growl emitted from his throat as he stalked closer.

Oh God. She cringed. At least it would be over soon. There was nothing more he could do to her now. She would bleed out any minute.

His sword clattered to the floor. His breath came in deep pants, flaring his nostrils with every exhale. No threats uttered from him as he bent over her. A deep rumble built from low in his chest and gained strength as their eyes locked.

Lindsay stared into the abyss, quite transfixed. The strange, ticking rumble reminded her of the purr of a cat. Louder, deeper, but somehow just as satisfying. She closed her eyes. If this was going to be the last sound she heard on this earth, she'd pretend it transmitted from some other source to lull her to the afterlife.

The devil was moving, but she didn't open her eyes to see

what he was about. Perhaps he was readying the killing blow. Perhaps he was leaving her to die in peace. Either way, it mattered not. Until a warm, slightly roughened cheek pressed against hers and he took in an endless breath against her hair, filling his lungs to the brink.

Was he... *smelling* her?

He exhaled a soft groan and drew back. His savage face appeared pleased as his gaze roamed every inch of her face, and then dipped lower. The rumbling grew louder.

Lindsay looked down to find her flesh very much intact, and very *bare*. Her bodice and undergarments lay flayed open all the way to her waist. Her breasts quivered with each of her shivers and drew his hungry gaze. Blood still stained her dress, but hadn't seeped to the clean skin beneath. Her flesh seemed to glow translucent in the dimness of the coach. She tried to grasp the sides of her bodice and pull it together, but he was on her before she could move.

She cried out in alarm as his hands pinned her wrists to the bench beside her. His hips forced themselves between her knees and she was so grateful he hadn't sliced through her skirts.

"Please..." she whispered as he brought his body close to hers, but didn't touch his stained armor to her exposed skin. "Don't kill me."

He shook his head slowly, an amused smile playing at the corners of his full mouth as he examined her like a rare specimen. Lindsay didn't understand his bizarre behavior, but couldn't bring herself to move. She had the distinct impression that if she ran, it would be like inciting a predator to the chase. He'd not harmed her. Yet. But perhaps he was more like a cat than the intense purr signified. Maybe he liked to play with his prey first before butchering it.

She swallowed hysterics that threatened to bubble into her throat.

He gave her hands a gentle press, as if to tell her to leave them where they were, then released them. Lindsay didn't dare defy him. He reached long, roughened fingers to her face, wiping at a trail of frightened tears she hadn't been aware she'd shed.

His hand snaked around to plunge into her loose hair. She

could feel how large it was as it cupped her head, and precisely how strong. He could crush her skull with one flex. He didn't, though. He just urged her, rather tenderly, toward him.

Lindsay's blood quickened through her veins. She had no choice but to let him pull her closer. Closer to those terrifying eyes. Closer to that blindingly exquisite face. Closer to his sinfully sensuous mouth.

So he *was* some sort of incubus. Even in these horrifying circumstances, with the blood of the freshly fallen at their feet, she couldn't prevent the thrill that shot through her.

If this were a reaper or a demon, surely *she* couldn't be the focus of his ultimate attentions. Lindsay gave a weak resistance in his unyielding grip as she frantically tried to think of anything she'd ever done that would damn her soul. She'd never been particularly obedient or subservient, but she'd only been quarrelsome if she was certain to be right and her opponent wrong. Which was most of the time. A few white lies might come back to haunt her, though she was pretty sure she'd confessed them at some point to father Vincent. Hadn't she? Vanity could be a marked weakness. Admittedly, she took pride in her long, thick black hair and kept her skin soft and fragrant. So would that be considered pride? Or vanity? Which one was the least egregious sin? She didn't always *mean* it when she said her prayers, but she dutifully said them, all the same.

Prayer. That was it. Demons could be repelled by invoking the holy spirit through prayer. Couldn't they?

"Hail Mary, full of grace. The lord is with thee…"

The demon's sinister mouth curled into a snarl of distaste. He didn't burst into flames as she had hoped, but he appeared somewhat uncomfortable. Oh, praise be! It was working.

"Um…" How did the rest of it go? Something about being blessed and Jesus and the fruit of her womb. Oh drat. At least she remembered the important part. The one she would need any moment now that she'd angered him. Her voice wavered. "Pray for us sinners now and at the hour of our death. Ame—"

He cut off her benediction with his lips.

Chapter Four

Many times the Ladies at court gossiped about soft kisses or a stolen passionate embrace. This was no soft kiss. And the dark sentinel looming above her stole nothing. He demanded. He plundered. He claimed.

Shocked and helpless, Lindsay didn't dare move. She hadn't a weapon and the idea of fighting him off terrified her. The beast was obviously being careful not to sully her with his blood-stained armor. This – *thing* might have single-handedly slaughtered a vanguard of more than twenty men. She shuttered to think of the sordid violence he could commit if she inflamed him by struggling.

For this could be no ordinary kiss. Something happened within the demanding contact of his hot, branding mouth. The swirling mist surged. The highland beasts quieted and took notice of a new variable in the world about them. Perhaps an alteration in the cosmos while something as intangible and exigent as fate shifted in a single moment.

His strong, warm tongue breached her mouth and explored the untouched recesses. Lindsay thought the creature should have tasted like death or brimstone. Maybe blood or damnation. He *did* taste like sin. Crippling pleasure paralyzed and shamed her. The expected anxious flutters or hesitant thrills didn't accompany this kiss. It went beyond that, instantly, to a curious burning sensation deep in her belly, radiating outward on a feverish pulse and culminating in a moist rush to her loins. Fear made the sensations sweeter and more terrifying. This was wrong. It was sinful. But she couldn't stop him if she tried. Her best chance at survival was submission.

His deep groan reverberated through her and then his hands were on her. Strong, demanding fingers gripped her shoulders, kneading them in rhythm with his mouth before trailing to her breasts. Lingering over their softness, his hands were gentle as they stroked and cupped the soft mounds. The rough pads of his thumbs abraded the sensitive flesh of her nipples and a stunned gasp of delight escaped her. The demon swallowed it and answered back with a fervent moan as his fingers continued to drift lower.

Here in the mist, Lindsay could forget where they were and what lay beyond the present. The future became a nebulous abstract, perhaps not even to be manifested. Only the next moment mattered, for it brought with it a subsequent untried sensation. The coach disappeared in the consuming fog and with it, all sense of time and reality. Perhaps, Lindsay thought, she was already dead. Maybe he truly did spill her blood and decided to follow her into the afterlife. Her very own reaper, easing the final journey by initiating her to passions of the flesh. Wasn't heaven supposed to be like this? Clouds. Beauty. Ecstasy.

Stroking her firm, trembling belly, he dipped below the rent seam of her dress. Her skin felt clammy beneath his warm, sure fingers. Moist from the frosty kiss of the vapor. When he trailed against the crisp hairs below her waist, Lindsay clutched at the wide shoulders as though to hold him in place. Of course, she realized the absurdity of the notion, but she would die if he stopped kissing her now. She couldn't look into those bleak, fathomless eyes. If she did, she'd have to admit that she took pleasure from the damned. That her soul might be as black as his.

Not that he gave any indication that he was finished. He drank from her as a parched man would from an enchanted well. It was as though he'd never drink again, and planned to gorge himself until he could no longer.

When his fingers dipped into her cleft, he found a river of desire. Breath escaped them both as he delved into the slickness and tested it against the engorged flesh aching to be touched.

Lindsay jerked against the movement. She hadn't even been aware her body could produce such a sensation. Perhaps it couldn't. Maybe this searing, aching pleasure was a manifestation of this man's dark power. Either way, it captivated her absolutely.

He barely had to move his hand, but only to hint at a pulsing circle, his knuckle pressed beneath the tight bud as his finger mimicked the movement of his lips. Soon, her hips moved with him of their own volition, riding the waves of pleasure like a horse racing out of control. She knew it carried her to a destination. That this climbing, overwhelming pressure couldn't continue to build. If she could just—

She crested in a wet rush of pure white fire. Her rhythmic cries followed the pulses of bliss centered in her core and were smothered by his relentless mouth. Her hips bucked beneath him but he held fast, driving her ever higher until she collapsed.

The black-clad beast drew back then, and the expression on his face terrified her. Absolute possession.

He ripped at the leather buckles of his armor, rending them with his bare hands, and tossed the chest-piece aside. A black tunic with a tear at the shoulder was all that stood between him and her bare breasts.

"Wait." Lindsay started to drift back into herself. The last pulsing vestiges of pleasure still thrummed through her blood. Her limbs felt heavy and soft, her thoughts muddled and slow to take form. What just happened? Had her very soul shattered and then been recaptured? She needed a moment to recover.

With a dark and anticipatory smile, he dropped his head to capture her lips in another searing kiss. This one left her feeling drugged and weak-limbed. Lindsay put her hand on his chest and pushed against him. This shouldn't be happening, should it? Why hadn't he spoken a word to her?

"I don't think—"

His tongue took advantage of her parted lips and she lost herself for a few more sensual moments before turning her face to evade him.

"I can't— Ohhhhhh."

He nibbled her ear. Licked at the sensitive flesh of her neck. Rendered her witless with his sinful, relentless mouth.

The cold air on her bare thighs dumped her harshly back

into reality. He'd pushed her skirts above her knees and had moved deeper between them. Lindsay grabbed desperately at her bodice and found it slick with a dead man's blood. She was going to be sick. What had they just done? With the blood of the freshly defeated at her feet and the corpses of innocent men strewn about outside her carriage? What sort of woman was she to act in such a disgraceful manner? Surely, he'd enthralled her, somehow. Bedeviled her into allowing him the most shameful of liberties. She had to stop this. Stop *him*.

"No!" she cried.

His head snapped up from her neck. Those ebony eyes snaring hers from a face so blindingly compelling she had to wrench her gaze away. She was in danger of being spellbound again.

"P-please... I—" What should she say? Would he kill her now?

His head dipped toward her once more, lips angling for her breast as he pushed her skirts higher.

"Stop," she commanded, twisting away from him and attempting to disentangle her limbs from around his strong trunk. At least she succeeded in grasping her bodice together. "I won't let you take me. Do you understand me, Demon? Y-you cannot. I'll die first."

His features darkened from bewilderment to anger in a moment. With a vicious snarl, he reached out and grasped her by the waist, hauling her against him.

Even knowing what he'd done, exactly how many people he'd killed, Lindsay had underestimated his sheer strength. Apparently, until this moment, he'd been treating her with utter gentility and painstaking restraint.

Not any longer.

Dragging her out of the coach, he held her body in an iron grasp even as she wailed and kicked and struggled with all her might. Lindsay was glad she couldn't see the carnage through the fog. But the metallic scent of blood hung thick in the air and the demon seemed to be picking his steps very carefully.

As he carried her a few spans, the mist began to dissipate and after an indeterminate time of her kicking at him and shouting obscenities, a brilliant sunset shone over the river Tay.

"Put me down!" Lindsay ordered. "I demand to be released."

To her utter surprise, the demon complied. Dumping her fully into the river and following in after her.

Chapter Five

The harsh chill of the water washed the blood away and blurred the sharp angles of grey from Connor's vision. The world melted back to the vibrant colors of autumn. Crimson was the first to return. He faded back into awareness while ripping a blood-soiled dress from soft, pale skin.

Woman's skin. *His* woman's skin.

"Christ!" he swore as he dropped her body back into the waist-high water, recoiling as though she were a hot coal scorching his flesh. The rent garments stayed in his grip, and he hurled them to the opposite bank in a fit of temper. "Fuck!" A mate? Now? How in the name of the Gods had this happened? He didna want her.

The woman surfaced, sputtering and flailing until she found purchase on the mossy rocks, and stood.

Connor blinked. Och, *that* was how. His berserker must have taken one look at the shimmering goddess in front of him and decided to claim her as his own. Straight, heavy raven hair clung to pert, high breasts and a firm, tight figure. She was a wee thing, finely-featured and delicately formed, but fire flared in her amethyst eyes.

Following the direction of his gaze, she looked down and let out a shocked squeak and covered her breasts, lowering her body back into the freezing water.

For a moment, they just glared at each other.

"Your eyes," she gasped. "They're green."

"Aye," he said moodily. "They've been since my mother bore me."

"Nay." She shook her head vehemently. "Nay, they've been black as pitch until now. Sir, you were possessed by...

some kind of demon. It made you do— well—*terrible* things." She regarded him with wide-eyed apprehension. "Don't you remember what you've done?"

He remembered it all through a murky shade of grey. Slaughtering Angus' rogues. The moment his beast had decided to claim her rather than kill her. The glow of her radiant flesh in the dimness of the coach. The hitch of her breath as he discovered the warm cleft between her thighs. The sweetness of her cries as she came for him.

The kiss that tied them together for eternity. That was, if he could get her to accept him as her mate.

"Goddamnit!" he hit at the water, showering the bank with a wave of his fury. He whistled for Colm, his Shire steed, and rubbed a wet and tired hand over his face. He was well and truly fucked.

Panic flared in her eyes as he stalked toward her, displacing the meandering water. She struggled backward against the current, but only stumbled and flailed.

"Yer coming with me," he ordered.

"W-wait!" She threw a hand up, effectively stopping him in his tracks. "J-just go. You c-can leave me here."

The hell he could. Her entire body trembled, and her lush lips took on a blue cast. He had to get her out of the water and fast. His ears pricked to the sound of Colm's galloping approach.

"It's too late for that." He reached down for her.

"I-I won't tell anyone what you've done." She cast her eyes toward the east, where the carnage from only moments ago was an acre away, still shrouded in a dissipating mist and tall highland grasses.

He let out an impatient noise. "Ye would rather me leave ye here, naked and defenseless?"

She looked at him like it would, indeed, be the safer decision. "I have a w-wardrobe, lashed to the coach."

"Aye, and do ye want to crawl over twenty dead men and as many horse carcasses to reach it?"

She paled, but then stuck her jaw out at a stubborn angle. "I-I would. I can't go with you. What if the... demon comes back?"

Connor reached down and wrapped his hand around her

thin arm, pulling her out of the water. "That was no demon," he ground out. "Only me."

Lindsay knew by now that resisting him was futile. Though she wanted out of the freezing river, she couldn't bear to be naked in front of him. Not after what they'd done.

What she'd allowed him to do.

She gave a token struggle, trying to disengage the hand clamped around her arm like an iron shackle. But the brute dragged her onto the bank, as a gigantic black shire approached at a gallop. Lindsay crossed her arms in an ineffective effort to cover herself and hunched down, feeling utterly humiliated and exposed.

The Demon used his free hand to snatch the reins and pull the prancing beast to a full halt before unlashing a bundle from the dark leather saddle.

"Here," he growled, unrolling a large, fur-lined cloak and settling it about her shoulders. He at least had the decency to avert his eyes from her nakedness.

"Thank you," she murmured, clutching the warm garment around her and trying to quell her violent shivers. It smelled of leather and musk with the sweet hint of frankincense. Like him.

Silently, he grabbed her by the waist and tossed her bottom onto the saddle, as though she were a sack of grain, and swung up behind her. An angry tension corded his thick muscles. She could feel it through the layers of the cloak and his still-wet clothing. A vein had developed a dangerous twitch at his temple.

"Where are you taking me?" she demanded.

Instead of answering, he reached around her and took up the reins with both hands, effectively securing her between his massive arms, and spurred the stallion into a gallop. Precariously situated as she was, Lindsay had no choice but to cling to him for dear life as they cantered north and west, plunging into the forest. She couldn't tell how far they rode, but the sun had completely disappeared by the time they left the trees, and he slowed to a trot in front of a particularly craggy outcropping of rock. Lindsay didn't see the cave until they were almost upon it.

The giant dismounted before the horse came to a complete stop, and drew his sword as he checked the cave for what she assumed were unfriendly inhabitants. If he thought she would be sleeping in a dank cave, he'd lost control of his senses.

Seizing the opportunity, Lindsay threw her leg over the other side of the saddle, took up the reins and kicked the horse's flanks with all her might.

The blasted beast didn't even move.

"Yaw!" she shouted and tried again. Her heart fell as the horse tossed his head and let out an impatient noise.

"Do ye think me dim-witted, woman?" He sheathed his sword and cast her an infuriatingly droll look as he patted the shire's thick neck. "Colm doesna obey anyone but me."

Of course he didn't. Lindsay narrowed her eyes, replying with more bravado then she felt. "I can't speak to your wits, but abducting me might just prove the most foolish mistake you ever make."

He shrugged. "Maybe so, but I had no choice."

Confused, Lindsay was about to ask him what he meant when he reached up and lifted her to the ground. Goodness but his strength was frightening. As was his size. She blinked up into his startling eyes. They were a lovely color, as vibrant as the highland grasses in the summer. Nothing at all like the fathomless abyss they'd been before when they'd—

Coughing, Lindsay looked toward the opening of the cave. Tucked behind some large boulders, it would appear to a passerby that two large slabs of slate leaned against each other and were buttressed by the mountain. Unless someone ventured closer, it would be impossible to see the depth of the resulting cavern about the convenient size of a small mire hut.

"I have to collect wood for a fire. Can I trust ye not to try and escape me, lass?"

Oh, there was no doubt about it; he truly was out of his mind. "You mark me, demon—"

"I told ye I wasna a demon," he said in a tone she could only have called long-suffering.

"I am Lindsay Stewart, niece of the Regent of Scotland, and I'm no one's prisoner. Even *you* can't be on guard all the time. The moment you turn your back, the first misstep you make,

I'll be gone. And when I return, I'll bring the wrath of the Stewarts and my betrothed Laird MacKay upon you and every corner of your house." Lindsay had seen such threats bring great Lairds and even English nobles to heel when issued by her uncle. She clung to the desperate hope that it would frighten this mean creature.

"Aye, I figured as much." His chest heaved with a beleaguered sigh as he unlatched a coil of rope from the saddle.

Chapter Six

"How can you say you're not a demon?" Lindsay spat as he set to lashing her wrists in front of her and securing the bonds to the exposed roots of a tree. Timber didn't grow tall or numerous in the western highlands, but the roots burrowed deep into the earth. This one must be old and hearty on top of the stony hill in which they dwelled, because the gnarled vines were as thick as her arm in some places.

"Because I'm no'," he answered simply.

"But all those men... you slaughtered them. And your eyes—"

"Those men have been burning, murdering, and raping their way across the highlands. They didna deserve to live."

So it was true. Angus MacKay was a warlord and a marauder. She didn't want to marry such a villain, but she couldn't stay with this... man, either. He posed too much of a threat. Not only in terms of her survival, but to her salvation, as well. Her body still warmed to his touch. She could still feel the press of his strong thighs against her flesh as they rode through the gloaming together. A dark and sinful part of her thrilled to his darkness and strength. "So, you get to decide who deserves to live and die?" she pressed, ignoring the heat climbing her cheeks. "What are you, some sort of avenging angel? A vigilante executioner?"

"Nay, just a mercenary."

"Well, that is even worse. What if any of those men were innocent of the crimes you butchered them for? What sins have I committed that I must be witness to such a massacre?"

He flicked her a glance from beneath thick, ebony lashes, and she might have seen regret soften his eyes before he turned his attention back to securing her bonds.

"You don't have to do this," she offered. "I'm no danger to you."

"I do what I must," he murmured, finishing with the knots and turning to face her. "And I canna let you go."

Lindsay knelt before him, all other options exhausted and a real terror building inside of her. Her wrists slid down the root but held fast. She'd never been tied up before, and considering what this man was capable of, it left her feeling utterly vulnerable. "*Please*. You can let me go," she begged. "I'm on my knees. I'll do anything."

Her captor's nostrils flared and, though his features darkened, a dangerous light illuminated his eyes. He took a step toward her, bringing the front of his damp trews to her eye-level. His mouth dropped open on a steadying exhale and his tongue snaked out to wet his lower lip. "I'll warn ye once, Lindsay Stewart, doona drop to yer knees and make such offers to me, unless yer fully prepared to accept my terms."

Lindsay trembled. She understood his meaning, absolutely. Her tongue wet her lips in a nervous gesture.

"What do you plan to do with me?" she asked, unsteadily. "Ransom me to my betrothed?"

He turned away from her and strode toward the cave opening. "Ye'll have no other betrothed. Not after I slay him."

No *other* betrothed? What could that mean? "My uncle, then?"

He shook his head. "Nay lass, yer coming with me."

"Where?"

"Castle Lachlan."

"Castle Lachlan, but—*Why*?" A dark fear curled deep in her stomach.

"Because yer to be my mate."

"Your... what?" That couldn't mean what she thought it meant, could it?

He paused, looking back at her with angry, glittering eyes. "My *wife*," he ground out before leaving her alone in the twilight.

———————⬤———————

He'd made a mistake leaving her to her own devices,

Lindsay thought as she used her bare feet as leverage against the rock wall. If he thought she would submit to being the wife of a demon – or – *whatever* he was, he could go straight to hell! Or, wherever creatures such as he spawned from. Pulling at the cords and tangles of roots with all her might, she felt her shoulder pop as her strength gave out. She collapsed to the ground, disheartened, but not defeated. If she could get free and gain enough distance on him, all she had to do was find the river Tay and could follow it east to Benmore. Her wrists hurt like the devil now. The rough cords of the rope hadn't been tight enough to be painful or cruel, but with all her struggling and pulling, she'd rubbed the skin so raw it bled in some places. That gave her the idea that maybe if she produced enough blood to make her slim wrists slippery, she could wriggle out of the knots and be gone before her captor returned.

It didn't work. Now the stinging and burning in her wrists caused tears of frustration and pain to spill down her cheeks. As she shifted on the ground, something hard dug into the flesh of her thigh. It was a small piece of shale but had a jagged edge to it.

Aye! Fate finally smiled upon her. Lindsay quickly went to work on the rope, clumsily sawing back and forth. Her wrists protested as her movements caused the coarse fibers to bite into her wounds, but she didn't care, she could taste freedom. To her dismay, the rope was well crafted and took longer to fray than she'd hoped.

It was almost completely dark in the cavern when she heard muffled hoof beats on the soft earth outside. Lindsay's hopes fell and despair threatened to choke her. No. It didn't matter; she'd hide the rock and wait for him to fall asleep, then she'd make her escape.

She gave him her back when he strode in, burrowing in his cloak and refusing to look at him. But her ears tracked his movement as he set to building a fire at the opening of the crevice. Soon the spark flared and threw her shadow against the stone wall. She hadn't heard him strike tinder, and yet the brightness grew as peat and kindling caught flame. The light bloomed brighter as he added larger, dry logs.

She tracked his flickering shadow as he approached her.

How did a man so large move so silently? His nearness made her uneasy, and she shifted within the cloak, painfully aware that she was naked beneath it. Adjusting the hem to cover her more fully, she heard his sharp intake of breath.

"Why do I smell blood?" he demanded in his cavernous brogue.

"I know not," she replied tartly, her heart thudding in her chest. "Maybe it's all the blood you've spilled coming back to haunt you."

He lifted her bodily from where she sat on the ground and parted the folds of the cloak to examine her wrists.

"Good God, lass," his voice was a tortured whisper. The pupils of his eyes rippled and then began to grow, overtaking the iris and spreading into the white. "What have ye done?"

Chapter Seven

Lindsay watched, stupefied, as man was replaced by creature. His muscles swelled and pulsed with blood. Granite black, humiliatingly familiar to her, encompassed his eyes. Lips pulled back from teeth that seemed to sharpen. She hadn't noticed that about him before.

He'd traded his black tunic and trews for a clean linen shirt and a deep blue and red tartan. The MacLauchlan colors. Somehow, the black had suited him, and had reinforced her idea of him as a demon. Now, dressed like a proper highlander, he seemed more terrifying somehow. More dangerous. Because she knew he was really a man, a MacLauchlan highlander whose soul melded with a monster or was possessed by a demon. Despite his claims to the contrary.

He didn't drop her wrists, but held them up as though to show them to her, his features sad and accusatory. An animalistic sound of distress emitted from deep in his chest.

"You're the one who tied me up," she defended her actions. "You're a fool if you thought I would stand for it. I'd be a worthless ninny if I didn't at least *try* to escape capture."

In this form, at least, he had the decency to look ashamed. He rent the ropes and tossed her bindings into the fire, then turned to examine her wounds.

Lindsay could only stare at him. What had he just done? Those ropes had been two fingers thick, at least, and he broke them in a different place than where she'd been fraying them with her stone.

Without a word, he swept her into his arms and carried her to the pallet of furs he'd lain out after setting the fire. Instead of placing her upon it, he sat cross-legged and nestled her onto his lap. He reached for a skein of water from his belongings close by and took one of her wrists from where she held them in the cloak.

Lindsay sat in wide-eyed passivity as he drew her wrists out over the packed earth and rinsed the blood from them with the clean, cold water from his skein. She winced, but the chill of the water seemed to dull some of the raw sting. This behavior was absolutely incongruous with what had transpired between them before. Yet this was the lethal warrior who'd slaughtered twenty men on his own. Here sat the sensual incubus who'd seduced her beyond her wits. Though now he treated her with careful tenderness and gentility.

She watched the firelight play off his brutal, enthralling face. His brows drew down with concern as he finished. Some of the cuts still oozed, so he ripped strips of clean linen from his own shirt.

"I cannot marry you, you know," she tried to tell him, keeping her mind off the pain. Perhaps the Demon was more reasonable than the man. "I'm betrothed to another. And even if you do kill Angus, my uncle would never allow our union."

He placed a soft kiss to her forehead and nuzzled her hair with his nose as though she were an adorable child, then proceeded to dress her wrists with the torn pieces of his shirt.

Lindsay could have laughed, really. Never in her life would she imagine this absurd situation. All but naked in the lap of a lethal reaper who tended her with gentle fingers, explaining why she couldn't become his demon bride. In spite of herself, a wry smirk played with the side of her mouth.

Once finished, he lifted her wrists and pressed the lightest of kisses to each one, as though offering a benediction. His lips paused above the line of the linen and kissed the sensitive skin on the underside where the pulse furiously leapt beneath his touch. Then he trailed kisses higher, and higher still. His full mouth worshiped her flesh. That predatory rumble vibrated through his great body and reverberated through her.

He pinned her with his unsettling eyes. She'd thought them fathomless and unreadable the first time they'd met. How wrong she'd been. Emotions and needs, primal instincts and a bottomless desire swirled within the pools of volcanic ebony. And her face reflected in their depths. Only her and never another.

The rumble intensified.

Lindsay broke contact by squeezing her eyes shut and shaking her head. How could she know that? What were these, desires of her own? Nay. She was merely frightened and weary. Finding meaning where none existed.

His lips touched hers. Not claiming or demanding, as they had before, but laced with a comforting, probing languor. She should have pushed him away, but didn't. Not because of the soft warmth that spread through her at his kiss. Not because his tender strength made her feel protected and treasured, which she hadn't experienced in a long time. But because he was a deadly hell-beast and she couldn't risk his ire. She was his captive. At his complete mercy.

And he could do whatever he wanted with her. Aye. Of course that was the reason.

To her absolute shock, he didn't press her further, but pulled away and wrapped the cloak more tightly about her body. Repositioning her, he stretched out on his side and nudged her to do the same. He created a pillow out of his bent arm and folded the fur upon which they lay over both of them.

There was no way she'd sleep tonight, Lindsay thought as her wrists began to throb. Fears of the coming dawn and what it would bring would surely keep her awake. As would plots of escape. Yes, she must focus on her getaway. At the very least it would distract her from the feel of his hard, warm body behind her. She tried to form a brilliant plan whilst listening to the rolling, content sound he made. It reminded her of an approaching sea storm, the heavy and expectant stillness in the air broken by a distant rumble. She had never slept so well as in a thunderstorm.

Connor always thought that women talked too much. It seemed they were bred with the need to discuss their every thought, desire, action and emotion. In the past, he found it irritating and would make a hasty escape when a gaggle of twittering ladies would cross his path. Now he'd give anything for a word from the lass who currently rode secured between his thighs. But, she'd clenched her pretty lips and refused to speak to him all morning.

He'd never been more disconcerted then the moment he'd awoken in the cave, her sleeping form curled against him. His blood had pulsed with awareness, with need. As had other parts of him. Though what astounded him most was the comforting familiarity of her proximity to him. He'd never be able to sleep again. Not without her beside him.

Dammit.

"We're close to Castle Lachlan." He gestured to the top of the gentle emerald hill they climbed. "It's just over that rise."

"What are you going to do with me once we arrive? Lock me in the tower until our wedding day?" Aye, her voice lashed with barbs, but at least she was speaking to him.

"Nay," he answered carefully, unsure of whether he headed into a trap of feminine designs. "Ye'll be allowed free range of the castle and the MacLauchlan grounds. My clan will welcome ye as one of their own."

"Really? Do they extend that courtesy to all the women whom you've captured and nearly raped, or do I get a special honor because you've arbitrarily decided to make me your demon bride?"

Her words should have angered him, but Connor felt startled amusement. A bark of laughter escaped him at the same time his blood heated at the memory of her responsive body in the mist.

"How many times do I have to tell ye that I'm not a demon?"

"Until Lucifer, himself, verifies the claim." She gave a saucy flick of her hair. "Or, until you tell me what you really are."

"I'm a Berserker."

"A Berserk—no, those are stories told by ancient bards and fishwives. There are no such things. Besides, Berserkers have to kill anything they come across, and you let me live."

"That I did." He smiled, if a bit smugly, very glad, indeed, that she lived. "'Tis why I have to marry ye. And, ye werena almost raped. Ye desired me in that coach."

She twisted in the saddle to pin him with an incredulous glare. "You're really so self-important to think I *wanted* that? You, sir, are sorely mistaken."

Of this, he could be certain. "Aye, lass, ye wanted it. For, a Berserker canna bring harm to his mate, he canna lay claim to her body unless she wants him to." He understood this painful fact all too well.

Chapter Eight

"Connor Douglas Gerard MacLaughlan!"

Lindsay watched with astounded fascination as a wide-eyed Evelyn MacLauchlan dropped her bandaged wrists and charged her captor with the incensed fury of a mother bear. "*You. Tied. Her. Up?*" She punctuated each word with a sharp swat on the arm with a wooden spoon she'd swiped from her apothecary table.

"Wha—she was goin'ta get away." He ducked her barrage, attempting an unsuccessful retreat around the large, round table.

So, his name was Connor. Lindsay never thought to ask. A name made him seem more real, somehow. More—human. It was a good name, too. Fitting, somehow, to the brutal handsome face.

"Out!" The woman pointed to the doorway, currently filled with the bulk of her husband, Roderick.

Connor rubbed at his abused arm, looking like a gigantic chastised boy. "But she's *my—*"

"*Out!*"

Roderick pushed his wide shoulder from the doorframe and clapped his elder brother on the back. "Come, let's let yer woman bathe and dress, we have much to discuss." In an identical move, both men looked back to where Lindsay perched on the window seat. She could only stare at them. They could have been twins but for a few minor distinctions. The same green eyes set in harshly-angled, handsome faces. Though Roderick's sparkled with an untroubled mirth and Connor's narrowed with defensive concern. Comparable bodies of pure sinew and strength draped with the Lachlan tartan drew an appreciative eye. Their hair was the same color of ebony, though Roderick wore his long and Connor cropped his almost to the skull. Lindsay thought it added an air of dangerous brutality to the elder brother. That, and the fact that Roderick seemed downright affable in comparison.

Connor looked like he wanted to say something to her, but he glanced at his brother and sister-in-law and stormed out.

Roderick turned and bowed to the ladies with a wide smile. "*Cuisle mo chroi,*" he crooned to his wife. *Pulse of my heart.*

"Thank you, my love." Evelyn winked and tilted her head to watch in appreciation as her husband ambled off in the direction of his brother. Once Roderick was out of sight, Evelyn set to work at the table, pulling jars and clay pots from various shelves. "I called for a bath to be brought. They should haul it up as soon as the water is hot. You just relax there and I'll make you something that will heal your wrists." She bustled about until she found a mortar and pestle. "I could just *strangle* Connor. I love him dearly, but sometimes that man is thicker than the walls of a mire dwelling."

Lindsay had liked the Englishwoman the moment she'd laid eyes on her, and her esteem had only grown within the last few moments. Though she was short and on the stout side of curvaceous, her golden hair and flaxen eyes set off the sweetest smile Lindsay had ever seen.

"Your husband, Roderick, is he—what I mean to say is—does he turn into..."

"A Berserker?"

Lindsay nodded.

"He does." Her lips tilted up in a secretive smile. "He's been teaching me some of the alchemic magic I'll be using to heal your wrists."

Now regarding the accoutrements with a dubious skepticism, Lindsay raised her eyebrows. Magic? Didn't the woman know she could be burned for speaking of such things? Of course, if she spent her days attached to the two Berserker brothers, what cause would she have to feel fear? Silently, Lindsay turned to look out the casement over Loch Fyne and the bustling, successful village of Strathlachlan. She couldn't see one church steeple in the entire valley. Did these MacLauchlans follow the old ways? Living as a far north and

west as they did, and isolated by the perilous terrain of
Scotland's highland lake country, it would be easy to hide
themselves from the eyes of Rome.

Evelyn startled her by picking up her hand and gently
applying a gritty yellow poultice to the cuts and irritated flesh
of her wrist. "I noticed your accent is different than what I've
heard," she said conversationally. "Mind you, I've only lived
here and Aberdeen besides London, but I can't place yours,"

Everywhere the poultice spread, the pain instantly cooled
and disappeared. Lindsay watched her gentle ministrations
with awe. "I hie from Glasgow, but I was educated in London
for a while where my father served as a Scottish emissary
before becoming Regent."

"That explains it then." The woman wrapped soft linen
around the first wrist and moved to the next.

"I'm inclined to believe this *is* magic," Lindsay moaned.
"The pain has vanished."

"My husband saved my life with this once. It was the day I
accepted him as my mate. His enemy slashed my thigh with
his sword and I would have bled out had he not treated me
with it. 'Twas a miracle." Evelyn smiled at the memory,
reaching for another clean linen. "Trust me, take those
bandages off tonight and you'll be good as new."

Lindsay sniffed it doubtfully. "What is in it?" It didn't
have a detectable scent, and the texture was unlike any she'd
felt.

"Like I said," Evelyn winked at her, finishing with a gentle
knot on the bandage. "Magic. One of the multitude of
advantages to being mated to a berserker."

"Indeed?" A bolt of curiosity snaked through her. She
hadn't been seeing her situation as advantageous in the least.
In fact, she'd been en route to one imposed, undesirable
marriage and found herself thrust into the path of another.

"Oh yes! Magic is just part of it. There's long life, for one.
You see, your life forces would be entwined and a berserker
lives maybe four or five times the length of an average person."
Evelyn talked as she tidied and Lindsay got the feeling she was
a woman who didn't like to be unoccupied. "My Roderick is
very attentive and thoughtful. He's blessed by a Goddess, you
know, so that accompanies unnatural strength and... stamina."

A pretty blush tinged her flushed bosom and crept into her cheeks, but she went on.

"He's very protective, but also learned and fascinating. Oh, you should see the MacLauchlan libraries. Being an educated woman and all, I'm sure you'll want to pass some time in there. That reminds me, be careful not to get those two into a political discussion upon which they disagree, because I just commissioned a new table for the great hall and I'm somewhat attached to the scroll work—"

"These are all qualities of *your* berserker," Lindsay interrupted the woman before she got too distracted by a tangent. It was easy to see Evelyn was happily matched. She glowed with an inner happiness and contentment that made it difficult to be in the same room with her for too long before feeling woeful and inadequate. And more than a little envious. "What about Connor? All I know of him is that he's a berserker mercenary."

Evelyn's face fell while she thought for a moment. "Connor's a very good man," she stated as though she had every confidence. "I admit, he tends to be surly and serious and more than a little high-handed, but he's been Laird of the Lachlan clan since he was sixteen. That came with a Baronetcy and an abundance of pressure and responsibility. Also, his father was a rather unpleasant sort who treated his sons abominably and killed their Mother in a violent rage. Roderick has told me that Connor protected him from his father's punishment many times when they were boys."

"I see." Lindsay studied her bandaged wrists, trying to ignore the pity clenching at her chest. She had to hold onto her righteous indignation. If she didn't she'd have to face her part in what they did together in that coach. And she couldn't. Not yet. "While that's very regrettable, I don't think it excuses him abducting betrothed noblewomen and forcing them into marriage."

A tin bowl made a loud clatter to the table as Evelyn stopped to face her, her eyes wide with incredulity. "He didn't explain it to you?"

Lindsay shook her head, a lead weight in her belly.

"Oh, darling, he can't force you to marry him. Once a berserker chooses his mate, it is up to *her* to accept *him*.

They're powerless until you do."

Lindsay's eyes narrowed. "Is that so?"

Connor paced the length of the armory, trying his utmost not to use his fist to wipe the obsequious smile from his brother's face with fists. Or something sharper.

He was familiar with every inch of this room, from the weight of each weapon stored at the stocks, to the family heritage of each coat of arms hung on the stone walls. Every kin and clan that claimed protection from the MacLauchlan house was represented above the weapons used against their enemies. It had been a prosperous time, of late, for the MacLauchlans. Though the clannish wars raged in the Lowlands, and noblemen fought for scraps of English favor like savage hounds, his valley had been protected from all that. Since the death of his warlord father, Connor had used his own reputation, forged on the battlefield, to create new alliances, broker peace and trade with neighboring clans.

Now, because of the actions of his berserker, he risked the ire of the great Stewart clan and the vicious MacKays. All for a raven-haired woman he did not want nor ask for.

Nay, he couldn't claim that as truth. He wanted her. He wanted her like a starving man hungered for a meal or a doomed man yearned for mercy. He wanted her with a great, yawning desperation that startled him with its savage intensity. He wanted her spread before him, beneath him, screaming his name loud enough to rouse the Gods.

A frustrated snarl escaped him as he ran a hand over his skull.

"I doona see why yer so provoked, Connor. A mate is a great boon to ye. In fact, with both of us mated, the magic we would wield would serve to mitigate the danger from the Norse berserkers who would see line of the Celts ended." Roderick leaned against the armory doorway.

"Do ye think that hasna crossed my mind?" Connor well remembered his brother's battle with Alrik the Blue, a frenetic berserker from the Norse lands. He'd taken Roderick's ability to speak, and almost abducted his mate, as well. It was Roderick's devotion to Evelyn and her acceptance of him that won Roderick the battle and the use of his voice.

"Well, then tell me why yer acting like hellhounds are nipping at yer heels ready to drag ye to perdition?" Roderick blocked his path, interrupting a perfectly good pace.

Connor growled at him.

"Ye've got a beautiful, fiery lass up there just waiting to be wooed. She desires ye, anyone can see that. In my experience, ye can use that to yer favor." He gave a lascivious waggle of his eyebrows.

Shoving his brother out of the way, Connor resumed his pace. "That's not an option," he insisted.

"Well, if yer preparing to win her with yer personality, I'd say my plan has a better chance, but I willna—"

"I'm not going to fucking win her!" Connor exploded. Grabbing a rack full of pole arms, he heaved it over. The weapons toppled out in dangerous directions, but none of them had a point for him. The outburst didn't aid the helpless frustration churning within him. Shoulders sagging, he let out a deep breath. "I should just pack her up and send her away," he muttered. "I was a fool to bring her here."

"Connor," he felt the weight of Roderick's hand on his shoulder and it only added to the load threatening to topple him. He didn't even have the strength to shrug it off. "Why don't ye tell me what this is really about?"

"You know what it's about." They both knew.

"Father?"

Connor glared at the mess of weapons strewn over the packed earth. "We've always been told that a berserker canna hurt his mate." He turned to face his brother, who regarded him with a concerned frown. "But a *man* can."

Roderick looked away, the pain of their mother's death still a fresh wound in his eyes. They'd both found their father that day, years past, when he'd struck their mother too hard while he'd been drunk. They buried their father that day, as well, and had never spoken of it again.

"Since ye've been mated to Evelyn, havena ye ever been afraid that ye'll—"

"*Never.* Doona even say it."

"Well *I* am, Goddamnit! I am afraid of the rage that burns inside of me. Not the rage of the berserker, but that of a man who carries an anger toward the souls who depend on him, this world who would strike him down, and the father who sired him. I'm fit for no woman, Roderick, especially not that infuriating lass upstairs."

"Yer not him, Connor," Roderick insisted. "Ye've proven it to everyone in the highlands but yerself."

"Not to myself. And not to Lindsay. You saw her wrists."

"You said she did that to herself," Roderick said.

"Aye, trying to escape me." He heaved a great sigh. "I made a vow that I woudlna take a mate, that I'd never kiss a woman. Just because my berserker bungled that doesna mean I have to break the promise. It's better this way. Safer."

"I suppose so." Roderick turned away from him, heading back toward the stone entry. "Per her betrothal contract, she'll have to wed the heir to the MacKay clan. I imagine she'd rather take Rory's hand than Angus's."

Connor grunted, a hollow emptiness opening up in his chest where his heart should be.

Roderick continued, his even voice a little too merry for the exchange. "Rory's a good man, if a bit foolhardy. I'm certain he'll tend to her needs... planting little MacKay babes in her belly night after ni—"

With a roar, Connor rushed his brother, pinning him against the armory wall by the neck. He could feel the air pumping though his lungs as his beast rushed to the surface, infuriated at the thought of another man touching his mate.

After a tense moment, Roderick only smiled at him, point made. "Ye canna let her go, brother. I doona think you realize the misery ye'd both be doomed to suffer."

Lowering his head, Connor released his brother. "Christ, I'm done for."

"Nay, this is just the beginning. Now, go hence and seduce yer woman. Win her love. Once ye have it, treasure it and make the choice every day to love her and treat her with kindness and respect. I promise she'll return the favor... and then some." Roderick smirked.

Connor heard the truth in his words. How did Roderick get so wise? Wasn't *he* supposed to be the elder brother, the Patriarch of the MacLauchlan clan?

He worked his jaw a few times, narrowing his eyes and

squelching his pride. "How does one go about seducing a woman?" Usually, willing lassies just made themselves undeniably available to him. Talking a woman into wanting him was uncharted territory.

Roderick just shrugged again, before leaning to pick up the wrack of pole arms. "I didna even have to speak to Evelyn, she was seduced just by looking at me." He threw his arms wide and looked down, as though that should be explanation enough.

Seizing the opportunity, Connor landed a punch in his midsection, knocking a breath from him. "I liked ye better when ye were mute," he muttered.

They strode from the armory out into the bustling sun-lit square of Castle Lauchlan.

"I've been told that from time to time." Roderick snatched an apple from a cart and tossed a coin to the vendor. "But that's usually when I'm right."

Chapter Nine

Connor wiped clammy hands on his tartan and paused in his pacing to stare expectantly at the bedroom door. She should return any moment now. After he'd given Lindsay the night to settle into her castle chamber, he'd suggested that Evelyn take her to the village. Harvest market had commenced a week hence and the ladies could peruse many local and imported riches. In her absence, Connor solicited the aid of the household staff in adorning her chambers in a manner would serve that of a noble bride. After much amusement on the part of the maids at his attempts to help, he was shooed away and assigned the task of making himself presentable.

To him, that had meant a through scrubbing and a clean tartan.

He had to admit, they'd done a fine job. Wreaths of flowers adorned the thick oak bedposts and any other previously unoccupied surface. Innumerable candles threw a golden glow about the room. He'd drawn the thick purple drapes to block out the sunset and amassed a light but decadent supper.

His eyes kept drifting back to the bed, spread with lush violet silks and a heavy fur blanket to ward against the autumn chill. It matched her amethyst eyes. She would look perfect draped upon it, her golden skin glowing in the candlelight, her hair tangling with the silk.

His body responded instantly to the image. Blood heated and sped through his veins, spreading the warmth through every extremity until he vibrated with anticipation. His cock became heavy and full, torturing him with an exquisite ache. Gods, he would worship her. Starting with that gloriously full mouth and reveling in a kiss he'd long denied himself. Then, her breasts would be his next conquest. He'd stroke and kiss them, awakening her senses and making her skin dance with sensation. Once she was begging, he would lay relentless siege to the sweet cleft between her legs with his hands, and then his mouth. He would pleasure her so thoroughly, she would lose all coherence. *Then*, and only then, would he spread her thighs wide beneath him and –

"What's all this?"

Startled by the pique in her melodic voice, Connor dragged his gaze from the bed to the very object of his fantastical musings. She was breathtaking. Even with her glossy hair captured in some kind of netted contraption and covered with a thin veil. His hands fisted at his sides, longing to release it and plunge deep into her soft tresses. She wore a borrowed gown of soft blue and lavender with a golden girdle at her waist, and an expression that could have frozen a charging stag in his tracks.

"Did ye enjoy yer visit to Strathlauchlan?" he asked, trying to ascertain the cause of her ire. If someone had mistreated her, he'd see them drawn and quartered, their limbs displayed in the castle square as a dire warning.

"It was lovely," she answered shortly. "Evelyn is marvelous pleasant company, in fact, the best I've encountered here." Raising a meaningful eyebrow, she examined the room through narrowed eyes, taking in the efforts of the afternoon.

His face fell, along with his hopes for the evening. The lass didn't seem in the least pleased; in fact, her chilly demeanor vexed him severely. He'd prefer her fiery temper and brash wit to this. Mayhap she was hungry. He tended to be a mighty bastard when famished, and she'd been out at the market for several hours. Gesturing to the spread of supper and surfeit of overstuffed pillows, he made a desperate attempt to salvage the effect. "I thought to join ye for a repast, perhaps we may better acquaint ourselves."

Her mask of indifferent scorn slipped a little as she glanced at the sea of candles and fragrant wreathes of Scottish primrose and heather before finally resting on the platters of fresh bread, cheese, fruit, smoked herring and a fine imported cask of wine. He glimpsed a moment of hesitant longing and his hopes rose again.

Until her features hardened. "This is how you were planning to do it?" she asked in a stony voice. "Lure me with practiced seduction so I will *accept* you as my mate?"

Connor wasn't sure he didn't swallow his tongue along with his shock.

"That's right," she hissed. "I know what you want from me, Connor MacLauchlan. I know that I must agree to be your bride before you gain more power."

Struck dumb, Connor just shook his head.

A mirthless laugh escaped lips drawn thin and white with anger. "I didn't believe it at first, when Evelyn told me about magic, despite what I witnessed of you on the road. Until *this*." She held out her wrists, free of bandages. Healthy, lily-white skin glowed in the candlelight, and where raw wounds had been before, fine blue veins pulsed with vitality beneath the translucent flesh. She'd healed overnight, as Connor had known she would.

"But, Evelyn also explained that, though I am your mate and you have brought me to this place against my will, I do not have to accept your hand unless I want to."

Connor saw now, that he'd made a mistake encouraging the two women spend time together. He'd thought that his loyal sister-in-law would work to soften Lindsay's heart toward him. Instead, Evelyn rallied to the side of her maltreated compatriot and gave her all the pertinent information with which to make a decision. Now Lindsay understood that, though she was technically his captive, she wielded all power over his future happiness.

Women! He ran a hand over his head, trying to figure his next stratagem. Gods but she was beautiful when angry. Her breasts heaved against the bodice of her gown, challenging the constitution of the seams. Connor blinked, forcing himself to concentrate on the problem at hand. If he wanted to do more than *look* at her beauty, he'd need to pacify her ire.

She had to know that he didn't just need her, he wanted her.

Planting her wee fists on her slim hips, she glared at him, the ice in her eyes at once turning to violet fire. "I refuse, Connor MacLauchlan, I refuse to be wed to a high-handed, mercenary, overbearing, tyrannical *brute* with more strength than wits, so that *you* may become a more powerful berserker."

A sensation akin to hurt lit a fire in his chest and anger thundered through the weaker emotion, ready to do battle. "When I found ye, ye were en route to marry Angus Mackay, the villainous, pillaging murderer of the Highlands."

"I had no choice in that," she spat. "And I only have hearsay and your word to his character, which isn't much to me at this point."

"Aye? And would ye rather me deliver ye into his hands? Perhaps *then* ye'd know the meaning of the word 'tyrant'." He advanced on her then, wanting to shake her until she came to her senses.

"The fact that you would even threaten that validates my opinion of you." Lindsay stormed to the door and threw it open. "Get out!"

Not a chance. He was Laird of this castle and he would be denied access to no corner of it. The lass was daft if she thought she would order him about. She may have found that she wielded a little more power in their damnable situation, but that didn't mean he'd let her lord it over him.

Crossing his arms over his chest and planting his feet, he towered over her, daring her to issue one more command, to push his temper one more notch.

"Very well," her eyes showed no fear, no hint of retreat. "Enjoy your evening, my lord, *alone*." With that, she stalked out in a pastel storm. The breeze created by the slam of the heavy door extinguished a preponderance of the candles, leaving his world infinitely darker.

Instant regret smothered the fire in his veins like a damp and weighty blanket. He may not have given her any quarter, but he certainly had not emerged the victor. In fact, he lost ground this night. Lindsay wasn't the only one who'd been forced into this situation, but, he had to admit, his shackles were sweeter than hers. He gained an exquisite, hot-blooded mate and the powerful boost to his abilities that would grant an abundance of safety and security to all those under his protection.

What did she get from the bargain? A fragmented and militant berserker with more growl than gentility. Well, there was a castle with plentiful coffers. But, no doubt, her dowry was enough to render that moot.

With a foul curse, Connor plucked up the cask of wine before searching out his own chambers.

Chapter Ten

The next night brought the first successful week of harvest market to a close. This was to be marked with festivities that would have invoked Mabon himself. Lindsay had strolled with Evelyn through fire jugglers and acrobats, bards and puppeteers, amusing herself despite the fact that she'd awoken to a dark mood. Distraction seemed to lift her spirits.

They wandered with the crowd toward the planks that had been assembled in a cleared field for dancing and carousing. The full harvest moon was bright enough to light their revelry and reflected off Loch Fyne with glittering brilliance. Long torches had been staked to the ground and lanterns corded around the makeshift plank floor casting dancing shadows about the night.

The evening was chilly, but hot food and free-flowing ale warmed the cheeks and blood of the Lachlan clan. Now they gathered about, their merry voices drifting through the night as the cheerful cacophony of tuning pipes, flutes, and fiddles rose in their midst.

As though drawn by an innate awareness, Lindsay immediately picked Connor out of the gathering crowd. He and Roderick stood at least a head taller than their kinsman who surrounded a massive barrel of ale perched on an oak table. Connor wielded a heavy mallet while Roderick steadied a tap at the base of the enormous cask, pretending to fear for the safety of his extremities. Riotous laughter ensued as Connor drove the tap home with a one-handed swing.

Lud! But his strength never ceased to astonish her.

Were they not afraid, these fierce highland warriors? Did they not worry that Angus might, even now, be plotting retribution? A tremor stole through her. What if she was the unwilling cause of a deadly quarrel of clans?

A brawny highlander handed Roderick the first tankard, congratulating him for his bravery with a hearty laugh. The next one was granted to Connor for performing the honors. He toasted his brother and tilted his head back and drank deeply.

Lindsay tried not to watch the cords of his neck work over the swallows, or notice the flex in his arm as he lifted the tankard to his lips. His impressive body was well displayed wrapped in a tartan and naught else but his boots. Across his chest, dark tattoos of knotted design spiked and wended through the cords of his flesh, branding him a chieftain in the old way. Likewise bands of knots encircled his biceps. They entranced her for a moment before she broke the spell with a blink. She resented her awareness of him and this vital, inescapable connection between them.

Evelyn linked arms with her and steered them toward the men as the music began in earnest. "They're magnificent, aren't they?" she purred. "I know you're cross with Connor at the moment, but I wish you'd at least lose yourself in the festivities." She cast Lindsay a suggestive look from beneath her lashes. "Berserkers are excellent dancers. It must be some primitive, innate rhythm they're in tune with."

"Indeed?" Lindsay didn't dare to think about it. Something about the words 'primitive' and 'rhythm' sent a dangerous thrill through her.

Roderick's entire demeanor lit from within as they approached, "Evelyn, *mo chroi*, I hope ye doona mind that I promised the first dance of the night to another." Several masculine sets of appreciative eyes turned toward them, and Lindsay ignored one burning glare, in particular.

"And who would that be?" Evelyn asked with a sweet smile as she accepted a sip of ale from her husband's tankard.

"This lovely lass, here, has requested a dance of me and she's so charming I canna refuse." He swept his hand toward a gangly girl dressed in a clean, but shabby dress. She couldn't have been more than eleven, and when she offered a shy smile a few spaces showed that she'd recently lost the last of her child's teeth.

"Well." Evelyn winked at the child. "I can't say that I

blame you, but don't expect me to be sitting here waiting for you to return to me. I'm going to accept the first invitation I have to dance!"

With a possessive kiss for his wife, Roderick swung his dance partner to the floor and opened the evening's festivities. Immediately, a handsome MacLauchlan cousin offered his hand to Evelyn and she succumbed to the call of the pipes and drums.

Trying her best not to feel abandoned, Lindsay offered a polite and inviting smile to the gathered Highlanders, still avoiding Connor who loomed like a threatening shadow. Perhaps one of them would offer an escape to the dance floor.

Instead, they simultaneously seemed to find something rapturously fascinating in their tankards. Mayhap it would be more decorous to stand with the women? Lindsay had noticed a rakish disregard for certain societal strictures out here in Strathlauchlan, but one could never be certain of which rules could be adhered to or discarded in the space of a few nights.

Wandering past the Laird she still refused to acknowledge, she ambled toward the opposite side of the floor where local and visiting ladies chatted and preened in hopes of catching the eye of a handsome reel partner. Though they gave her a few curious looks or polite smiles, the women weren't abundantly friendly. In fact, Lindsay felt a distinct chill from more than a few, especially those wearing the Lauchlan colors.

She looked down at her borrowed gown of deep, royal blue. In honor of the Clan Lauchlan, she'd wound red ribbons in her hair. She hadn't donned their tartan, as she was still a Ross and *not* wed to a MacLauchlan, but she'd thought the gesture of wearing the colors had been a friendly one.

Feeling uneasy, she turned toward the dance floor and sought Evelyn. To everyone's riotous amusement, Roderick reached out and swatted his wife's backside as they crossed each other on the floor. Before she could exact her revenge, their partners swung them wide and they were lost amongst the dozen or so other couples. Lindsay joined in the laughter, thoroughly charmed by the happy couple. A melancholy weight kept her from completely enjoying herself. What Roderick and Evelyn shared was rare and magical. She'd never been destined for anything like that.

Her eyes flicked to Connor before she could stop them. He was watching her, not bothering with discretion. The firelight cast shade in the deep groves of his muscle which cut an imposing figure melded from light and shadow. Those compelling green eyes of his glittered across the entire dance floor, pinning her where she stood. The music retreated and people blurred into a cheerful mélange of faceless color. For a single moment, her world consisted of the unrequited desire she read in his relentless gaze and she was transported back to the dark carriage where he'd found her. The things he'd done to her. Not just to her body, but to her soul. Lindsay found herself inexorably altered by his skillful touch. She'd spent the past nights in sleepless dishevelment, tossing restlessly with fevered need. When she closed her eyes, the blackness reminded her of his stark, possessive eyes as she'd shattered beneath him.

How had he played her so easily? How had he turned fear into desire and then intense pleasure? She was so ashamed. Not only because of what she'd allowed him to do, but because of what she yearned for him to do again.

Overwhelmed by the thought, she broke their connection with a prolonged blink and focused her gaze on the distant lake, hating herself. Hating him.

"Can I take ye round the floor, lass?"

Stunned, Lindsay turned toward the masculine voice. It belonged to a light-haired, stocky young lad she recognized as one of the castle men-at-arms. "Oh, I—"

"Of course ye can, Jamie, I've been making eyes at ye all day." A hand snaked from behind her and clasped Jamie's. Smiling, the man pulled a young maid, who'd been standing behind Lindsay, toward the dance floor.

Embarrassed, Lindsay shook her head and tried to focus on the merriment around her. She avoided Connor's eyes, they held too many of her secrets to acknowledge right now.

As the night wore on, ale and whisky flowed freely, causing men to become bold and wend their way to claim a dance from a willing lass, and more if they were lucky. Time and time again, Lindsay watched with a desperate hope that one of them would offer her the kindness of his hand. As it stood, she was fair certain she was the only woman under four score who'd yet to take a turn. It was as though each of the men went out of their way to avoid her eyes, nay, her very vicinity. In fact, other women had seemed to realize as much, and inched away from her to increase their chances of acquiring a partner. Heart pounding, Lindsay watched the steadily increasing berth around her person widen. What was this about? Had she offended the highland Lachlan's in some way she couldn't have foreseen? In ballrooms from London to Glasgow she'd always been a highly sought-after dance companion. What was wrong with these people?

Balancing on tiptoes, she scanned the crowd, hoping to find the safety of Evelyn's company. But, the woman was nowhere to be seen. After several rounds of frolicking, she seemed to have disappeared. Roderick's broad form was likewise missing.

"Och, newlyweds." The familiar graveled baritone caressed her ear and sent shivers of aroused awareness coursing through her entire frame. Hot breath teased at her ear causing her to want to arch like a cat seeking a fond stroke.

Connor.

Hadn't he just been across the way? How *did* a man so large move with such stealth?

"It's rude to sneak up on someone," she scolded, turning to face him. "Especially in the dark," she told his chest. "Aren't you supposed to be over *there* lording over all you see?"

"I didna sneak." He sounded amused again. Damn his eyes. "Ye would have noticed me if ye werena trying so hard not to. Everyone else did." A furtive glance about verified that the assemblage seemed either very interested in what was going on with them, or trying equally hard *not* to appear so.

Lindsay had to step back from him, the proximity was making her light-headed. The tension coiled in his muscles caused an irrational fear that he might just throw her over his shoulder, carry her into the castle and spend the night ravishing her.

She risked a glance at his face and her mouth went dry. Judging from the storm in his eyes, they might not even make it to the castle before the ravishment commenced.

"Dance with me, Lindsay." It wasn't a question.

She shook her head, trying to capture her wits more than

refuse him outright. Her name sounded like a sin on his tongue and a traitorous part of her wanted to do anything he commanded as long as he said her name like that.

"Ye doona have to talk with me, ye can even stay angry with me if ye like. But I can see ye've been aching to dance."

Was she so transparent? Had the men who'd avoided her company this night sensed the desperation from her and been repelled?

"Besides." He closed the gap between them and pressed against her. Their breaths sped in tandem and she felt as though she could hear her heart beat in her ears. Or was it his? "Our bodies seem to communicate better than our mouths."

He was right. About all of it. But she couldn't bring herself to tell him so. Instead, she put her hand in his and followed him to the floor. The crowd made ample space for them, and they faced each other while the musician began the reel.

Connor bowed to her and she forced herself to return the favor. She'd be damned before showing him any fealty, but the dance dictated it, so she acquiesced. The intricate steps took much of her concentration and Lindsay was grateful she could focus on them instead of the dangerous currents jolting her wherever their skin touched.

"My colors look good on ye, Lindsay." The possessive authority in his voice piqued her simmering temper. She looked up at him sharply. He really must desist saying her name as though it were a provocative word. It was merely a *name*, an ordinary one at that, and it passed from his lips like a delicious profanity.

The dance circled them away from each other to momentarily trade partners. The bearded man in front of her took her hands in a hesitant grip but refused to meet her eyes as he spun her. In fact, he cast anxious glances at his Laird until he could hand her back to him, shoulders sagging in relief.

Lindsay frowned. "You say that as if one could declare dominion over a color, my lord." If anyone would be foolhardy enough to try, it would be the warrior in front of her.

"'Twould be easier to claim than ye've been, lass," he said with a teasing smile.

Despite her ire, Lindsay's heart stopped. Momentarily

fascinated by the uncharacteristically boyish dimple in his left cheek, she didn't notice how closely he'd moved until their bodies almost melded.

"A clever man would have given up by now," she pointed out, a bit more winded than she would have liked.

His large hands spanned her waist and she found herself breathless for the second time that night as he lifted her in a spin. She had to admit it delighted her to be lifted higher and more effortlessly than the other women. Locked in his grip, she felt absolutely stable. There was no danger of him dropping her— or letting her go.

"Well," he said as he deliberately slid her down his hard, warm body. "I've always been attributed with a great deal more brawn than brains."

Lindsay found herself smiling at that, and she reveled in the answering glimmer in his eyes. She supposed she could relate. He had a strange way of stoking her temper, then disarming her in a way that left her completely bewildered and off balance. The longer she remained in his arms, the less capable she felt of making rational decisions. It seemed she could dissolve into an absolutely primitive creature, unaware of reason or consequences. A creature of pure physical instinct, only concentrating on fulfilling the next primal need.

"Besides," his voice deepened. "I canna let you go. Not ever. Not only because of what I am, but because of *who* ye are."

"What do you mean?" she asked, suddenly catapulted out of her body and firmly back into her mind. Did he only want her because she was a Ross? Had his aim been political all this time? Damn but she was tired of being pursued because of who her father had been and who her uncle was now. As Regent of Scotland, they'd have the ear of the King. Who wouldn't want those connections?

Connor was silent for a long time. Say what he might, nothing but sharp intellect shone behind those clear green eyes, and he was calculating something. The worth of her dowry, perhaps? He seemed to come to a decision, his eyes hardening with resolve.

"Because, whether ye've accepted me or not, I've publically claimed ye as my mate. Ye belong with me, Lindsay."

"Excuse me?" she asked, trying to disengage from his arms. He held her fast, not giving up the steps of the dance.

"No man in the highlands who valued his life would dare to *touch* ye. At least not without my permission."

"What?" Aghast, she just blinked up at him, all the charm of the banter vanished, replaced by incensed shock. "Is that the reason I've not danced all evening?"

Connor shrugged. "Aye, they know we've not been wed as of yet and that any approach would be seen as a challenge for what is *mine*."

"Wed as of...*Yours*?" That was *it*! Lindsay wrenched herself from his grasp, not caring if she disrupted the dance. "Do you have *any* idea how lonely and humiliating tonight has been for me?" she hissed. "How *dare* you! How could you even presume that I would consider accepting you as a husband, Connor MacLauchlan? You've never even *asked*!"

She stormed away from him, grateful the crowd parted to let her pass. They might be afraid of their berserker Laird, but they loved him too. She couldn't have borne it to look at him for a moment longer.

His dark, weary stare tormented her enough as it was.

Chapter Eleven

A pervasive restlessness stirred Lindsay's blood as she wandered through the hallways of Castle Lachlan. Raising her candle to light the shadows, she crept as silently as the rushes allowed. Midnight had chimed not too long ago, and most of Straithlachlan slumbered. She'd spent the last two nights locked in her chamber in a self-imposed seclusion. Ignoring the pleas from Evelyn, the entreaties of Roderick, and the loud but empty threats from Connor, she'd only opened her door to allow in the maids and the meals. The Laird of the castle and his kin had been respectful enough not to force their way into her rooms and she suspected the maids reported that Lindsay hadn't made an attempt at escape.

Nay, she'd been thinking this entire time. Pondering the expansive paradigm shift she'd just experienced. Everything she'd known about this world had changed in such a short amount of time.

Everything. Magic was real. The old Gods existed. Men of the land were blessed with celestial powers. One of them had claimed her as his own. And it was up to her to decide her fate.

And his.

For a woman of her station, such decisions were never expected to be settled on her shoulders. Her dear father had loved her, yet had signed a contract with the MacKays sight unseen and without discussing her feelings on the matter. As a woman she'd been considered chattel, a commodity to be traded and disposed of, entirely dependent on a man as her liege-lord. And that had brought her nothing but misery, loss, and peril.

For two days she'd paced and pondered, obsessed and

weighed options. Should she attempt escape and try to reach her uncle and throw herself upon his mercy and beg for protection? Or upon her successful escape, uphold her contract with the MacKays? Their lands were close enough by horseback. In the likelihood that Connor killed Angus, his twin brother Rory would be Laird and Lindsay had heard he was a fair and kind-hearted man. She could carry out her duty to him and try to make a good life for herself...

Connor.

Could she stay here with him? That seemed to be the most dangerous decision of all. Connor didn't just pose a threat to her safety, but also to her heart. She'd always strove to maintain an emotional distance from any decision made for her, promising herself that whatever happened, she'd maintain her pride, her will, her poise, and her spirit.

Connor threatened all of these. He frightened, overwhelmed, and infuriated her. He enthralled, pleasured, and intrigued her. The path he represented was uncertain. Dangerous, even. The man was a mercenary, a beautiful, masculine mercenary. The servant to a warrior Goddess who demanded offerings of blood. And her berserker—er—*the* berserker was steeped in it.

Thus, after two full days of drowning herself in a sea of possible outcomes to hypothetical decisions, Lindsay could stand it no longer. She'd given sleep its due diligence, thrashing about in her bed for an hour or so. Agitated and unable to shake a lonely chill, she threw on a shawl and ventured forth into the night. Evelyn had mentioned an impressive library the day they'd met, and Lindsay felt certain she could find it on the lower floor of the west wing. A book might be just the thing to offer her a much needed escape from her situation.

The faint strains of a lute caused her to pause half-way down the stone steps. Straining to catch the melody, she could barely feel her toes touch the cold flagstones as she stole down the rest of the staircase and peered around the corner of the long left hall, at the end of which,   was the library.

Firelight spilled into the hall from the large library archway. Golden light and inky darkness bent and danced with each other to the solitary tune of the lute. Lindsay felt herself floating toward the melancholy sound, drawn by a melody so breathtaking and disconsolate that her heart bled.

Blowing out her candle, she peeked into the doorway and had to clasp her hand over her mouth to stifle a gasp.

Connor's bulk, silhouetted by the flames in the man-sized hearth, rested against a heavy study table situated in the middle of the library. Propped by a haphazard chair, his strong leg supported the negligible weight of the lute that wept beneath his deft fingers.

He glanced up sharply at her movement, the song dying on an abrupt *plunk*.

She couldn't make out the exact expression on his face, but Lindsay assumed it was any variant of displeasure. The thought made her sad. Though, she supposed, she was still angry with him. Wasn't she?

They stared at each other for a still and silent moment. He looked out of place here, in this room filled with brittle, oxidizing scrolls and well-worn books. The delicate baubles and keepsake treasures that rested on stone columns or wooden shelves sometimes caught the light of the flames and Lindsay worried for them. They were breakable. What if they didn't survive the presence of this volatile force of a man?

What if she didn't?

He stood, breaching the moment. His massive shoulders seemed to bow beneath an overwhelming burden and his brow tightened. "I'll leave you."

Her eyes rested on the fragile instrument resting in the clutch of his massive hands. Instead of crushing it with his brutal strength, he'd coaxed the softest melody from it. One that she wanted to hear again.

"No." She put a hand out, as if to stop him. "No. Please, continue. It was lovely."

For an uncertain moment, he paused and Lindsay held her breath until he sank back against the table. Positioning the instrument, he inhaled audibly and resumed the lyrical tune.

Prompted by her cold feet on the stones, Lindsay padded the few paces toward him.

Likely due to the autumn chill, Connor wore a loose black shirt beneath his tartan and still wore his boots, though the laces had been loosened. He smelled of firewood, hearty scotch, and clove spice, as though the autumn sun perfumed his skin.

Lindsay swallowed convulsively as saliva flooded her mouth. Why was her blood quickening when the mellow strains of the lute should be soothing her restlessness? She tentatively moved a stack of books and a magnifying glass out of the way before taking a perch on the table next to him, but not close enough to touch. If he noticed or cared, he gave no signal.

After several measures he asked, "Were ye lookin' for me, lass? Is there something yer in need of?" He never looked up from his nimble fingers. Her notice was arrested by them, as well.

"I couldn't sleep," she answered honestly. "I came in search of a book."

He nodded, his jaw grinding a bit as his throat worked over a swallow. But his fingers never paused, though the melody dropped into something like a mourning song. "I couldna sleep, either."

Linsday realized she'd never seen him like he was now, loose-limbed and intent on something that required a delicate and practiced proficiency. Never would have thought he had something beautiful in his heart as the music drifting from his instrument. In this moment, he wasn't a domineering baron Laird or a lethal berserker. He was just a man, concentrating on something that brought him solace and sometimes joy. Something he'd had to have done many times, judging by his considerable skill.

The size of the hands and the girth of his wrists astounded her. Sinew danced beneath the thin skin of his wrist as his fingers changed their positions on the strings. Lindsay had never thought of those fingers as elegant or particularly dexterous before. Brutal, maybe. Strong and skilled in clutching a weapon or meeting out death or punishment. But, she supposed, her very first experience with his hands should taught her exactly how varied his skills were and how expertly he applied them.

Her traitorous body warmed at the memory. Though his eyes had been demon black, those hands had manipulated her flesh as expertly as any responsive instrument. He'd used them to coax unfamiliar sounds from her, a climactic song of pleading and pleasure. He'd tuned her most sensitive peak, thrumming it in a percussive, throbbing rhythm until the crescendo had left her breathless and forever altered.

Yes, she should have already known he was a musician.

Letting a captured breath out on a shaky sigh, she shifted uncomfortably and squeezed her thighs together. She'd bloomed at the memory, her soft woman's place becoming as slick and aching as it had been for him that terrible day. Her nether regions flooded as she replayed the images of what had transpired between them. What could have happened had she not stopped him. Memory and fantasy melded until she wasn't sure where the lines blurred and what reality contained.

His tune had sped a little without her noticing much until he stopped altogether. The wood of the lute's neck protested as he squeezed it in a white-knuckled grip. Every muscle tensed beneath his clothing and he became utterly motionless but for the flaring of nostrils and heaving of breath.

"You canna do this to me, woman," he growled. "I can smell..." His mouth opened on a tortured pant and he wet his lips with his tongue.

Lindsay hopped off the table in alarm and retreated a few steps. "What?" she asked. Could he smell her arousal? Nay, that was impossible. He'd have to be... preternatural to do that. Closing her eyes, she berated herself for her stupidity. Her pride would never allow words to be betray her, but her body already had; and his perceptive senses knew exactly what she wanted. What would happen now?

"Ye haveta leave," he barked. "If I look at ye now, I'll be upon ye before ye can scream."

If possible, she became even more wet.

"*Lindsay*," he warned.

"But you said a berserker can't have me without my permission."

"But *I* can." This was growled between clenched teeth.

He could have? All this time? He could have broken her door in with naught but a little will and what was, to him, nothing more than a slight shove. But he didn't.

The thought held a dark and violent appeal.

The neck of the lute shattered beneath his grip. "Run from

me, Lindsay," he begged. "While ye still can."

Heart racing, Lindsay stared into the fire behind him. It licked at the man-sized hearth, spitting hungry embers onto the stone floor from time to time with a loud crack. Her soul had felt like that fire for untold years now, contained within the cold recesses of stone walls, only allowed to burn bright enough to be enjoyed by those who needed its warmth and utility. Perhaps it was time to give it enough fodder to consume them both.

"No," she whispered.

Chapter Twelve

Connor was only distantly aware of the crash the lute made as it was discarded. Firelight glowed off the white nightshift she wore and her hair was a straight, inky waterfall that flowed over her breasts that ended just above her hips.

Grabbing her around the waist with one arm, he pinned her against his body as he plunged the other in her hair and held her head prisoner. Capturing her lips was the sweetest plunder he'd ever wrought. She wasn't pliant, either, in this endeavor. She met his invading tongue with her own, sparring with him and stroking him wetly. Gods, her mouth. Could there be a sweeter place to reside in all the world?

He could think of only one.

Growling at the thought, he released her head and reached down to grab a handful of her tight arse. Without breaking the hot contact of their mouths, he lifted her against him. She had no choice but to wrap her long legs around his hips. She complied, locking them together and winding her arms about his neck. Between the layers of his kilt and her thin nightshift, his aching length cradled itself against her warm cleft and pulsed with an exquisite pain.

Soon.

He couldn't believe she wanted this. Couldn't believe it was happening. Hadn't he come in here to whittle away some lonely, aching hours? Wasn't she still angry with him for being a high-handed incomparable ass?

Maybe. But the scent of her honeyed provocation against him was undeniable. Regardless of what she felt, his mate needed him to pleasure her again. In this, he would not fail her.

They wouldn't make it to a bed. And he knew that in his state, he'd break Evelyn's favorite chaise. Stepping to the table, he held her negligible weight with one hand as he used the other to swipe books and various paraphernalia out of his way. They didn't just fall to the ground, some items flew spans across the room. A magnifying glass shattered somewhere in the distance. He didn't care, except that her feet were bare. He wouldn't allow them to touch the floor until every shard was cleared.

She broke the kiss with a gasp and blinked as though a spell had been broken. Her wide, violet eyes took in his face, which was now turned toward the fire. He knew what she read there, and she gasped in response to its intensity. She was a little afraid.

She should be.

Claiming her moist lips once again, he set her on the very edge of the table, so her core still came into contact with his cock. Splaying his hands between them, he spread them up her ribcage, past her breasts, and gripped the front of her shift.

Ripping it from her was the most satisfying thing he'd accomplished in his lifetime thus far. And it was just about to get better.

Her skin glowed a pale cream against the dark wood of the table. Her hair pooled in the shadows. Once she was bared to him, Connor reluctantly conceded the sweetness of her mouth for the call of other tantalizing regions. Trailing his tongue down the slight column of her neck, he licked at the pulse that fluttered an irregular beat against his mouth, before dipping lower.

Her breasts were impossibly pert and firm. Securing her arched back with his forearms, he feasted on them. Licking at the thin, sensitive skin beneath her rosy areolas he denied the puckering nipples his attention. Lindsay's hands roamed and dug into his scalp and neck, demanding satisfaction. Little insistent mewls burst from deep in her throat. Connor found himself lamenting that his hair was too short to pull, though every inch of his skin reveled in her touch.

She deserved this torment. Latching on to her nipple, he flicked the tip with his tongue and she gifted him with her first moan of the night. Oh there would be many to follow.

He thrilled to the challenge.

Leaving the nipple moist, he drew back and breathed on it. Goose pimples erupted over her whole body and she gave a little whimper. He could feel a wicked smile tilt his mouth as he moved on to the other breast. Reveling in the sweet and salty taste of her skin, he laid her back on the table, freeing his hands to roam her body.

He'd wanted to go slower than this. To explore every inch of her, to touch and claim every part. But he was too hungry, and her scent was too tantalizing. Connor's fingers found the sweet triangle of curls immediately and, as he dipped in to coat his finger with her moisture, his teeth gently dragged across her nipple.

She gasped his name.

Yes.

It had been well done of him to keep his clothing on through this. At the sound of his name leaving her lips he would have thrust into her and blindly driven himself into oblivion. Not yet. He had to taste her first. To drink from the well that sprang for him. He couldn't deny himself that right. He couldn't deny her that pleasure.

Though he bent over her, his left hand came up to splay across her chest and hold her down. "Lie still," he commanded, then sank to his knees on the rough stone.

"What are you—?" Her small, breathy voice cut off when he wrenched both of her legs wide with his hands, pinning her to the table.

He growled at the sight of her. Slick, glistening, and pink nestled in a bed of glossy ebony curls. He'd never seen anything so beautiful.

"Connor I—I... Oh God!"

The first taste of her was ambrosia; the second catapulted him to heaven. Nothing could have prepared him for the softness he found, the pliant flesh that yielded to his lips and pulsed against his tongue. He explored her mercilessly, enjoying the quivers and jerks of her strong, lean thighs beneath his palms. Her legs were fighting his effortless imprisonment, struggling to close around his head and retreat from his relentless mouth. Or to hold him prisoner there.

Her moans and pants and cries were the sweetest music

he'd ever heard, deep and throaty with enough entreaty to stoke his manly pride. Tracing her inner petals with his tongue, he avoided the tight bud that was the center of her sensations. He sucked those folds of flesh into his mouth, flicking at them playfully and following the rolls and jerks of her hips. Denying them both, he dipped lower, probing at her core with his tongue. He was rewarded with a rush of her desire that he lapped up with an appreciative groan.

His body was wound tight as a fucking bow string. He needed inside of her. And fast. He started to wonder if he was going to survive this. Fire thrummed through his veins and his berserker simmered too close to the surface. What if he hurt her?

"Connor... please." Her desperate plea pulled him out of his head. "I need—"

She needed a climax, and he needed to give it to her.

Her moan was raw when he latched onto her; it grew to a cry when his tongue went to work. He settled his shoulders into his occupation and allowed her to rest her feet upon them. He drove her to edge again and again until her skin shimmered with sweat and her legs trembled with effort. When her voice became hoarse and her pleas weakened to painful groans, he released her and reached beneath her thighs to span her waist with his hands.

Here, mo chroi, he thought, *I give you this, along with my heart.*

Her shoulders arched off the table and she screamed. Connor followed her bucking hips with his mouth, determined not to yield her flesh until he'd wrung every last quiver of pleasure from her. Her hands gripped his forearms, fingernails biting into his skin. God he loved this. He could spend the rest of his life here, if she'd only let him. He wanted to close his eyes, but couldn't, the beauty of her coming for him awed and stimulated him. He was so fucking hard his cock wept beneath his tartan.

But he didn't want this moment to end. Didn't want the rapture on her face to die. He had put it there.

And he already wanted to do it again.

When she collapsed back to the table, little quakes of aftermath quivered across her belly, she released her death-grip on his arms and let out a long and shaky breath.

Connor didn't move though, after he pulled his neck away from her. He couldn't. He'd been locked into place by the sight of the one thing that could threaten this perfect moment.

Her nails had made him bleed.

Lindsay lay in a boneless puddle on the hard table, as little tremors and pulses of pleasure still snaked through her at various intervals. Glancing down, she could only see the top of Connor's head between her shamelessly spread legs. Then he started to rise into her line of vision.

The black eyes came into view first, and then the berserker towered over her prone body, his muscles twitching with ready urgency.

In truth, any fear or uncertainty melted away. She knew this gentle beast. Connor was hard, proud, stubborn, and authoritarian, but his berserker, while primitive and uncouth, had treated her with tender gentility. The irony was not lost on her.

And she was beginning to understand them both.

He reached for her, and she rose to him. His unfathomable black eyes tracked her every move like a rapt predator as she carefully unlatched his brooch and let his tartan fall from his shoulder and down lean hips. He stroked her hair and caressed her shoulders as she unlaced the front of his shirt and revealed the dark tattoos on the massive expanse of his chest. When she pulled the shirt toward her, he obediently lifted his arms so she could ease the garment over his head.

No words were needed between them, as he didn't speak in his death-dealing form. Lindsay knew he could read her every intent. His dark purr flared deep in his chest and Lindsay felt a smile of pride and pleasure reach her heart.

The firelight burnished his skin a dark bronze. Lindsay couldn't stop the tremble of her hand as she reached out to explore his awe-provoking body. The muscles of his chest were hard and warm beneath her hand, but the skin was utterly smooth. He hissed in a breath when her other hand joined her first in their bold investigation.

God, but he was huge, and the thought of all this barely contained power unleashed on her body spiked with an urgent need that had been banked by her first climax.

His hard stomach heaved beneath her hands as she drew them lower. It never occurred to her to be shy, not after what he'd just done. Instead, she wanted an equal part in this. She wanted to give what she received and claim the pride that he displayed at her pleasure.

When she wrapped her fingers around his sex he growled and gripped both of her shoulders. His preternatural eyes rolled back and disappeared into his skull. His lips curled away from sharpened teeth, but she still was not afraid. This part of him was beautiful and mysterious. Lindsay wondered what it felt like for him, locked and pulsing with blood beneath her hand. Did it please him like his touch had pleasured her?

She moved her hand from the thick base of his shaft to the plumb head where she discovered a slick bit of moisture clinging to the opening. This was his desire for her. This was what he would release deep inside of her when the time came.

All right, maybe she feared that a little. He was so big, so hard and heavy and hot as a branding iron. He could split her in two.

His grip contained more pressure as he guided her to lie back. His lips were suddenly everywhere. Her jaw, her mouth, her neck, nibbling at her ear, returning to her mouth. His urgent need stoked the fire within her. His lips burned her skin as though branding every inch they touched as his.

And she was his.

Though she'd tried her best to fool herself. Fought it, and him, since the beginning. Pretending she was the mistress of her own fate. From the moment she'd met the abysmal gaze of the beast and he'd decided to spare her, she'd been helpless against her primitive answer to his absolute claim.

A relentless throbbing had taken residence in her sex and, as he pulled her hips closer to him to position himself against her, the heat of his cock against her most sensitive flesh promised satisfaction. But he could not have what she did not expressly give.

"Take me, Connor," she commanded. "I am yours."

Baring his teeth again, he joined them with one powerful thrust.

Chapter Thirteen

The berserker remained bent over her body, soothing and distracting her with enticing licks and hungry kisses. He throbbed inside of her, hot and pulsing, but refused to move until she relaxed beneath him.

After the stinging pain passed and her body accepted him, she nudged at him with her hips and kissed him deeply.

With his inner rumble vibrating through her, as well, Connor began to move. Slowly at first, with absolute care, stretching her tender flesh around him as he almost withdrew, then plunging forward again, gaining ground within her. She moaned his name. He growled his pleasure.

She should have known that growl was a warning.

The rhythm intensified then, as though he tried to rally the last vestiges of his self-control. But the dam had broken and the flood of passion engulfed them both. Before long his hips pumped into her with wild abandon. Some thrusts angled so deep, he touched her womb. The sensation rocked her, causing her to cry out each time.

Wild, deep, elusive pressure built inside Lindsay until she clawed at him in desperation. Her nails scored his back. Her teeth sank into his ear, his shoulder, his neck. His grunts and growls spurred her on as his skin stretched tight over straining muscles.

With a ferocious snarl, he reared back. Crushing her to him with one arm he lifted her leg high against his waist with the other. This angled his cock impossibly deeper and touched something inside her that catapulted her into the stars. A burning and potent ecstasy jolted through her with such intensity it would have thrown her back had Connor not had such a strong hold. Her whole body convulsed, possessed by a demon of unrelenting lust, indulgence, and bliss. She cried his name to the skies, a supplication for mercy or a plea for fruition, she couldn't be sure. She didn't care. White-hot pleasure like this couldn't go on forever. It would swallow her into the abyss that swirled in her lover's eyes. Mortals weren't supposed to comprehend the divine, but in that moment, Lindsay was certain she stared into the face of his Goddess and was blessed.

His thunderous bellow permeated her haze and grounded her into the moment. She felt him swell and kick deep inside her body, releasing a warm rush against her womb. He was most beautiful in this moment, coming apart in her arms, his eyes containing the two halves of his nature.

When the storm passed, they stayed locked together for an endless span of time. His panting breaths hit the top of her hair and hers broke on the tattoos of his chest where she rested her cheek.

"Did I hurt ye, Lindsay?" Connor's deep voice held a hint of terror. His release must have freed him from the Berserker's hold.

She tested her muscles with him still inside her and enjoyed his breathy hiss.

"A little," she admitted with a smile against his skin.

"Ohh... Christ..." he let out a tortured groan and withdrew from her.

Lindsay tilted her head back to look at him. He was looking from her torn and discarded nightgown back to the fireplace as though he didn't know whether to cover her or hurl himself into the flames.

She took his face in her hands, forcing his tormented gaze to meet hers. "Take me to bed, Connor MacLauchlan," she ordered. "I want to look into your green eyes the second time."

With tenderness born of incredulity, he lifted her into his arms and wrapped them both in his tartan.

Lindsay stirred alone in her bed, surrounded by violet and sunshine. A luxurious stretch brought twinges to muscles only recently awakened and awareness of a sublime satisfaction emanating from within. She hadn't felt Connor leave this morning. Though after conveying her to her room, he'd exhausted her with his tender and passionate mouth. She barely remembered falling asleep against his chest. Hardly a word had passed between them that wasn't command or plea in the darkness. They hadn't spoken of the future. They didn't profess to love. But they set aside their insecurities, fears, and aspersions and gave themselves over to the intensity of emotion and sensation flowing between them.

Energized at the thought of seeing him again, Lindsay threw her covers off, bounded out of bed, and dressed. She made it through her morning toilette in less time than she probably should have, and left in search of Connor and breakfast.

As luck would have it, she found both in the same place.

Breakfasts were simple and held in a sunny nook off the solarium overlooking the loch. Evelyn sat at the square table, flanked by the hulking Lachlan brothers, looking fresh and lovely in a bullion kirtle that matched the rope of golden curls braided down her back.

"Lindsay! Wonderful of you to join us." Her face was full of warm delight as she rushed from her seat to pull her into a tight hug. "I've set a place for you at every meal, just in case." Evelyn motioned to an empty seat directly across from her. Hearty bread, oils, fruits and cheeses lay out in abundance. An empty goblet stood where she was to dine.

Despite her unorthodox circumstances concerning her status as a "guest" in castle Lauchlan, Lindsay was shamed by her discourtesy to the lady who'd shown her nothing but sweetness. "Evelyn... please forgive me for—"

"Speak nothing of it," the woman cut in with an insistent wave of her hand, "Just sit down and balance the conversation."

Feeling suddenly shy and demure, Lindsay sat and smiled at Evelyn as she took her adjacent place. She also cast a polite smile at Roderick to her right, but was unable to look above Connor's forearms, which rested on the table. Instead, she studied the four neat crescents her nails had marked the previous night and tried to suppress a blush.

"Good day, my lord." She tore a crust of bread and poured

nectar of pear into her goblet to dip it in. "I trust you slept well?"

"The night passed very vigorously, my lady." His murmur was a rumble of amusement.

Linsday coughed and dropped her bread in her lap. "Is that so?" She retrieved the crust and fidgeted so that she didn't touch her cold hands to her burning face. "And this morning?"

His dark chuckle washed over her. "I spent the morning in the library, cleaning the remnants of a hasty occupation."

Lindsay risked a sharp glance at him then. His eyes sparkled at her, much like the sun off the deep loch. He looked younger, somehow, relaxed and at ease. In the white light of morning, his strong, tanned face took on a boyish cast as he quirked a mischievous smile at her.

Suddenly she couldn't catch her breath.

"What kind of occupation?" Evelyn queried, her eyes narrowing on the both of them.

"A rigorous study in conquest, you could say," Connor answered, his hot gaze never breaking from Lindsay's.

Lindsay bit back a discomfited smile. "I've become quite fond of your library, sir." Popping a grape in her mouth, she rolled it about with her tongue before biting down. "So far, I've found it quite gratifying."

Connor's hand fisted. "I should show you the old Rectory, I can promise a *religious* experience."

Roderick made a choking sound around a mouthful of smoked fish.

"Just promise me that nothing happened to my chaise." Evelyn managed to look horrified and pleased at the same time. "I imported that from the continent! I won't even let Roderick have me on it."

Roderick swallowed, smirked, then said, "Ye would if I tried."

Evelyn swatted him.

"Actually," Connor addressed his brother. "It was your magnifying glass that didn't survive the night."

The younger berserker's brows drew together. "What... were you doing with my magnifying glass?"

"Nothing, it just got in the way," Connor shrugged.

Lindsay hid her abashed smile behind her hand. How

could this family discuss such things at the breakfast table of all places? She took some responsibility for her banter with Connor, but here they were, easy as you please, reporting the casualties of their new-found passion.

She'd never been so mortified in her life. But neither had she never been happier. Nothing could ruin such a perfect moment.

"My Laird, I have a missive from the MacKay." Jamie Dougal, Connor's man-at-arms unceremoniously strode across the solarium. A solemn expression sobered his animated face. "Angus is calling for your blood and demanding his bride."

Chapter Fourteen

Two days, eight hours, and twenty seven excruciating minutes. Lindsay calculated the time since Connor had strapped his sword to his waist, his double-bladed axe to his back, and kissed her good-bye at the gates of the stables.

"I have things to say to ye, Lindsay, but I doona want them punctuated in the blood of your betrothed." His gaze had been intense, meaningful.

She'd fingered his scorched black leather armor, unwilling to let him out of her sight. "Will you not take Roderick with you?"

He shook his head, "Angus wanted me to bring Roderick, which makes me worry that he's planning violence against castle Lachlan. I canna leave ye unguarded, ye've become too... precious to me."

He hadn't looked at her as he'd said the words and Lindsay understood that such declarations were alien to him.

"Roderick would lay down his life for my mate as well as his own; ye'll be safe with him."

Heart full, Lindsay hadn't been able to say the rush of words bubbling up her throat either, for fear she'd beg him to stay with her. He couldn't do that. He wouldn't put the people of Straithlachlan and the surrounding clans under his protection in danger on her behalf. And it would stain her soul to ask it of him.

He'd meet Angus on MacKay lands, and there her vile betrothed and his remaining band of pillagers would meet their deaths at the hands of his berserker.

She grasped his neck, pulling his head down to meet his lips with her own. Throwing her maelstrom of emotion into the kiss, she pressed her full body against the hard leather of his armor and he crushed her to him in an almost painful grip. Yes, their bodies did seem to be able to convey what their words could not.

"When will you return?" she'd asked breathlessly when they broke apart.

"I'll revisit your bed in two night's time." he promised, before mounting Colm and galloping south, toward MacKay lands.

Lindsay kept herself busy in the apothecary with Evelyn, or out in the market with Roderick. She enjoyed an easy rapport with Connor's younger brother, appreciating his quick wit and easy smile. Though evening meals with the three of them were full of lively conversation, an undercurrent of tension laced through every moment their Laird was absent. Lindsay tried to fill it by slaking her curiosity about their kind.

"Do you and Connor ever fight together?" she asked. "Or would you end up trying to kill each other, as well?"

Roderick smiled, his dimples identical to his brothers, made her miss Connor all the more. "Nay, in fact, Berserkers recognize each other, and were bred to fight alongside one another in battle. It is very difficult for us to slay another of our kind."

Evelyn had reached out and caressed her husband then, gratitude shining from her golden eyes.

"In fact," Roderick continued, after kissing his wife's hand. "It's unlikely for a berserker to kill those of his own clan, who he's sworn to protect, unless they provoke him."

"Provoke?"

"Aye, kind of like beating a hound. He'll be loyal until he rips out yer throat."

Lindsay nodded with a relieved smile. "I'd wondered about that, fearing for every child about the keep who'd skin a knee."

"Actually, once a berserker is mated, he has more control over his change, and his magic. I've heard tell that he could even learn to will the change regardless of blood, though I've not had chance to test the theory." Roderick shrugged, as though completely comfortable that the time would come.

Lindsay had looked for Connor's return that night, readying herself with a fragrant bath and brushing her hair until it shone a glossy black and crackled beneath the comb. Her body warmed with anticipation of his touch, of his possession. Sitting on the edge of her casement, her ears had strained to hear the sounds of his stallion's hooves carrying him back to her arms.

The night had been long and darker than any other in Lindsay's entire life.

"He's been late before," Roderick soothed her at breakfast the next morning. "We both have. Besides, he'll skin my corpse and wear it if I leave the two of ye unprotected."

"Castle Lachlan is a sound keep. You have the men-at-arms," Lindsay had argued. "And the added hands of the men at the market, should something happen."

"Tell that to Connor if he returns and finds me missing," he'd said wryly. "Doona worry lass, if he's no' home by tomorrow morning, I'll go after him."

Lindsay had remained perched upon the library table for untold hours watching the slow progress of the morning sun through the sky.

Something was wrong. She felt it in her blood. In her very bones. Her stomach churned with dread and something akin to pain. She wasn't merely worrying. A sick and terrible knowledge tingled at the base of her skull causing her head to ache and her heart to pound.

"You have to go to him." Stunned by Evelyn's voice, she looked up to see the woman framed in the grand archway, a frown lining her forehead.

"What?"

"Connor. He's in danger. If you don't go to him tonight, he's going to die."

"Have you word of him?" Lindsay launched off the table and hurried to Evelyn, looking for a missive. "What has happened?"

"I can't be sure." Evelyn worried her lower lip. "I know

this is going to sound unorthodox, but ever since I was a girl I've been able to foresee the deaths of others." She grasped Lindsay's hands in a desperate grip, her earnest gaze burning with veracity. "He's trapped at Dun Keep almost a day's ride from here."

Lindsay looked at the sun as it rode high in the noon sky and her heart plummeted. "You said he would die tonight? It's already too late for me to make it."

"You might have a chance if you ride like a demon. Leave now. Take one of the Arabians." Evelyn turned and they sprinted through the hall in a frantic dash for the stables.

"We should get Roderick," Lindsay called.

"*No*," Evelyn cried. "If Roderick goes, the same fate awaits him. It *must* be you. In fact—" Her soft brown eyes lowered to the floor. "I didn't tell him."

"I understand." Lindsay blindly followed Evelyn as she was pulled down hallways barely familiar to her. "What do I do to save him?" Frantically, she considered her aspects. She knew nothing of combat. She'd never been attributed with an abundance of intellect or a head for stratagems. She was neither strong nor particularly courageous. In fact, her arsenal had only ever been a pretty face, a self-serving wit, and a sharp tongue.

"That, I cannot say." Evelyn led them through the stone square that separated the keep from the armory and the stables. "All I know is that you're his only chance."

Lindsay froze in the doors of the stables, watching dumbly as Evelyn ordered and oversaw the preparing of her horse.

Of course she was going to go after him. To question that never even entered into consideration. She wasn't going to let him die. He still had 'things' to say to her. Apologies to make. Undying devotion to pledge. He'd promised to return and she'd hold him to that promise even if she did have to go after him and drag his lumbering, oafish arse back to Castle Lachlan herself.

Connor MacLauchlan wasn't dying this night. There was no way he was getting out of this that easily.

It caused her some pause, though, wondering what could possibly be fearsome enough to endanger the life of her ferocious berserker. She was about to find out, and she was his only chance.

"Lord help us both," she whispered.

Chapter Fifteen

Only five men held the chains to the iron clasped about his throat. Five. Connor scoffed at their underestimation of his lethality as he allowed shackles to be clamped about his wrists. He tugged on the left one with a flex of his arm, dragging ragged chains through both hands of one of his captors. The skin of the man's palms broke and he had to turn from Connor in order to hide the wells of blood.

Connor bared his teeth in a sneer. Bloody idiot should be wearing leather gauntlets. Obviously, he'd slaughtered the most elite of the MacKay warriors at the river Tay, and Angus was left with this sorry lot. He almost felt sorry for the bastard.

But the villain didn't deserve a moment's pity.

The sharp sting of a cane broke on Connor's bare back, and he swallowed a curse. It would welt and bruise, but wouldn't draw blood. Angus was more clever and maniacal than his father had been.

"Get the fuck out of here before he sees ye bleed," Angus ordered to the injured man as he strode into the tiered stable. His dirty grey eyes narrowed in his severe, thin face as he watched them spread Connor's arms wide and chain him to the thick loft beams. Folded pads of linen were shoved between the manacles and his flesh, to prevent them from cutting him. Not as a courtesy, but as a precaution.

Connor snarled at Angus, but didn't lunge at the man. For behind him, a heavy warrior held a dirk to the neck of a trembling six-year-old girl. If her blood was spilled, Connor would berserk, and would not only rip Angus's limbs from their sockets and beat him to death with them, he would systematically massacre the forty or so innocent highlanders huddled in the corner of the stable.

One of which was Rory MacKay.

Sometimes the berserker was a blessing; other times, like this, a curse. He'd failed his charge to Rory. Distracted by the needs of his heart, he'd procrastinated coming after Angus and endangered these people. He should have known, should have foreseen that Angus would have no problem using his own divided clan to achieve his ambitious ends.

He wanted to apologize to Rory, who stood in front of the unarmed cluster, as though he could single-handedly protect them. Held at sword point by a score of soldiers, the crowd, comprised of mostly women, children, and the elderly, couldn't tear their eyes from the child held hostage in front of Connor. Sometimes, they'd glance at him in fear, crossing themselves against his pagan evil. Sometimes they looked to Rory for hope, or to Angus for mercy. But most of their collective notice remained on the frightened hostage as silent tears streaked her wee cherubic face. Her hair was a mass of glossed ebony, just like Lindsay's. If their love ever produced a sweet lass, he imagined she'd look something like this angel.

Connor closed his eyes against a yawning ache in his chest. He'd never spoken to her of love. He should have before he left. He should have told her what he'd begun to want. To look forward to.

To feel.

He couldn't take his eyes off the child.

"Do ye know why yer not dead yet?" Angus leaned in close, secure in his false assumption that he'd leashed a berserker.

Connor didn't dignify his question with a response, but promised a slow and torturous death with his glare.

Angus's lips parted in a nasty rendition of a smile, revealing a mouth full of crooked, unkempt teeth. He was leaner than his father had been, built with wiry strength and thinning copper hair. "Because I'm using ye to set a trap for yer brother. Not unlike my own brother used ye to set a trap for me." He motioned to Rory, who looked ashamed but furious.

"Let them go, Angus. They're yer people. Ye are their Laird." Rory pointed to his brother. "This is between us."

"They supported yer mutiny," Angus hissed.

"They challenged yer tyranny," Rory fumed. "But why punish the lassies and the wee ones? This is no way to—"

A cane crack to the back of the head dropped Rory in an unconscious heap of armor and limbs. Angus sneered at his brother's limp body and turned back to Connor. "After I dispense with you and Roderick, I'm marching my men north to Straithlachlan to rape his new wife and raze yer castle to the ground. Then I'll take back what ye stole from me."

Now secured to the beams, Connor tested his iron shackles. They held fast. "Why?" he demanded. "Why attack my people?"

"Because yer brother murdered my father. Because you slaughtered my men and captured my Ross bride, who was my only connection to the monarchy. Yer crimes must be answered for!"

"What about *your* crimes, Angus MacKay?" he spat. "The blood of yer people cry out for vengeance. Yer father was a traitor. He'd have been burned by the Stewart had he survived the battle. Roderick did him a favor by relieving him of his head."

Anger turned the man's grey eyes silver before he reached up and kneed Connor in the gut, again careful not to spill any blood.

Connor laughed, if somewhat breathlessly. "Ye'll never lay yer hands on Lindsay Ross you filthy fuck. I'll have yer head first."

Knowledge flared in Angus's eyes and a slow smile spread across his cruel face. "Soft on her, are ye? Perhaps you've already claimed her as a spoil of yer victory against my men." He leaned a little farther forward, lowering his voice to a murmur. "Let yer last thought be of me between her legs, night after night, erasing yer memory from her mind. Whatever she suffered at yer hands, she'll suffer three-fold at mine. Mayhap I'll have to raise a berserker bastard as my own." He barked out a laugh as Connor lunged at him, only to be pulled short by his iron shackles. "Aye, can ye imagine that?" Angus turned and petted the little girl on her dark head before reaching for a thick cane. Her reedy whimper left a gaping hole in Connor's heart.

A sharp pain tore through his arm, as Angus brought the

cane down on the bend in his elbow. "Avoid his kidneys," he ordered his men. "I doona want him pissing any blood."

Connor kept his eyes fixed on the terrified gaze of the child as Angus and his men began to beat him in earnest. "Look away, wee one," he gasped. "Doona watch."

Unable to turn her head, she squeezed her eyes shut and Connor was able to relax a bit. No stranger to beatings, he gritted his teeth and tried to formulate a plan.

Night fell. Hours passed. Panting and bruised, Connor had begun to despair of finding any scenario that wouldn't end with these innocent people dying along with the MacKay soldiers. He couldn't live with that stain on his soul and he knew Lindsay would never be able to look upon him without seeing a monster. Their delicate, blooming bond would be severed and he would be crushed under the weight of his sins. He studied the little girl again, who'd cried herself to exhaustion and now lay limp in her captor's hold.

There *had* to be another way.

As he shifted most of his weight on one knee, as the other was likely broken, a terrifying tingle of awareness coursed up his spine.

Lindsay.

She was close.

"This little bird is demanding an audience with ye, Laird." A fat, dirty man with soot in his graying beard held Lindsay's arms in a brutal grip as he led her to stand beside the mean bench that Angus had converted into a table.

"*No,*" Connor breathed. At the sight of her, his soul reached out, dragging his body to lean against his chains with all his strength. "Lindsay. No." His voice sounded dark and low, even to his own ears, laced with a desperation that had never been a part of him until now.

She didn't even glance at him.

The Laird of the MacKay clan didn't look up from the quail he was tearing apart with his fingers and shoving into his mouth.

"Throw her in the corner with the others," he commanded.

"But, sir, she claims to be—"

"I am Lindsay Ross, daughter to the former greatest Regent of Scotland and niece to the man who currently holds the title. I *demand*, in the name of that great station, that you release every one of these people at once." Her eyes flicked to the small girl who'd stirred at the commotion of her entry and was again threatened with the edge of a blade.

Connor remembered a similar threat she'd meted out to him when they'd first met. He loved the sound of her haughty, superior tone. He loved the strength of courage that held her posture ramrod straight. He loved the violet retribution blazing in her eyes. He loved... her.

A fear, dark and bitterly frigid, washed the pain from his body, dousing him in bleak, numb impotence. He knew at once, in the darkest recesses of himself, that he would die for her, kill for her, slay everyone in this room and be denied the glory of her company, just so she could live on unharmed. Part of him was ashamed. Part of him thirsted for blood.

After a stunned moment, Angus stood, wiping the grease from his thin, cruel mouth with his shirtsleeve. Possession gleamed in his eyes as he scanned her from the top of her shimmering raven hair, to her generous mouth, to the curves displayed by her velvet purple dress. She'd donned the color of royalty.

Clever lass.

She didn't shrink from the lascivious perusal, but gave as well as she got, making it perfectly clear that she remained unimpressed.

"How bold of ye, lady Ross, to make such demands." Angus towered over her, crowding her with his body.

Connor let out a low warning growl.

"Release them, eh? Even yer berserker captor?" Angus tracked her every response very carefully.

Faltering for the first time since she'd entered, her gaze fluttered to Connor and her poise slipped for the slightest instant before she jutted out on obstinate jaw. "I said *everyone*."

With a snort, Angus paced back behind her, breathing into her ear. "And what would I receive in return for meeting your conditions?"

"Safety from the wrath of my clan, from the arm of the

king."

"Ye'll have to do better than that, my dear. The berserkers have sealed their fates, but if ye want to save these people—" He swiped with is hand to the frightened occupants of the room. "Ye'll have to honor our betrothal contract."

"Don't ye dare!" Fury coursing through him, Connor forgot his injuries and lunged toward Angus. The beams groaned and protested beneath his struggles, but the shackles held fast.

Lindsay shot him a quelling look, but a telling blush crept up her chest and colored her cheeks. "I've already been deflowered by Laird MacLauchlan. Our betrothal contract is then considered void, as I am no longer in possession of my virtue. Surely you'd want someone else."

Angus smiled and wrapped his oily fingers around her shoulders. "You know nothing of my desires."

"Take yer fucking hands from her," Connor raged. "Mark me, Angus, I will bathe in your entrails."

The little girl let out a soft cry as her arm was wrenched painfully behind her. Lindsay reached forward as though to stop it, but was held captive by Angus's hands on her shoulders.

"Calm yerself, MacLauchlan, we doona want any unpleasantness to befall the lassies." Angus turned a wide-eyed Lindsay to face him. "As I've already explained before ye appeared, I doona mind if ye bless our clan with a berserker. Be he bastard or no, he'd become mine by law, and he'd fight for my clan."

"He'd always be a MacLauchlan," Lindsay spat. "They would come to claim him."

"They could try," he shrugged. "But I canna say I mind that your channel has already been shaped, my dear. I only care that I'll be the one fill the void from now on." Angus lowered his head and dragged his lips across Lindsay's neck.

Connor snarled as his gaze tracked the shudder of revulsion that trailed down Lindsay's spine. He was going to force the man to eat his own heart *after* he peeled the skin from his body.

With a visible swallow, Lindsay forced out a laugh. "I highly doubt that, my Laird, it would rather be like a twig trying to fill a tunnel shaped by a timber log."

Angus's head snapped up. "Mouthy bitch!" He back-handed her with such force she lost her balance and fell to the ground.

Connor's ferocious roar caused his own ears to ring.

Lindsay looked up at him, a triumphant glimmer shining in her eyes. Her lip had cracked beneath the blow.

The tiny drop of blood was all Connor would need.

Chapter Sixteen

The berserker emerged. His demon-black eyes swept the room as muscles rippled beneath muscles, pushing the veins pulsing with blood and power to the surface of his skin.

Mouth open in a terrifying roar, the sharpened teeth gleamed in the torchlight, causing some of the women to cry out in horror. His answering cry silenced them all as he stepped forward and pulled on his bonds. The woadish tattoos on his chest furrowed and the cords of his shoulders and arms strained against the beams. A reference to Sampson came to mind as Lindsay watched the entire structure of the stable shift.

The wood gave a sharp crack as a warning before the entire loft collapsed, burying at least three of Angus's men beneath the wood, heavy oak casks, and bales of straw that weighed as much as a man.

Unleashed, Connor wasted no time further terrorizing his prey. He had blood yet to spill. Hurling the chain that hung limply from his shackle at one soldier, it hit the man with the speed of a whip and crushed his face. He circled the warrior on the adjacent side in a blur of movement and stilled just enough for them to see the heavy chain wrapped about the man's throat. The berserker decapitated him with a mighty tug.

His eyes fixed on the soldier who held the little girl between him, Angus, and where she'd fallen. Lindsay realized she had to do something or the sweet child would die.

Leaping from her spot on the floor, Lindsay snatched the little girl from the slack-limbed man the instant before Connor ran his own knife through his voice box. The girl wrapped her tiny, trembling body around Lindsay's and burrowed her face into her neck. To spare the child from having to witness any more of the absolute destruction, Lindsay turned to face the carnage and walked backwards toward the large stable doors. The panicking MacKays pressed as close to the walls as possible, but Lindsay knew that once Connor had finished his slaughter of the soldiers, he'd turn his voracious blood lust on the women and children.

The door she'd entered was now blocked by debris, leaving the wide livestock entrance the only means of escape.

"Run," she commanded over her shoulder. "Open those doors and flee."

"Aye, my lady!" A chubby older woman, and what appeared to be her stout daughter, ran to the crossbeam of the stable door and struggled to lift it from the hitch. It took several of them a desperate try before they hefted it free. The sound of their struggles were drowned out by the death moans of massacred men.

Lindsay kept her eyes on what Connor was doing, watching her tender lover of the previous night exact punishments so violent she could barely reconcile it.

It seemed as though he was saving Angus for last.

The door only opened a crack before heaving a loud protest and catching on the stone. The collapse of the loft had compromised the entire structure, which had been of simple craftsmanship to begin with. The adults began to thrust the children through the man-sized opening one at a time. The older woman attempted to pull the child from Lindsay's grip, but the girl wouldn't let go.

"I know her people, lady, I'll see her home." The apple-cheeked woman put a gentle hand on her arm, though her eyes tracked the progress of the berserker, but her movements remained brusque and efficient. One didn't get to be her age in the highlands without seeing a life's share of bloodshed.

Unlatching the child's arms from her neck, Lindsay kissed her. "Run, little one," she urged, as the other woman shoved her through the door into the waiting arms of her daughter.

The cacophony of bloodletting began to wane until one terrified masculine plea remained. Lindsay turned to see Connor slowly advancing on a retreating Angus. He'd picked up a heavy, broken beam from the floor, implausibly holding it with one hand. He crushed the tyrant's legs first with a one-handed blow, ripping a high-pitched scream from the villain's throat.

Lindsay had to admit that her own heart thrilled to the sound. When evil bled, it was difficult for even the softest heart to mourn. The second blow crushed Angus's chest in, and the third flattened his head with a sickening crunch.

Finished with his warrior kills, Connor turned his attention to the last few of the women filing out behind her. With a hiss he charged them, angling to leap around Lindsay and crush them into the walls.

Lindsay backed closer to them, throwing her hands wide. "Connor, no!" she cried. "Let them leave." He pulled up short, snarling. Though, when he looked down at her, his black eyes went to her lips and they softened. At least, she would call it that. Grunting, he lifted a finger to wipe at the tiny trail of blood that had leaked from her wound. He made a soft sound of regret.

"I'm all right," she crooned. "Let's—"

A moan sounded from behind him, and Connor's head whipped around.

Rory had stirred and struggled to push himself from the earthen floor. With a massive effort, he achieved a sitting position and held his head with another beleaguered groan.

The berserker leapt for him at the very same instant that Lindsay lunged for the chain that still hung from the shackle about his neck. She dug in her feet and tugged, desperate to save the new Laird of this decimated clan. Her feeble strength wasn't enough, and her feet made shallow trails across the packed earth.

"Connor, stop!" she cried to no avail. "Connor I... I accept you!"

He froze.

"I accept you as my mate. You hear me?" His shoulders rolled and a force of some kind seemed to ripple through his great body. "Now... don't kill anyone else or I shall ..." how did one punish a berserker? "Be very cross with you if you do," she threatened. There, that should strike terror into his heart. She rolled her eyes at her own ineptitude.

Suddenly, an elated sensation stole her breath, and though

her soul soared, it seemed to bind to his with links stronger than the iron chains she clutched. It was as though they'd been weaved into the ether with the fibers of the strongest silk, unable to be rent apart by any force imaginable.

It was fate. It was choice. And he was hers.

For a moment, no one breathed, then he turned to her, his green eyes shining with incredulity and, for the first time since she'd met him, aching vulnerability.

"Tell me you meant it," he breathed. "Tell me you accepted *me*, Lindsay, not just to save those people."

Lindsay looked at Connor and truly saw the man within him for the first time. His eyes, raw with unchecked emotion, glimmered with affect she'd never seen before. Hope. Trust... Love. It *was* love, fledgling but pure that pulsed between them and she was humbled by the gentle, unstoppable force of it.

"I accepted you the moment I accepted you into my body," she admitted. "I just lacked the courage to say it until now."

He lunged for her, pulling her against his body and searing her soul with a kiss. She didn't even notice the pressure on her cut as their mouths fused. He devoured her with a frantic desperation until she placed her hands on the sides of his face and softened the kiss before pulling back.

"You're going to have to stop getting blood on all my fine dresses," she teased. "At least, this one's borrowed."

He let out something between a groan and a laugh. "I love ye, Lindsay Ross. Having ye as my wife and my mate will complete my life. My very existence will belong to ye. My body, my soul, my magic and my beast will—"

Lindsay put her finger over his lips, lifting an eyebrow at him. "I may be your mate, but it's not certain I'll be your wife, Connor MacLauchlan," she quipped.

"Why?" he asked, nibbling on the tip of her finger. Her body warmed to the movement of his lips.

"Because." She extricated herself from his grip and took hold of the chain about his neck. Tugging him toward the door, she threw a saucy look over her shoulder.

"Ye still haven't asked."

UNWANTED

A Highland Holiday Novella

Chapter One

The Scottish Highlands, Winter 1411

The high-pitched wail tangled with the scream of the wind whipping over the rocks. It surely wasn't human. What in the name of man or beast could make such a noise?

Without his preternatural hearing, Finn wouldn't have been able to hear the reedy sound over the cacophony of the storm. Nor could he heed the pants and yips of the starving wolf pack tracking him through the snow.

He drew his sword and hatchet. Whatever it was, he could kill it.

He pointed his sealskin boots and jogged toward the racket with anticipation. What danger would he vanquish in the Solstice storm? The Highlands were steeped in tales of shape shifters and vengeful faeries. Perhaps a demon?

Finn's purpose on this isle was a lethal one. To prove himself to those at the temple of Freya who would doubt his lineage and loyalty. But a good fight would warm his blood.

He bared his teeth in a snarl as he leapt atop and over one of the giant stones that littered the Highlands. Landing in a crouch in the snow, Finn spun to face the creature, his weapons raised for attack.

And froze.

Limbs straining against their bindings and a face as red with rage as he'd ever seen, the wee babe squalled at a pitch Finn would never have imagined humanly possible.

He made a face. Did all babies make such a horrific noise? If so, how did the world ever come to be populated? Perhaps this was why women cared for little ones. A man would likely murder his own progeny after ten minutes of such a sound.

He knew they were surrounded before the scrawny wolf leapt between him and the infant. The beast's intent was the child's soft fleshy neck. Finn kicked his hatchet out of his belt and embedded it into the animal's jugular before it could lunge for the kill.

The child was lucky that only human blood brought out his Berserker lust. Running the few paces toward the squirming bundle, he snatched it out of the gathering snow. Spinning about, he locked eyes with the alpha and snarled. They stayed like that for a moment, each beast sizing up the other.

The alpha was a female, large and strong, with dark grey and white fighting for supremacy in her winter coat. She rippled with aggression.

Any other day, with any other opponent, she would have ordered her pack to slaughter, and she would have emerged the victor.

Not this day, Finn thought, and growled again.

Lowering her head, the alpha turned, and she and her pack disappeared into the wind like a lethal mirage.

Finn looked around for any sign of the child's people. The storm was such that he couldn't be certain if snow fell from clouds or if the wind whipped the deep drifts about to beat at whatever would dare to stand against it. He could see for some distance, but it was all arctic wilderness.

Maybe he should leave the babe to its fate? He knew all too well how cruel the world would be to a fatherless child. But his hand had already killed to save it. And the thought of discarding this life made him as cold on the inside as the merciless storm.

He looked around in desperation one last time before studying the purple, contorted face of the child who hadn't let up its angry yowling.

Retrieving his axe from the dead beast, he swiped it through the snow and then returned it into his belt, all the while holding the tiny burden in his other arm. Finn tucked it into his cloak, hoping the warmth would shut it up. Somehow, that seemed to make it angrier.

The Gods must be punishing him.

He'd been following the shores of Loch Fyne for a time,

and could see the lights of Strathlachlan grow closer when he crested each small hill. At its edge, Killrock Keep, also known as Castle Lachlan, glowed like a beacon in a sea of white.

Finn ran through the snow, grateful now more than ever for his supernatural speed and endurance. The faster he could divest himself of the burden, the better. He didn't stop until he reached the outskirts of the village. The town square had been forsaken due to the storm. Solstice dawned tomorrow and townsfolk still reveled in the warmth of their neat row houses and cottages. The strain of lutes, pipes and song accompanied by the roar of laughter tangled with the wind. Finn sank further into his furs, though the chill that snaked through him had nothing to do with the weather.

The trade street had been locked down, and each stall or business sat dark and deserted. The only light spilled from the large inn and tavern where cheerful sounds of drunken revelry filtered through thick, sturdy walls. Finn tried once again to quiet the baby's cries. Which is to say, he ordered it to cease its yowling. It only squirmed harder within its meager wrapping and found an entirely new octave in which to suffer.

Letting loose a string of curses in English and then his own Nordic language, he pounded on the door to the inn hard enough to shake the rafters.

The door swung open immediately and the smell of ale, roast mutton, and copious unwashed bodies assaulted his senses.

"Got no rooms left," a heavy, aging wench hollered at his chest over the din of the common room. She looked up when he pulled the hood of his furs back. Heat and interest sparked in her dirty gray eyes. She thrust a hip to the side and narrowed her shoulders, creating a deep groove in her already cavernous cleavage. "Even for the likes of ye, love, lest ye want to warm *my* bed."

The child started screaming in earnest. This time he agreed with the whelp.

"Wot's this then?" Her thick brogue, deepened by libations, muddled the words.

"I found it in the snow."

"Then the poor bastard's hungry."

Finn flinched at the word *bastard*, but the woman didn't

seem to notice. The look on her ruddy face told him that she was reconsidering her offer.

"He needs a woman." Finn shoved the bundle toward her.

"He needs a *nurse*." She recoiled, swinging the door toward him. "Ye canna leave him here."

Finn blocked the door with his fist. "Then where do I find a nurse?" he growled through clenched teeth.

Her eyes went round as saucers and the sharp tang of her fear filled his nose. "A-at the end of the row on the left," she stammered.

Finn turned and pulled his hood back over his head as the heavy door slammed against him. He had to leave this babe with someone tonight. For on the morrow he must carry out his holy charge.

To assassinate Connor and Roderick MacLauchlan.

Chapter Two

By the time she'd finished her hip bath, Rhona McEwen shivered so violently her muscles protested. It felt as though they would lock her joints down and she would become a standing statue of ice and pain.

Casting a baleful look at her dwindling cache of wood, she decided to go without a fire again tonight. She hadn't the coin to buy any more from the woodcutter and she didn't want to consider the alternative means of payment. The next time he came by, she might have to take him up on his salacious offer.

The only ray of hope in her frigid world was the request from Castle Lachlan. Lady Evelyn MacLauchlan was in the middle of a difficult pregnancy and she wanted to meet with Rhona on the morrow and maybe appoint her services. The prospect thrilled her, but she'd have to figure out how to survive in the months between now and the birth of the Laird's niece or nephew.

Shivering into her best stockings and shift, she regretted the bath to her very bones, but she couldn't think of presenting herself at the castle smelling like she slept next to the goats and the chickens.

The flame from her lone candle flickered in drafts from the howling wind that leaked through too many cracks in her walls. In the unsteady light, she searched her one-room dwelling for her kirtle and skirt. She could have sworn she'd stretched it out next to the hip bath to smooth the wrinkles. It wasn't beneath the furs on the small, under-stuffed mattress, nor draped on the lone oak chair next to the fireplace. She rummaged through her ancient trunk and found only her other soiled shift, a lone pair of shoes and patched wool cloak. Those were the whole of her belongings if she didn't count the cupboard where she kept extra supplies for any babe that might be left with her.

She could have sworn she hung it up by the... Oh Lord. She braced herself and turned around.

The garment lay crumpled inside the fireplace, its dingy grey melding with the ashes. Blast it! She must have disturbed it while dragging the hip bath into the corner by the annex opening to the stables. Of all the fool things to do. Maybe she should have lit a fire on the eve of such an important meeting, if only to make sure she could see her surroundings properly and avoid such a disaster.

Retrieving the garment, she sat on the edge of the bed to inspect the damage. Ash and soot smudged one entire side of the bodice and sleeve, though the skirt was relatively unscathed. How could she show herself at Castle Lachlan dressed in this? Surely such fine ladies would turn her away. It was too late, and too cold to wash the garment. It would never dry in time.

Sinking to the bed on trembling legs, Rhona considered giving in to the exhausted, frustrated sobs trembling in her throat. She couldn't just yet. She still had to express her milk before going to bed or she'd hate herself in the morning.

Even more than she already did.

A pummeling knock almost shattered her door. She shrieked with surprise and leapt to her feet. Her heart threw itself against her ribs. The pounding repeated, this time shaking the rafters of the stable.

"Who's there?" she called, hating the terrified catch in her voice. Rhona was answered by a sound she was all too familiar with.

The wail of a hungry child.

"I'm coming." Discarding the kirtle to the trunk, she grabbed one of the furs from the bed and threw it around her shoulders before lunging for the latch.

She only opened the door enough to block the wind with her body, afraid it would blow out her candle.

But she needn't have bothered.

The man at her door was the size of one of the boulders that were scattered about the Highlands like ancient, hulking guardians. His enormous body buffered her doorway against the wind and snow.

Rhona gasped and craned her neck to look up into the shadow of his hood where his face was hidden. She could only make out a strong chin and hard mouth drawn into a tight frown. A thrill of fear raced up her spine. In this storm, no one was about to hear her scream.

"It won't stop."

Rhona jumped as heavy arms thrust a wailing, wriggling bundle at her.

"Are you the nurse?" The voice was deep, cavernous, with a guttural accent Rhona had never before encountered.

Still unable to completely recover her wits, she nodded and opened the door to grant him entrance. It may not be the most intelligent thing she'd ever done, letting this unknown giant into her home, but he might have coin. Also, she couldn't bring herself to turn away a hungry infant in distress.

He had to bend at the waist to enter. After Rhona secured the latch, she turned and jumped to see him holding the baby out to her like an offering. Though the infant had to be at least a month or two old, he could cradle it in his gigantic hands.

Rhona just blinked at him dumbly.

He dressed like a barbarian. A cloak of speckled white and silver fur hung to his knees from shoulders as wide as an aged oak. Warm, fur-lined boots, the likes of which she'd never seen, wrapped about his calves.

He didn't just take space, he claimed it. His form dominated her tiny dwelling, filling every free corner with his essence, if not his own heavy limbs.

"It won't stop," he repeated in his smooth baritone, breaking her trance.

"O-of course." She snatched the baby from his hands, careful not to touch him. If the barbarian noticed, he didn't comment.

Rhona carried the sodden bundle to her cupboard, where she extracted clean linen for changing and another for swaddling. The babe's blanket was much too thin for such weather. She looked down into his angry wee face and murmured to him, not that she expected it to make much of a difference until he was changed, warm, and fed. Cheeks that needed fleshing out were chapped and red with cold. The little body was quickly losing strength, its angry struggles becoming weaker, the cries thinner.

"Hold on for me, dear heart," she crooned, then glanced toward the man whose back was to her as he inspected her modest home. He'd pushed his hood off his head, exposing long, straight hair that would have been as white as his cloak were it not for threads of gold brought out by the candle's flame.

Rhona had to avert her eyes lest she be caught staring. "Where's the mother?" she asked.

"I found it in the snow by the Loch," he said gruffly over the cries of the babe. "You live in a stable."

Rhona frowned while she worked, not appreciating the disapproval in the stranger's tone. "I do not. I live in a room off of a stable. The stable master's home is attached to the other side of the building." Perhaps her room had once been a spacious stall, but it had a fireplace now and she wasn't about to concede the point to him. Not when he used that tone of voice.

"What is through there?" He was examining the rickety, half-sized door through the wall next to the fireplace and adjacent to her front door.

"My goat and chickens," she explained, hating that she sounded so defensive.

He grunted.

"And you found *him* in the snow," she corrected for good measure, as she tied the new nappy on and disposed of the soiled one.

"What?"

"*Him*. The child is a boy."

He didn't answer her and she didn't know if she cared for him to. She rubbed at the baby's freezing limbs, hoping to improve the circulation. She stood and tucked him into the fur with her, hoping to warm him with the heat of her body.

How could someone abandon such a helpless wee creature?

Rhona looked up into the face of the enormous stranger and lost her ability to think. Nor could she breathe. Their proximity was too close, though he stood across the room.

He leaned against her small fireplace and scrutinized her from eyes so intensely green and beautiful that she could barely fathom it. Something about his stance belied the relaxed posture. A leashed violence vibrated in the air around him sending tendrils of energy reaching for her. He made no move, but Rhona still felt the urge to back away. Strong, perfectly formed bones structured a visage that could have only been sculpted by a master. He was the image of an archangel, surely. Only those brutal, wrathful heavenly warriors could dare to possess such golden masculine beauty.

"It's not working." He thrust his strong chin to the screeching, wriggling body beneath her fur. "I'll give you this if you can make him stop." He took a coin from a pouch hidden in his cloak.

Rhona's mouth went dry. She couldn't exactly tell from where she stood, but it looked like gold.

She dared not hope.

"Please blow out the candle and sit there," she murmured, gesturing to the chair.

His cruel brows drew together in a scowl. "Why?"

"So I can feed him."

His eyes dropped to her breasts and he squinted, as if he could see them hidden beneath her fur. He swallowed, frowned, and then gave a curt nod.

Divesting himself of his heavy cloak, he uncovered a tunic the color of the sea in a storm and soft-looking, animal-skin trews. Strapped over his mesmerizing hips were weapons so large and frightening that if they hadn't been hidden at the time, Rhona may not have let him past her threshold.

Not that she would have been able to stop him.

Her heart threatened to escape her, again, and she clutched the babe closer to her. Lifting his eyes to hers, the barbarian reached out and snuffed the candle flame with his palm, drenching them both in stormy darkness.

Chapter Three

Finn tested the strength of the rickety chair before settling the whole of his bulk upon it. He couldn't take his eyes off the woman as she blindly stepped to her trunk and sank across from him, still clutching the noisy child.

She couldn't know that her request to snuff the candle was meaningless. That he could see her in the darkness. He could study her soft features as intently as he wanted.

And he *wanted*.

The instant she'd opened her door, with her wild copper curls glowing in the light of a lone candle, his body had responded to her. He'd initially planned on abandoning the babe to her care with some coin and being about his business.

Instead, he was furiously trying to figure out how he'd let himself become folded into this ridiculous chair.

It had to be her voice.

Soft and husky, with a touch of rasp escaping through a lilting Scots accent, her voice held him in a thrall that was at once mystifying and disturbing. Until now, he'd never met a woman who'd dared argue with him, and this lady had yet to offer him an agreeable word. Even still, her voice thrummed a vibration so deep within him that his Berserker purred with it.

And demanded more.

She shrugged off the fur that protected her from his view and it pooled around her.

Finn forced a swallow around his dry tongue.

Apparently confident that she was shrouded from his view by darkness, she reached her free hand up to her shoulder to unlatch the buckle on her threadbare shift and let it fall to her lap.

Any other time, he would have been ferociously aroused by the sight of such full, creamy breasts. In fact the sight of this woman, bared to the waist, ignited warm embers of desire low in his gut. But a fascinated awe superseded the provocation as he watched her position the child at a plump nipple.

"Here you are, sweeting," she murmured. "This will keep you."

Miraculously, the bairn's angry squalls faded into a series of frantic grunts, an impressive sigh, and then blessed silence.

The miracle woman parted her lips on a soundless breath and closed her eyes, as though feeding the babe gave her great relief.

Would that he could incite such a response.

Finn balled his hands into a fist, feeling like a foul intruder on a soft and intimate moment. But he couldn't bring himself to look away, so he craned his neck to watch a ritual as old as time, but completely foreign to him.

The child had burrowed his hand into the generous flesh above where he took greedy pulls at her breast. A little ring of moisture gathered at the corners of his mouth, as if he took more than he could swallow. Now that the whelp wasn't splitting his ears, Finn didn't mind the look of him so much. His eyes were too big for his skinny face. All the babies he'd had chanced to see, which he had to admit hadn't been many, were fat-cheeked and dimpled.

Finn frowned, a cold pit forming in his chest. His nostrils flared and anger simmered to the surface. How could someone just discard a helpless life such as this? He wouldn't let the boy starve. The babe would be sheltered from the gnawing desperation of an empty stomach. He'd never smell the scent of plenty and be denied because of the circumstances of his birth. He wouldn't have to fight the dogs for the scraps of a meal.

This Finn vowed.

"Where do you hie from, stranger?" Her question surprised him. He'd never conversed with a woman before. He did little in the way of talking at all. He had his sword. And his axe. He had the respect and fear of those beneath him and the derision of those above him. What use was conversation in either case?

"North," was the best he could come up with.

Her eyes shifted restlessly and she chewed her lip. It seemed as though his answer unsettled her. "What brings you to Strathlachlan? Are you here for the Solstice or perhaps for Yuletide? Are you visiting someone?"

"I am duty bound," he responded honestly. *To murder your Laird.*

"Oh?" A wet, sucking sound came from the bundle and she reached a hand in to make an adjustment. "There are no markets or fishing this time of year. All the animals are scattered to the valleys so you're neither trader, fish-monger, herder, nor farmer."

"I am none of those things." *I am a death bringer.*

She furrowed her brow. "You are a soldier, then."

"I am a warrior." *I am a Berserker.*

What was she doing to him? That voice. It soothed him, absorbed him. Piercing the shades of silver and shadow that was his perception of darkness, it wrapped about him like a velvet cloak. It calmed the monster inside of him, stroking over his skin until he wanted to purr like a weak and sated kitten.

He was a warrior.

But *she* was dangerous.

Finn stilled as she lifted her free arm to her other breast. She cupped the full weight gently, testing it with a slight squeeze, then feeling her way around the side, running a finger across the rosy nipple.

The chair's arm split beneath his grip.

She paused, lifting her face blindly in his direction. "Are you all right?"

"Aye," he forced out. Of course he wasn't fucking all right. Desire slammed into him with the violence of a war hammer, stealing the breath from his chest. All the blood warming his body collected in his cock until it throbbed along with the desperate pounding of his heart.

Was this permissible? Did it mean he was depraved? There was a child between them, a helpless creature that she nourished with her body. Why, then, did the sight suddenly inflame him beyond all reason? Of course she had the most beautiful breasts he'd ever laid eyes upon. And, granted, the sight of a woman fondling herself was a most luscious and fantastical thing to behold. He realized she did it for practical purposes, safe in the assumption that she was hidden from his view. She meant not to tempt or tantalize him, but here he was, tortured beyond his physical capacity.

The child let out a disgruntled squeak as she pulled him from her breast and readjusted him to the other side.

"Don't you fret, wee one," she murmured. "There's plenty to fill you."

And I've plenty with which to fill you, he thought, and ground his teeth together hard enough to make his jaw pop.

"What is your name?" she asked, turning her attention back to him.

"Fionngall. Finn." His throat felt tight as he watched her eyes in the shadows. He remembered their color in the candlelight, the same as the shifting northern lights of his homeland. Prismatic and iridescent blues, greens, and golds accompanied by surprising hues spanning the entire spectrum.

A man could lose his soul in those eyes.

Her generous mouth lifted with amusement. "That makes sense, I suppose."

"How?"

"The meaning of your name."

Finn's brows drew together. "I was not aware my name had meaning."

"Of course it does, especially to me. It means 'fair-haired stranger,' which you are." She smiled in the darkness, as though it was directed somewhere close to his shoulder. "Every name means something. Mine's Rhona McEwan, for instance. Rhona means 'wise' or 'ruler' though, sadly I am neither." She gave a wry laugh.

Finn's mother had told Finn once that he'd been named by his father, before he discarded her to fend for herself. His mother had hair the color of cedar barrels. Finn knew all too well that he resembled his father. She told him that through her tears while dragging him through the winter snows toward the temple of Freya. His features had been the reason she'd abandoned him to his fate. But a Gaelic name, one with *meaning*?

"Rhona." He forced the memory from his mind and tested

her name on his tongue. It tasted sweet and guttural. Like mead and sex.

"Yes." Her voice sounded warmer than before. Huskier.

"You have a man... a child?" If she did, he didn't provide her with much. Finn frowned with disapproval. And, where else would he be on a night like this if he could be wrapped in her soft embrace and nuzzled against those generous breasts?

He could smell the dramatic shift in her emotions before she spoke, and knew he'd made a grave mistake in the asking.

Rhona's stomach gave a jolt of unease that spread through her bones. She had nothing. No one. But how did she say so without leaving herself utterly vulnerable? Of course, she was naked to the waist and completely at the mercy of the warrior. If he wanted to hurt her at any time, she would be powerless to stop him. Even if Eoghan still lived, she doubted that he would have been much of an obstacle to whatever this giant of a man took into his head to do to her.

Swallowing her apprehension, she decided that she'd sealed her fate one way or the other by opening her door to him. She had a job to do and he had gold. If he paid her, she could survive a little longer. For whatever that was worth.

"I have no husband or child," she told the darkness, squeezing the wee babe closer to her bosom. "I mean, I-I did, but I don't anymore."

"Why?" His cold voice held no trace of sympathy nor cruelty. In fact, the inflection rarely changed. It unsettled Rhona, who was used to passionate, raucous Highlanders with booming, melodious brogues. This man, Finn, was stoic and cold, leaving no hint to his emotions, or that he even possessed any. He seemed as arctic as the far-north from whence he traveled. And just as lethal.

"They were... taken from me," she answered carefully.

"When?"

"A year or so past."

"How?" His voice sharpened with something akin to interest.

Rhona blinked, shocked at his audacity. Did he want to rip open the scars of wounds too freshly healed? Was he truly so pitiless, or just ignorant?

"What bold questions you ask." She threw as much censure into her voice as she could muster.

He was silent a moment. When he answered he sounded truly puzzled. "It takes boldness to defeat your enemy or challenge your leader. It takes no boldness to ask a woman a simple question."

So it was ignorance, then. Did he ever have a lot to learn.

"In any case," Rhona continued sharply. "It's not a story you want to be hearing."

"It is," he insisted. "I do." A loud creak split the darkness as he adjusted himself, and Rhona worried about the structural dependability of her poor chair. "I find I want to know how you came to live in this stable. Why you're all alone on the eve of the Solstice." The newly discovered desire didn't seem to please him, though he didn't sound particularly angry either.

She was equally conflicted about his confession.

'Twould be most helpful if she could see his features and gauge his reactions. Rhona remembered that his face was chiseled with planes and angles by the hands of a master. That his immense body was wrapped in the finest, strangest clothing she'd ever seen and he carried gold from the continent in a heavy pouch. This kind of man would make her most uneasy in any circumstance. In the past, she'd never bring herself to meet his eyes, let alone carry on a conversation with him. In truth, she'd always been shy and demure, terrified of conversation, let alone confrontation. She'd been a mouse. A rug for others to tread upon.

But loss and desperation changed everyone, didn't it? It was difficult to dread disapproval, censure, or humiliation when you no longer even feared death. There was something of a liberty in that. What else could anyone do to her now? What mattered but the next meal, or finding wood for warmth? Why should she care if this fair-haired stranger was offended, disgusted, or simply bored by her tale?

The expectation emanating from the darkness gave her a sense of anonymity. He could hear her words, but could not see her shame. It felt as though she was in confession and could finally voice her sins. For they were many.

"My father was a cruel drunkard who died of a diseased

liver when I was six. My mother worked as a seamstress for the wives of rich merchants in Glasgow and I helped her with her sewing." She shifted, somehow compelled by his silence to tell the entire truth, not to coat it with honeyed words as she was wont to do. "That is to say, she made me sew until my fingers blistered or bled every night and I very much hated it."

"What is sewing?" he asked, his voice becoming even more arctic. "Why does it make you bleed?"

"Clothing," she explained. "I made and repaired clothing. In fact, I did it long enough to know that your tunic is loom-spun, not wheel spun, and the stitching is double-threaded crossed stitch, same as your trews. Though I don't know how they managed it with the animal skins."

Rhona decided to take his grunt as a sound of amusement and kept going.

"Before he died, my father signed betrothal papers between me and the son of a good friend of his. I married Eoghan McEwan upon his father's death and he moved me to his farm, in Argyle."

"This did not make you happy," the darkness rumbled.

Rhona had thought that she kept her voice light and monotonous, as though telling a story about someone else she'd once known. Some unfortunate woman whom she pitied. She could feel the tightness of the muscles in her face, the lines of stress about her mouth.

"My few short weeks of marriage were probably the easiest of my life, though I was unhappy at the time. My husband was neither cruel nor lazy, nor was he kind or attentive. But there was plenty of food, the house was comfortable, and the work bearable. I just wanted..."

What had she wanted? Love? Deference? Someone who didn't expect her to wait on him hand and foot? Rhona remembered how worthless she felt when Eoghan would criticize her to his friends or neighbors. *"She canna cook a decent stew or handle the animals,"* he'd say. *"But she's a bonny good tup and will bear me strong sons."*

His boast of her skills as a lover always embarrassed and puzzled her. She merely did what he commanded her to do while she gritted her teeth and bore his attentions.

Eoghan had told her that it would only hurt the first time,

but he'd been wrong. Every single time she'd lain with a man, had been excruciatingly painful in some way or another.

"Well anyway," she continued, "He was called to fight for the Stewart against the Donald in one of the early skirmishes and he was defeated in the battle. Laird McEwan's soldiers came to claim the farm in his name some days after."

"But it was your farm." Bless the warrior for sounding incensed on her behalf.

"Women cannot own property in this country," she explained, trying to keep the bitterness out of her voice. "And I had no heir with which to hold it."

He grunted again, this time less amused.

"The McEwan soldiers who bore the news offered to take me back to my mother in Glasgow so I...went with them."

Suddenly the storm outside seemed angrier, the screams of the wind became war cries or death knells. The darkness was no longer a cloak in which to hide, but full of shadows and danger. Of foul-smelling sweat, smothering heaving bodies, and bruised, torn flesh.

"They...took me to an encampment outside Inverary, told me I had to earn my passage by becoming their whore." Sometimes when she thought of this, Rhona struggled to breathe. She had to stop and take in a few shuddering gulps of air. "There were three of them, who kept me for a week and then dumped me here when they were called away."

The babe's feeding rhythm had diminished and he squirmed again in her arms. Poor lad must have eaten too fast. Pulling him from her breast, Rhona lifted him to rest against her shoulder and rubbed and patted his back while she rocked her body. She couldn't be quite sure if she rocked herself or the child, but it was comforting nonetheless.

The man in the darkness remained silent, motionless. She couldn't hear him breathing. Perhaps she'd even put him to sleep. But now that she'd started telling her story, it felt as though she purged some kind of poison and she couldn't stop until she'd wrung every last bit of it from inside her.

"They never did pay me." The plaintive afterthought still bothered her, but she decided that was all she was going to say about that week of sheer hell.

"I found work with a local seamstress at the market, here,

Mrs. McConnell. She paid well and the hours were good. She liked to tell people she took in an unfortunate widow, and I didn't mind her saying so. I had no pride left at that point, for I realized some weeks after taking up with her that I was carrying a child." A wry laugh wrung through her swelling throat. It sounded more like a strangled sob when it escaped.

"I lived for that life inside me," she admitted. "I loved it. Sang to it. Talked to it while I worked. I said I didn't care if it came out a boy or a girl, that he or she could be anything they wanted to be and I would do all to help them safe and happy."

"Mrs. McConnell was a deeply religious woman. She saw me come into the village with the soldiers, as did some others. Once she found out about my condition, she said that it was apparent I couldn't be sure of the baby's legitimacy. So she dismissed me. My mother also denied me aid for the same reason. My reputation was as soiled as my body."

Rhona remembered how hard those months had been, trying to make her last wages stretch until the birth. She paid the midwife first and the busy old pagan woman had been kind and patient with her, teaching her about self care and the care of infants. She even fed Rhona at night if she would do her dishes and help with soiled laundry after other births.

"I gave birth in October, more than a year ago, to a daughter, Miorbhail. Though I just called her 'Mira'."

"Did *her* name have a meaning?" His disembodied voice caused her to jump. It sounded different than before. Lower, the words more clipped. Somehow the air between them had changed. An undercurrent of hostility and anger radiated through the darkness and Rhona couldn't be sure if it emanated from her or the warrior.

Rhona hadn't even been certain he'd been listening. He was so quiet, unnaturally still. She was such a terrible fidget, she couldn't believe that someone could make themselves as motionless as a stone in such an uncomfortable chair.

"Miracle. Her name meant miracle." She wiped at a stray tear and tried to swallow around the emotion lodged in her throat. "But she only lived for a fortnight. I still don't know what took her. She wasn't sick. She was eating enough, growing chubbier than this lad is. The midwife said that babes just... die sometimes. That there's no reason for it. She said that it was probably best given my circumstances."

Her voice hardened and her tears dried. Most of her grief washed away in the river of tears she'd cried already, leaving emptiness occasionally filled with impotent anger.

"I would have found a way, no matter what my circumstances. I would have kept Mira safe and fed and warm. I would have sewn a thousand dresses, washed a thousand sheets, or fucked a thousand men. It was *not* better that she died."

Silence roared in her little room after her passionate words landed in the darkness. She still rocked the boy in her arms, thumping his back a little harder than before. "Does that shock you, sir?" she asked, daring him to condemn her.

"Yes," he answered, with more vehemence than she expected. The word was so tight, so full of a leashed meaning that she couldn't identify.

"Well you can go—"

An impressive belch against her ear silenced her and the baby squirmed and fussed in her arms. She brought him back down to her breast so he could have his fill. She wondered how close the warrior truly was. Would their knees touch if she stretched them toward him? Would he rescind his payment now that she'd shocked him?

"What happened after?" he prodded.

It was Rhona's turn to be shocked. Why did he want to know all this?

"There isn't much to tell after Mira... a woman at the market brought her grandson to me. His mother had died in childbirth. I nursed the babe for several months. The woman's husband was a beast-keeper and he gave me my goat and three chickens for payment. After that, the woodcutter's wife had their fifth child and her milk dried early. I nursed her baby daughter for a few months, and they sent me dinner and wood to warm me. But her child started on solid food almost a month ago..." Rhona trailed off. The stranger, Finn, knew everything about her now. More than he probably wanted to. But she felt surprisingly better, unburdening herself like that. Lighter, somehow.

"You didn't hate your child?" Finn asked bluntly. "What if her sire was one of those men who—" He didn't finish his sentence, and Rhona was glad. She didn't want to hear the words on his tongue. She didn't want to actualize the thought in his mind, not while they were alone and she was so exposed.

"Nay," she murmured. "None of that was her fault. She was an innocent gift born of all that ugliness."

The sudden sound of movement startled her and she had the distinct impression that the giant had stood. Surprisingly, it didn't disrupt the baby who had fallen asleep at her breast.

"Someone's here," Finn's voice didn't sound alarmed, but still held an intensity that worried her.

"How would you know—"

The second insistent knock of the night tested the meager strength of her door.

Shocked that the noise didn't wake the sleeping child, Rhona gingerly set the babe on the bed and rushed to buckle her shift. She stood and turned to grab her fur, then backed into something so solid and warm that it stunned her into stillness.

She hadn't known he stood so close. Her breath quickened pace with her heart. "Please don't show that you are here," she whispered. "It would be disastrous for me."

"I won't." His breath warmed her ear as he bent to whisper to her and gooseflesh broke over her skin. She didn't want to open the door. She didn't want to move. His chest was so solid against her back. So stable.

The knock sounded again, this time louder, and the babe let out a muffled squeak that spurred Rhona into action. She lunged for the rickety latch and pulled the door open.

James MacLauchlan, the woodcutter, loomed in her doorway, smelling as though his most recent bath had been in Islay scotch. Even the strength of the wind couldn't whip the overpowering scent away from her.

She stepped onto the stoop and closed the door behind her, the cold stone freezing her bare feet.

He leaned down to her and Rhona shrank from the grimy unmentionables caught in his dirty, russet beard. "I noticed yer chimney was cold. I've brought a full load for ye." He took his time running his eyes over her, noting the thin hem of her shift peeking from beneath the ratted fur she clutched about her shoulders. He staggered a bit when he motioned to the wood piled haphazardly in his cart and covered with a skin to protect it from the storm. It would be enough to warm her for at least two weeks.

"I'll be taking the payment we agreed upon now." His hand snaked out and grasped her elbow.

"Wait." She made to pull her arm away but kept her voice low, hoping the storm shielded their words from Finn. The stranger knew too much of her shame already, and she depended on his gold for survival. "I've taken a job. I have a babe in there with me and enough to pay you. If you come back tomorrow night, after I've changed the coin with the smithy—."

His grip became painful and he pushed forward, as if to force her inside. "My wife is invalid after the birth of this babe. It's been months since I've lain with her and I havena the coin for whores."

Rhona's heart dropped into her stomach. How was she going to get rid of him? "I'm sorry, but I'll pay you—"

"Ye promised me a tup for a fire and I mean to collect what's owed me." He reached over her and pushed the door open, making to shove her inside.

Rhona resisted, but paused when she saw his eyes widen in shock. Her instinct told her to scramble out of the way seconds before the heavy woodcutter flew several feet backward into a bank of snow.

Chapter Four

Finn did, indeed, appear the avenging angel as he stalked the woodcutter. Rhona inched toward the door, squinting against the stinging crystals of ice cast at her by the storm. The barbarian all but disappeared into the snow with his light furs and fair hair.

James sprawled on his back in the bank, moaning and cursing.

Finn said not a word as he lifted his gigantic boot and stomped on the woodcutter's chest. It seemed like he used little effort, but James folded in on himself and rolled to his side, his mouth gaping and closing like a fish starved for water.

Rhona gasped and covered her mouth with her hand. Part of her wanted to stop Finn. What he did would bring dire consequences upon her head. The whole of the village would surely turn against her. But God help her, she could do naught but watch, hoping that his punishment was indeed as painful as it looked.

Finn moved behind him, his features contorted with satisfied wrath as he delivered vicious kicks to MacLauchlan's middle and lower back. This man knew exactly how to wreak pain and did so with brutal efficiency. Though James was a large man with a body honed of hard work, Finn didn't once unsheathe his weapons, as though the woodcutter didn't pose enough of a challenge.

Something dark and violent rose within her belly as Finn's boot covered the side of James' neck as the man curled into himself. Rhona couldn't call it excitement, per se, but it was a thrill so foreign that it frightened her. It spread a trembling, moist ache deep into her womb and caused her feminine muscles to clench tightly.

"When you are again able to breathe, you will crawl home to your *wife*." Finn's voice was chillingly soft, but it somehow reached her through the howling of the wind. She saw James's head move in a frantic nod and his neck was released.

Instead of coming toward her, Finn marched to the cart and started stacking wood into his arms.

"Wait," Rhona cried. "I don't want anything from him. I'll find another way."

Finn shook his head and wordlessly continued stacking an impossible load of wood into his arms. When he could no longer see over, he hefted it to rest against the dry part of the stable building, moving as though the burden didn't impede him in the slightest.

"Did you not hear me?" Rhona followed him, ignoring the biting cold on her feet. "I told you I did not want it."

Finn cast her an indecipherable look and didn't pause in his work. "He was defeated."

"What does that mean?"

"It means that what was his now belongs to you."

"That's ridiculous," she gasped.

"*That* is the way of things." Finn stood and tromped back into the snow for another enormous armful of firewood. Honestly, a man shouldn't be able to carry so much. It was unnatural.

"I appreciate you defending me, I really do." She moved to block him from a third and final trip. "But he's going to claim that I stole it and that will be no end of trouble."

Finn stepped around her without even breaking a stride. "No he won't." He spat in the direction of the now gasping woodcutter and loaded the last of the wood. "He'll be busy pissing blood for the next few days." It appeared the prospect very much pleased him.

"And what about after that?" Rhona burrowed deeper into her fur. "What about next time, when you've moved on and no one is here to protect me?"

The barbarian paused, holding a stack that would have taken three normal men to carry, and considered her question. His face remained impassive, as though it were set that way. "There is no other woodcutter in the village?"

Rhona shook her head. "I would get firewood on my own if I had any boots to wear in the snow. As it is, I'd lose my toes to frost if I tried."

Dumping the last bit of firewood, Finn looked down at her bare feet as if for the first time. Letting out a foreign, ugly curse he lifted her into his arms before she could protest and carried her inside.

Finn leaned against the door and used his elbow to secure the latch. For a woman living alone, the door didn't lend much in the way of security. He remembered being afraid he'd shatter the rotting wood when he knocked. It left her so vulnerable. Defenseless. That would have to be remedied if he were ever to get a peaceful night's sleep again.

"What are you about? Put me *down*," the woman demanded in a loud whisper, glaring blindly at his chest in the darkness.

Finn frowned. He didn't know what he was about. Some sort of unraveling was taking place within him. When he'd noted her feet, bared and red in the snow, his only instinct had been to shield her from pain. He'd not thought past picking her up and taking her inside.

She smelled like juniper soap and cinnamon. Finn leaned down to breathe her in. He'd been able to control his inexplicable desire for her, so far. But having her in his arms like this, at his mercy, caused his control to slip in dangerous increments.

"Shh. You'll wake the baby," he whispered back, reluctantly setting her wriggling form on the cold floor. He liked the feel of her curves through the furs so much that images of what they would look like bared to him formed in his mind. "Don't move," he commanded her.

"I can't see anything." She sounded nervous. "What are you doing? Lighting a candle?"

Finn walked to the bed where the baby slumbered in his bindings. His tiny eyelids fluttered with dreams and his nostrils flared with every deep, strong breath. Finn lifted the tiny creature and cradled him in one arm and retrieved his fur cloak with his free hand.

"Did you really offer yourself to that man for firewood?" he murmured, staring down into the cherubic little face while he crafted, out of his cloak, a warm bed for the babe between the mattress and the wall and stabilized on each side by his sword and axe.

It took her a long time to answer and he worked silently until she did, tucking a flap of the softest snow-hare's fur over the child.

"His last delivery was my final payment for feeding his child. He was late and I went three days without a fire." Her voice dared him to pass judgment on her, but a small thread of pleading wound through her words. "I was freezing and desperate. You can't know what it was like. I would have done anything."

Finn tensed. He did know what it was like. He'd suffered for days and days naked and shivering without hope for any warmth. But he was a Berserker, bred in the frozen north to withstand the cruelest of elements. It was impossible for him to freeze to death.

She was a delicate woman. And he should have beaten the woodcutter to death regardless of a thought for his family.

Finn stood, satisfied the child was secure and warm. "How desperate are you now?"

"I beg your pardon?" Despite her incensed question, her face told him that she knew exactly what he was asking. Her full lips drew into a tight line, like it was wont to do when she was displeased. Her brow fell, creating two distinct grooves over the bridge of her pert, lightly freckled nose.

Finn's heart started to pound. Much like the moment before swords clashed in battle, a release of excitement surged through his veins. "What if I paid you enough gold to keep your fire lit for a year?" He stalked her in the darkness, watching emotions play across her beautiful face. Her cheeks were more gaunt than he liked, her eyes plagued with dark circles and wariness. Even so, she had somehow become the most desirable woman he'd ever known.

"For what?" she breathed.

He came to stand in front of her, studying the subtle curves of her features painted in shades of grey by his night vision. "You know for what," he murmured. "For a night with me."

She suddenly became very still and Finn knew he was a merciless predator who'd ensnared a soft, tempting rabbit. She was in his clutches and his instinct demanded that he make a meal of her. Blinking rapidly, she took in a few frantic gulps of air.

"Why?" she finally asked with a tremulous breath.

Her question astounded Finn. "Because I want you."

A hand fluttered to her chest, then smoothed her riotous curls, and landed in her mouth so she could chew at a nail.

"You really don't," she informed him, fisting her restless hand in her fur. "If you're looking for... amusement, you can search out Francesca at the tavern. She's lithe and exotic. Italian, I believe. I've heard she's very skilled."

"I don't want Francesca." Finn had availed himself of a hundred Francesca's in his lifetime. He didn't want lithe and exotic. He wanted curved and freckled.

"Brigid, then." She reached for her hair again, twisting a curl around her finger while she shifted from foot to foot. "She's very young and known for being adventurous. Golden-haired, like you."

"I don't want Brigid." Resourceful tenacity and gentle warmth appealed to him much more than youth and daring. As for golden-haired, Finn found that he'd lately developed an acute interest in red.

"Well, you don't want *me*," she backed up a bit, forgetting to whisper.

He blinked. "I don't?"

"No." Her voice trembled the more adamant she became. "You look... well... like you do." Her arm swatted toward him as though his features were a major fault. "And I look like... I look like I've birthed a child. Like I've been nursing for a year. It makes no sense."

She had it right on the last point. The woman wasn't making any sense. "The woodcutter offered for you," he countered. "Why deny me?"

"Did you not hear what I said?" she asked. "I'm accessible to men like James MacLauchlan but not to someone like you." She pressed her palm to her forehead and let out a beleaguered sigh. Even in the darkness, he could detect the flush in her skin as it glowed brighter.

His eyes narrowed as Finn bristled at her rebuff. Crossing his arms over his chest he asked, "And what am I like?"

"Like Adonis, that's what," she spat. "Like... the most... Well you're so... bloody *handsome.*" She finished the word with a gesture of exasperation.

A grin spread across his mouth. She thought him handsome, did she? Most women did, seeking to entice him by means he often found humiliating for all involved. But Finn hadn't thought he'd appealed to Rhona. She'd barely even looked at him. She'd gone out of her way to make it clear she didn't desire him to touch her.

"And?" he prodded, waiting to hear her reason for them not to lie together.

"And nothing," she groaned.

That was it? Because he was handsome? Perhaps the woman was a wee bit daft. Beautiful. Adorable when piqued. But maybe a little off. "You find me handsome, so you refuse to lie with me?"

"I didn't *refuse.* I—"

"So you *will* let me have you."

"*No.*" She frowned. "Maybe. I don't..." Two delicate fingers pinched the bridge of her nose.

Were all women this confusing? How could he be so thoroughly aroused by her and completely puzzled by her at the same time? Was this some kind of female game she played? Finn acutely felt every bit of his ignorant upbringing in this moment. Aside from his mother, he'd never even met a woman until his seventeenth year when Olaf had taken him to meet with some whores who would chance to service a Berserker. Sometimes it was dangerous work.

Finn took a steadying breath. Rhona had just said 'maybe', and that meant he had a chance. "You. Don't. What?" he asked very slowly.

"I don't want you to make this offer for me out of charity or pity." She dropped her hand. "I know how wretched I am."

Aghast, Finn thought she must have been joking, but for the earnest, vulnerable anxiety shimmering through the tears in her eyes.

He reached out and grasped her hand, placing it on his trews where his cock strained against its bindings, desperate to be between her legs. Between her fingers. Her lips. Her breasts.

"Does *this* feel like pity to you?" he hissed. "Because I've been in this way since you opened your door to me."

Chapter Five

Rhona struggled to free herself from his unyielding grasp. The length he pressed against her hand flexed and pulsed, its heat radiating through the thin barrier as though to entice her to accept it. She'd never felt a man so large before and his proposition suddenly frightened her.

His groan sounded more like a growl, rumbling from a place so deep that it reverberated in the air around her. Unwittingly, her own body responded with a soft, moist ache that bloomed in her belly.

"Does it?" he murmured against her ear. His nearness was overwhelming. Even in the darkness she had a sense of his sheer size and unmitigated power.

"No," she whispered, going still in his grip.

"What does it feel like?" His voice had changed again. Tinged with something wild and dangerous, it slid along her senses like a bedeviled snake. Tempting and repelling all at once.

"Like... need."

"Let me have you," he pressed. The growl was deeper now, an inch away from a command. "I vow not to leave you wanting."

Rhona didn't understand what he meant. Was he promising to pay her? She was always wanting. Wanting for shoes. Wanting for warmth or food. Wanting to seek some idle pleasures instead of devoting her every hour to work and survival.

"I—" With the gold he offered she would not want for any of those things. Not for a long while. She knew she could survive the brief and vicious moments of his pleasure. She just couldn't seem to bring herself to say the words.

Finn released her hand and wrapped strong fingers about her shoulders. "I'll not be a brute to you, not like those fucking soldiers, if that's what you're afraid of."

Rhona pulled her hand away from his sex.

She wasn't afraid. God help her, she should be. But she'd survived it before. And from what she remembered, before a man took a woman in violence, there was a subtle shift in the air between them. An evil, expectant vibration that should be a warning yet was so easy to ignore.

Rhona felt none of that with Finn. The man had already protected her from suffering such a fate. And if he'd wanted to take her against her will, why offer her coin? He could have had her at any time and she'd be powerless to stop him.

No, she wasn't frightened of his lust. It was his aversion or ridicule that caused her apprehension. It mortified her that she'd told him as much.

Finn was the embodiment of physical perfection, and the contrast made her feel inferior. No matter how she looked, she couldn't find one flaw. One blemish to mar his beauty.

Rhona bore tiny marks on her hips and belly from where her pregnancy had stretched her skin. She knew her breasts were no longer as pert and high as they'd once been. Her hips were wider then when she was a young lass, her bottom more round. She couldn't bear for him to see and compare.

"I'll consent to your offer on one condition."

His grip tightened on her shoulders.

"You can't light a fire, not even a candle."

"You want it to be cold?"

"No." She took a shaky breath, hardy able to believe what she agreed to. "I want it to be dark."

"Done." He sounded pleased. "Though I have a few conditions of my own.

Her stomach clenched. She should have known he'd have demands.

"Yes?"

His hands trailed from her shoulders down her arms, drawing the fur along with them, exposing bits of skin to the cold.

"You belong to me tonight." His voice maintained that

growling timbre, as if some terrible beast lived inside of him and would take its pleasure from her, as well. "You must let me have you as I wish to."

A flurry of moths erupted within her stomach. Trepidation washed over her with the force of a frigid, powerful ocean wave. This was a dangerous demand, made in a dangerous tone. The treachery lie within the wicked spark his words ignited within her. An ember of something she didn't understand writhed through her blood, causing her limbs to twitch restlessly.

Desires she couldn't identify flooded her senses as if her soul was trying to compel her to an end she couldn't predict. And as her mind recoiled from this devil's bargain she made, somehow her body anticipated it.

This frightened her most of all.

"Very well, warrior." Rhona closed her eyes. "Do with me what you will."

--------------------●--------------------

Finn watched Rhona's throat work over a swallow. Her nostrils flared with quick, anxious breaths and when her eyes opened, they darted blindly about.

Several tense moments passed as Finn grappled with his urgent need. She was now his to do with as he pleased. Too many images, desires, and appetites thundered through him. He stood paralyzed for fear he would fall upon her like the ravenous brute he'd just promised not to be.

"What... do you require of me?" she asked in a halting voice.

He wanted her to talk to him, to direct him to her pleasure with that husky brogue of hers. He wanted to hear her moans and screams of pleasure, but he dare not wake the babe.

"Just stand where you are," he commanded, letting her fur drop to the ground.

She let out shaky sigh when his fingers moved to the ribbon holding the front of her thin shift around her shoulders. Finn could just make out the protuberance of her pink nipples against the fabric and was assaulted by another wave of lust. He took a steadying breath and forced his trembling fingers to be deliberate as he pushed the shift off her shoulders and let it join the fur at her feet.

Finn couldn't hold in his moan as he took in her nakedness. In the entirety of his life, he'd never beheld such beauty. Even in the darkness, Rhona covered her breasts with her arms and crossed her legs in a vain attempt to protect her modesty. The shy action caused possession to scream through his veins.

Mine, his Berserker demanded.

Could she be?

He jerked free of his clothing, unable to take his eyes off of her as he stripped and discarded his things to the chair.

Now there stood no barrier between her flesh and his.

She looked ripe and round and soft like a fruit ready to be plucked from a late summer tree. Riotous curls framed her wide eyes and spilled down her delicate shoulders. They helped her arms to hide her breasts from view.

Finn's hands curled into fists as his gaze followed the indent of her waist to the dramatic flare of her hips and the subtle curve of her belly.

Her thigh blocked her sex from his view, but Finn didn't mind. He'd keep this image of her with him always to take out and savor in the lonely cold nights that dominated his life.

She started when he reached out and brushed her hair back, exposing a pale shoulder. He circled her, breathing in her musk of spice and winter. No matter what his body demanded, he couldn't rush this.

And didn't want to.

Rhona had promised herself to him for the rest of the night, and he planned to siphon every last pleasure that the stormy darkness had to offer.

Finn reached for the curve of her waist, sliding his hand around to her back and pulled her to him.

She gasped and lifted her hands to press against his chest.

"Did I hurt you?" he whispered, allowing her to create space between them, though his mouth found the shell of her ear too irresistible not to taste and nibble.

"My breasts...They're tender from the feeding."

His abdomen flexed with a rush of desire as the words left her mouth. Her breasts. Full and lush with rosy nipples. He ached to touch them, to test their weight in his hands and taste their sweetness with his mouth. But he'd not cause her pain for the entire world.

"Here then." His hands traversed her supple flesh as he continued his moist exploration of her soft lobe. He could feel her skin blooming with goose pimples against his. She softly pressed her head closer, letting out a trapped breath.

So it seemed her ear was a weakness. One he planned to exploit.

His hands dropped from her back to shape the sweet curve of her bottom. He kneaded it to the rhythm of the blood pounding lust through his veins. Then he pulled her against him, allowing her hands to control the pressure above her waist.

She stiffened as his cock pushed against the soft skin of her belly, but made no noise. He did his best to distract her with his mouth on her ear, her neck, the smooth skin of her shoulder.

The contact of their skin overwhelmed him. The difference of her softness against his hardness. Her rounded curves against his sharp angles. It took his breath away and brought years of forgotten needs and desires roaring to the surface.

Finn had always thought of his life in uncomplicated terms. Hard and cold, brutal and merciless. His every triumph built upon the blood of his innumerable enemies. His every defeat celebrated by those he would seek to call family. His cursed beast raged inside of him, more lethal and ferocious than any other, and yet survival was an endless battle of pain surmounted only by force of will.

The soft creature in his arms was the antithesis of all that. Her body was lush and warm. Inviting and pliant. Instead of seeking vicious domination, she survived only by means of enduring. Her hands were clean of blood. Her heart was free of vengeance. And in spite of her own difficult battle for survival, she nourished the weak with all she had left to give.

It wasn't only his body that ached for her, nor merely his Berserker that roared to possess her. It was his stained soul that reached for the purity of spirit that pulsed within her. If he could meld with that, if only for the span of a stormy Solstice eve, then perhaps he could taste that purity and carry a piece of it with him always.

The soft hitches in her breaths and restless movements told him she would respond to his mouth, but he couldn't yet smell what he needed from her.

She wasn't ready for him yet.

But she would be. He wanted her slick and wanton, writhing and begging for him to give her release. He wanted to erase the memory of any other man from her mind until he consumed her like her very scent was consuming him. Somehow within the space of a few dark hours, Rhona had claimed a piece of him.

It was time to stake a claim of his own.

Rhona swallowed a moan of protest when his lips left her ear. The innocent attentions he'd paid her there had felt like a sin. As stoic and accommodating as she planned to be, the wet play of his tongue followed by the soft scrape of his teeth on her earlobe caused a cold fire to race along the surface of her flesh.

She was alive with sensation, her every nerve vibrating with awareness of him. His skin was warm against her body, contrasting with the wintry air. The rocks of his chest pressed back against her resisting hands, the bands of muscle rippling along his torso unrelenting against her stomach.

And his sex pulsed like a hot brand against her belly.

It was a weapon. Just as fearsome as any of the others he'd brought into her home. He'd penetrate her with it, stab her. Not just once or so like a sword or dagger, but many times. Why, then, was he prolonging her torment with soft, wet nibbles and sensitizing caresses? Why force her to stand and endure this antagonizing anticipation of his inevitable intrusion?

At least his hands were gentle. Despite the rough calluses on the skin of his palms, he touched her with the utmost care. It was as though he was aware that his immense strength could break her, and he focused very carefully on not doing so.

At least of that she could be grateful.

The feel of his hands on her backside was an intimacy she wasn't used to. Each time he cupped the pliant flesh and kneaded, cold air hit the quivering place between her legs.

Rhona shuddered. She'd never been much aware of that place before. It caused her shame. It caused her pain. It brought life into this world. But she'd avoided it for everything but to clean and care for.

How puzzling, nay, *alarming* that she should be so aware of it now. A feeling of restless emptiness that bordered on a stinging ache had settled there. With each brush of his mouth against her ear or neck, with each exploration of his fingers, the awareness increased until she felt the need to squirm.

His hands drew away from behind her, following the curve of her hip to dip between their bodies.

Though she could see nothing in the absolute darkness, she squeezed her eyes shut, waiting for the humiliating intrusion of his rough fingers. Instead, he paused at her stomach, tracing the small swell that had never disappeared after her child's birth, then the indent where her hip met her thigh.

"What are you doing?" she asked, unable to stand it any longer.

"Learning the feel of you," he murmured, his hot breath teasing the fine hairs at the nape of her neck.

"Why?" According to previous experience, he should have pushed her onto the bed by now and pried her legs apart, thrusting between them until he spent himself. "Shouldn't you just... get on with it?"

"Nay." His fingers trailed against the curls above her sex and a jolt of charged energy sliced up her spine. "I need you ready to take me inside you."

She couldn't see his face, but the dark need in his voice caused a shudder to quake her very bones. The words spoken in his deep tones did something disturbing to her insides. Didn't he understand? She'd never be ready. She'd never want this.

"Please. I don't—"

His finger snaked between the folds of her sex. He hissed a breath through his teeth and groaned.

But Rhona had forgotten how to breathe entirely. A stab of sensation jerked every muscle she possessed tight as a bow string. It was a lightning slash of pleasure that disappeared as soon as it registered.

Finn hadn't lingered in that spot, but dipped lower to the very entrance to her body.

Rhona bit her lip. A small amount of slick moisture encountered his exploration. She vaguely remembered her husband asking her why she couldn't get wet for him. It had been his only complaint in that regard, but it seemed to irritate him to no end.

"Not enough," he rumbled.

Her heart pounded. Finn was already displeased with her. Oh God. How had she thought she could do this?

The mountain that was his chest lowered beneath her hands. He was kneeling? Did he mean to take her on the cold floor?

She clenched her legs together, suddenly very aware of the cold now that she was not pressed into the heat of his skin.

More fingers invaded the lips of her sex, parting her and exposing her core.

Rhona whimpered, suddenly feeling very lost and vulnerable, as though the storm raging outside was about to break in and batter her exposed skin. Did he mean to humiliate her? Would he hurt her now?

"I must taste you," he growled. "You're so fucking beautiful."

There was not light by which to see her. How could he know she was beautiful? *Taste her?* He couldn't mean to...

"No—"

Her protestation died on a strangled breath as a long, strong lick split apart the very center of her. A foreign, frightening needle of pleasure shot through her with such incredible force that her knees weakened.

As if sensing her imminent collapse, Finn's strong hands gripped her hips and held her aloft. His mouth remained where it was, buried within her core, his lips exploring the pliant ridges of her sex, teasing around the center of her burning loins.

This was nothing like she'd ever experienced. Rhona couldn't be certain it truly was happening. Was this lethal stranger really on his knees before her, tasting of her womanhood? No one had ever done such a thing. The very thought scandalized her. The action nearly sent her into conniptions.

In contrast to his callused fingers, his tongue was smooth, hot, and deliciously wet. It slipped among increasingly slick flesh leaving sweet trails of pure, aching pleasure in its wake.

Shocked beyond comprehension, Rhona's fingers sought and dug into his muscular shoulders. Her toes curled in on themselves and a trembling began so deep that it must have come from her soul.

A tide of need and pressure released from her belly as she felt her sex bloom and open beneath his expert mouth. It was as if all her blood and awareness surged there, to be part of this dangerous, delicious experience.

His moan was muffled by her skin, and his fingers dug almost painfully into the meat of her hips. He left no question that he was pleased by her body's innate reaction.

Now, more than ever, she was grateful for the cover of darkness as she couldn't seem to process the absolute intimacy of what he performed on her. Instead of recoiling from his wicked mouth as she was first inclined to do, Rhona pressed herself forward against him.

Heat and instinct melded somehow within her, pulsing pleasure through her blood with the beat of some ancient rhythm. The sounds of the angry storm outside retreated until she could only hear the desperate pant of her breath and the soft, wet sounds he created.

She seemed to be reaching for something, something she couldn't name and didn't understand. Her body strained for it, her hips searched for it, riding his mouth as though she were a woman possessed. In truth, she couldn't recognize herself as she was now. Reduced to a creature of wanton need. Bereft of pride or fear or dignity, begging to be set free from this passionate torture.

As the warrior rolled his tongue over her and his lips nipped at her flesh, he seemed to be aware of what she required, but unwilling to allow her to have it.

"P-Please," she whimpered. "Finn... I can't..."

He groaned again, and plunged his tongue against the sensitive bud that was at the center of her burning need. As he ground against it, her entire body convulsed. In that moment, she understood her fair-haired stranger was something other than a mere man. As she shuddered and melted into the wave of pure, wet-hot pleasure that engulfed her, he supported her entire weight with his outstretched arms, all the while continuing his relentless conquest with his tongue.

Rhona had to bite down on her tongue to keep from crying out. The pain seemed to heighten the intensity of the pleasure pulsing from her sex and reaching to every recess of her being. A few helpless sobs escaped her as the sensations rolling off of his tongue reached a peak so incredible that she wasn't sure she could contain it.

Just as she felt as though she might be overwhelmed, his lips retreated from her.

It was all Rhona could do to inflate her chest and depress it. She was naught a mass of throbbing, wet satiation and trembling limbs. She couldn't seem to let go of his shoulders, and he didn't release her hips as he rose in front of her. If he did, she would surely sink into a puddle of boneless nonsense.

She'd had no idea her body had been capable of such bliss. That in the right hands, she could be played like an instrument to crescendo to such a tremendous peak.

"You are ready for me now," Finn informed her. He seemed so certain. His voice tight and laced with need.

Tension and dread crept back into Rhona's pliant muscles. He'd only just given to her the sort of pleasure that he wanted to take. For that, she could be thankful. For that, she would submit to anything he wanted of her. He would be kind as he climbed on top of her and painfully slaked his lust.

And she would endure.

Chapter Six

Finn wiped the taste of her from his lips. Nothing could compare to the sweetness of her nectar. Nothing. As she'd trembled and pulsed in his arms, he'd taken as much pleasure from her release as he'd ever taken in his own. He could have spilled his own seed with the lightest of touch, he was so fucking hard.

He needed inside her. Now.

Bending down, he swept his arm behind her knees and lifted her. He took pride in how her legs trembled. In the astounded glaze covering her heavy-lidded eyes. He loved how her breasts bobbed with her every move.

Depositing her on her back, he followed her down on the bed, covering her body with his.

Her eyes widened and her breath quickened. Her muscles, once replete with pleasure became instantly rigid again.

Yes. She was ready.

The urge to kiss her knocked the wind out of him. He wanted to claim her with more than his body. He wanted her to taste herself on his lips and understand the sweetness that was her essence. He wanted to bind himself to this woman for the rest of his unnaturally long life.

He shook his head, focusing on beauty of her pink-tipped nipples instead of her parted lips. What he wanted was a fool's wish. He couldn't hope to have something as pure and beautiful as her for more than tonight.

But tonight he would have as much as she could give.

"Open your legs," he prompted, unwilling to take his eyes from her glorious breasts.

She complied, creating the sweetest cradle for his body.

Her fragrance surrounded him, winter spices and musk. He was about to sink into bliss and ride them both to the edge of heaven. He positioned the head of his throbbing cock at her entrance; reveling in the abundance of moisture her body had gifted him with upon her release.

And then it hit him.

A cloying, sour note mixed in the bouquet of her intoxicating scent. One that grew stronger with each moment he hovered above her.

Fear.

Finn drew back and truly looked at her. Though it was dark, Rhona's eyes were clenched shut. Her hands burrowed into the mattress and clutched the faded, tattered linens in a white-knuckled grip. The muscle of her delicate jaw flexed and her pulse leapt against the straining skin of her neck.

He'd been so mistaken. She wasn't ready for him to take her. She was bracing herself against it.

Gritting his teeth against a slew of curses, Finn fought the murderous urges battling with the lust in his blood. Those fucking soldiers. Maybe he'd coax their names from her lips and hunt them for sport. They would fight and kick like rabbits in a snare before he gutted them. He would feed them their own entrails before the lights went out of their eyes.

Struggling to contain the violence pounding in his heart, Finn dropped his head into her fragrant hair and took three deep, centering breaths.

She continued to lie absolutely still beneath him.

"Wrap your legs around me," he commanded, more brusquely than intended.

She whimpered, but complied, hooking her ankles at his back.

Finn burrowed his arms beneath her and lifted her off the bed and stood.

Her eyes flew open and she held tightly to his shoulders. "What are you doing?" she asked. "I thought—"

"Oh, I still mean to have you." He turned his body and sat on the bed, settling her onto his lap with her knees split over him.

"But... how?" The heat from her core beckoned to his cock, which seemed to stretch toward her of its own volition.

Finn took the curve of her hips in each hand and lifted her away from him, positioning his throbbing column against the opening of her body, once again.

"Like this," he grit out. "But you have to do it."

Her eyebrows shot up. "What?"

"I won't hurt you. And I'll not take what you do not freely give me, Rhona," he vowed. "*You* take *me*. Take me inside you."

She blinked, her chest lifting and falling with her labored breath. Finn watched a myriad of emotions play across her face before her eyes closed once again. Hands resting on his shoulders, she lifted herself on her knees, then exhaled and slowly pressed her body forward.

The slit of her body was wet and tight as it stretched over the blunt head of his sex. He knew he would stretch her. He was an uncommonly large man. But the feel of her flesh slowly accommodating to him had to be the sweetest sensation of his long life.

And it was going to kill him. His lust and instinct pounded through him demanding that he thrust and dominate. It took such incredible force of will for him to remain still, that his muscles began to quiver.

It was her eyes that saved her. They flew open, filled with astounded wonder as she sank in torturous increments. Her lips parted and the warm rush of her astonished sigh hit his face. Finn tempered the surges of need by intently watching each sensation flow through her expressions. What he saw there awed and humbled him. Relief, pleasure, curiosity, utter vulnerability.

Rapture.

His heart contracted. This moment was crafted for them. For him. If he did nothing good in his life, he did this. He brought this woman satisfaction, and for that he was saved.

When she almost had him inside her, she paused, looking troubled. "I don't think I can take any more," she whispered.

"You can," he gasped. Clutching her hips, he lifted her until he almost withdrew, pulling a ragged sound from them both.

She began her descent again, this time faster, wetter, and with more confidence. She did not stop until he was buried inside her to the hilt.

Sweat broke out on his forehead, his restraint stretching to impossible lengths.

She held still, letting their breath tangle in the darkness. Finn dared not move either, for fear that he might lose this perfect place. He fit inside her like she'd been a warm sheath crafted only for him. When she adjusted herself, testing her untried muscles, a raw moan ripped from his throat before he could call it back.

"Did I hurt you?" she asked, lifting some of her weight off of him.

He gasped out a chuckle, gripping her hips even harder. "Nay, but I fear that I may be unmanned."

"I need... something." Her whispered carnal confession caused ripples of an orgasm to clench low in his belly. "What is this need?"

Fin dropped his forehead to hers and gulped in a breath, praying to Freya for strength.

"*This.*" He lifted her hips and brought her slick weight back down upon him, impaling her with his shaft.

When she gasped and grasped his shoulders, he did it again, and a third time watching her eyes stretch impossibly wider with each invasion.

"Am I hurting you?" he returned her question.

"No," she whispered. "It feels... good."

The surprise in her voice broke what little control he had left. He lifted her tempting arse in a solid rhythm now. Before the night was over, she'd have a few other words than "good" to describe how she felt.

He loved the feel of her fingers gripping his shoulders, and her sex likewise gripping his as he pumped her body above him. She tried to help by bracing her legs against the mattress, but Finn knew that for all the control he'd meant to give her, this was his job now, to set a rhythm that would catapult them both into the stars.

Her soft gasps turned into startled whimpers as he quickened their pace. Her bottom slapped against his thighs, creating the most erotic sound he'd ever hope to hear again. He could feel the clench of her muscles, and the strain of her body as it reached for the release hovering above them.

"Finn." She groaned his name in her husky timbre and it was nearly his undoing. Her lips, moistened with her pink tongue, almost collided with his, but Finn plunged his hand into her hair at the last moment and pulled her in close to his body.

"I'm going to..." As her intimate muscles clenched around him, her teeth sank into the meat of his shoulder, muffling her cry.

The sharp pleasure-pain of her teeth dumped him over the edge. Burning fire shot from his spine through his cock and exploded inside of her in long, sharp spurts. His seed coated her womb and further eased his thrusts through her pulsing sex. Her convulsing muscles milked from him the most powerful orgasm of his life. As soon as the initial implosion subsided and Finn rode the throbbing waves of intense pleasure, he understood that this moment of joining with her had forever changed them both.

When the last of her pleasure had wrung from her, Finn caught her as she collapsed against him.

"Who are you?" she panted against his ear. "*What* are you?"

Finn closed his eyes, savoring the feel of her body held against his. What was he? He was a warrior. He was an assassin. He was templar and priest. He was prisoner and servant. He was hunter and executioner. He was lover and worshiper. He was a bastard in every sense of the word.

"I am a Berserker."

Chapter Seven

Rhona had heard the word before, she'd grown up with the bedtime stories and myths sung by old bards.

Berserker.

It was whispered in awed tones whenever the imposing MacLauchlan Laird and his brother were about. They moved with a primal rhythm through the town like two huge dark sentries, surveying their land and people with severe, protective scrutiny. The fantastical stories that followed in their wake had been impossible to believe. However a shadow of precipitous danger chased the brothers like a biblical scourge, and Rhona had taken care to never garner the notice of a Berserker. Fabled or not.

And now she was wrapped around one who remained buried deep within her body.

"What did you do to me?" she breathed against his neck. "Was it some kind of Berserker magic?"

His chest vibrated with a soft chuckle. "Nay, I was just a man taking pleasure with a beautiful woman."

Pleasure *with*. Not pleasure *from*. Rhona found she liked that very much.

"But I've been with men before and nothing even close to that has ever happened."

Finn drew them apart as if to look at her, but that was ludicrous as the night was black as ever. "You never found pleasure with a man? Not even your husband?" Pure astonishment crept into his voice.

"Not once," she confessed. Did that mean something was wrong with her? Was she defective somehow?

"Then they were not men," he scoffed. "They were no more

than rutting animals."

Rhona supposed she agreed. But she didn't want to think about any of that now. Not in the aftermath of what they'd just done. Reluctant to leave his warmth, she wriggled off of his lap.

He let out a groan but allowed her to stand. She felt blindly in her familiar room for her cupboard and extracted a cloth to wipe herself before handing it to him.

Finn took it before she could say, "Here."

"How do you do that?" she asked.

"Hmm?" Languor dripped from the sound.

"How do you know that I was holding something out to you? Come to think of it, how did you know that the woodcutter had arrived before he knocked at my door?"

"I see you," he answered her with few words, as was his way. "And I heard him."

"That's impossible. It is black as pitch in here and the storm is so loud that it sounds as though a herd of wild ponies are stampeding through the village."

Rhona nearly screeched with surprise as she found herself being lifted in his strong arms as though she weighed as much as the babe had. It was the reminder of the sleeping child that killed the sound in her throat. He walked them to the bed and laid her upon it.

"I can see you now." Rhona frowned at the smug pleasure in his words. "Your breasts are beautiful."

Her arms clamped over her breasts.

"No you can't," she protested, her mind unwilling to process his claim. But then, he had just effortlessly found her in the dark, lifted her and made his way to the bed without error.

"Stop doing that," he commanded, his strong hands encircled her wrists and gently pried them from the front of her.

"Then stop calling me beautiful," she shot back. "It's cruel." He'd seen her the *entire* time? While she'd been standing in front of him? While his mouth had—?

Dear sweet Jesu, she was going to die of mortification.

"You *are* beautiful," he insisted, joining her on the bed and covering them both with her insufficient furs. He lay on his back and pulled her against his chest.

"I'm not beautiful," she countered, "I'm invisible. Sometimes I feel that I could stand in the middle of the square and scream and thrash about like a wildling, and no one would notice."

Finn pulled her in close, tugging on her knee until she had it resting over his muscled thigh and trapped between his legs. "People don't see you because they don't want to see you. If they did, they'd have to admit that they ignore your bare feet or your tattered clothes. They'd see the loss in your eyes and realize they've mistreated you." His voice was harder now, cold, like it had been when he'd first entered her home.

Rhona swallowed a lump that formed in her throat. "But you see me?" she asked. "Even in the darkness?" She wasn't sure how she felt about that. Though the darkness could be a dangerous place, it could also offer safety. He was one man from which she could never hide.

Finn's arms enfolded her. "How could I not?" he murmured. "To me, even in the shadows, you're illuminated. Unlike any other."

"Really?" A stray tear escaped the corner of Rhona's eye and she had to catch it with her hand before it fell onto his chest. She allowed herself to sink into his warmth, reveling in the feel of his hard, naked body. For one night, he would ward off the constant permeating chill. For this one night, she'd be safe and protected. Instead of utter, empty loneliness, she had two people for company, each with their own joys.

Each with their own needs.

"I've never seen anything like it," he admitted.

"So," she rested her cheek against his chest, listening to the strong, steady rhythm of his heartbeat. "You can see at night, you can hear as well as woodland predator. Is everything they say about Berserkers true?"

"What do they say about Berserkers?" his amused words sounded as though they came from the deep chest against her ear instead of his mouth.

"They say all kinds of things. Like you have to feed on blood and it'll make you strong as ten men. I've heard the blood will also cause you to go mad until you kill everything in your path, whether it be man, woman, or child."

Finn grunted, but it wasn't a displeased sound. "I don't feed on blood, I'm not a Demon."

Rhona waited a bit. "But... what about the rest?"

Her head lifted with a shrug of his shoulder. "If blood is spilled before me my Berserker is unleashed. He is a beast of rage and destruction. He is stronger than *twenty* men, faster than a pack of wolves, and without the ability to feel fear or compassion. It is his duty to annihilate anything that lives." It sounded as though he recited a creed.

"Duty?" she stiffened. "Duty to whom?"

"To Freya, our Goddess of battle."

"This Berserker is a curse? It lives inside you?" Disbelief curled inside of her. Because of her circumstances, she'd never put much thought or stock in one god or another. Blessings eluded her, no matter how long she spent on her knees begging for help. And she worried far more about the immediate pain and punishment exacted my man then the vague possibility of a vengeful deity. Why blame God or Demons for one's misfortune? People were capable of enough evil on their own.

"A man is born a Berserker. It is what I am. It is what my father was." He sounded resigned to the fact.

Would he kill her for slicing a finger? Or a child for skinning a knee? Rhona tried to reconcile this fearsome, compassionless creature to the considerate lover that held her so snugly against him.

"Freya." She tested the foreign name. The names of the Celtic Gods slid through her mind with familiar ease. Her father was a deeply superstitious man who adhered to the old ways, though her mother clung to the Christian faith now dominating the Lowlands. "What sort of Goddess is she to create such a lonely existence for a man?"

"She is a Goddess of the Northmen. Only her people can claim the Berserker." His voice warmed a little, as though Rhona had pleased him, somehow.

"That's not true." She rubbed her hand across the smooth span of his chest, finding the flat of his nipple with her palm. "It's widely said that our Laird, Connor MacLauchlan and his brother Roderick are Berserkers. And they're as Scots as there ever was."

He stiffened against her. "Do you know them?" The

question held an intensity that alarmed her, but she dare not move away from him.

"Nay," she answered honestly. "I'm not the kind to socialize with nobility, though I'm summoned to the keep in the morn."

"What do they want with you?" Suspicion deepened his question to a growl.

Rhona shook her head against him. "It's not the men who summoned me. Lady Evelyn MacLauchlan was going to discuss retaining me when the child is born in the spring. I had some dried herbs I was going to take her that might help to soothe her morning ills that won't abate even after all these months."

"One of them has a mate?" His voice shook with astounded outrage, louder than it had been since the baby had fallen asleep.

"They're both recently married, if that's what you mean." Rhona lifted herself onto her elbow.

"*How* recently?" he demanded, sitting up and unsettling her.

Rhona didn't understand what could possibly have made him so angry. Did he know them? Were they his friends? Enemies?

Had she put herself in danger with the only clan that would have her by sheltering him?

"Tell me!" he took her elbow in a firm grip. A jolt of alarm stabbed through her.

"I-I don't know exactly. Roderick brought Evelyn home in the summer, she was already pregnant. And the Laird married Lindsay Ross rather quickly, I believe, just after Samhain."

A slew of guttural words flowed from his direction. They sounded like curses. Like the kind of incantations that blighted entire bloodlines.

"Please," Rhona begged. "You'll wake the—"

A reedy whine preceded a plaintive cry from over her side of the bed. Rhona sighed as she extracted herself from his grip and rolled over to retrieve the wriggling bundle from his nest on the floor. Worry curdled like sour milk in her stomach as she soothed and bounced the child.

Had she called more trouble and tragedy upon her house

by allowing this stranger into her bed?

Finn crouched and added another dry log to the blaze he'd crafted in the fireplace. He'd checked to be sure that the woman was fully absorbed by the babe so that she wouldn't notice that he'd ignited it without tinder.

She couldn't have understood the impact of the information she'd given him.

As a final test of his strength and loyalty, Magnus the Elder had sent him on a holy quest solicited by Freya herself. Upon his success, he was to be inducted into the order and adopted into a bloodline. The holy blood of the Berserker had somehow leaked into the Celtic Isles. There were two men unworthy of the blood, and therefore had to be eradicated.

Finn was to be their executioner.

Magnus neglected to mention that Connor and Roderick MacLauchlan were mated, a position which increased their power tenfold. They would be unstoppable. Lethal enough on their own, even for him, but with two of them?

Finn heaved out a great breath, squinting at the flames as though they held the answers to everything. He was such a fool. The Goddess and the elders of the temple hadn't sent him on a quest.

They'd sent him here to die.

The dulcet sounds of Rhona's soft hum to the suckling child combined with the dancing flames mesmerized him. One threw enough heat to singe his skin; the other ignited a warm glow deep in his being.

He couldn't look at them. Not now. Not with the emotion gripping his chest. He had to wait for the implacable cold to come back. He was too raw. Too exposed.

Somehow, over the course of the night, the ice blockade he'd built around his heart had thawed. At first, Finn thought it was a consequence of the intensity of heat created by their passion. Now he had to admit it went beyond that.

When he'd first glimpsed Rhona in the light of her one lone candle, something sparked between them that bespoke of providence. While he'd watched her succor the abandoned child, that spark fanned into glowing embers, fed to flame by the force of her abiding spirit and selfless love she'd proclaimed for her own child conceived through misery or brutality.

The inferno created by their shared passion had consumed him, leaving him no choice but to burn as hot as the laws of nature would allow. In the aftermath, he'd expected the flames to die out, leaving nothing but cold stone and charred ashes. Like always.

Instead it remained, much like the fire he'd just built, spreading warmth to every dark and shadowed corner and creating a bed of coals that would endure countless bitter nights to be fanned into a strong blaze at the slightest provocation.

A woodchip burst and sparks showered toward his legs. Finn was grateful that he'd donned his trews in order to gather the wood.

He needed this moment to collect himself, to examine the turmoil tearing his insides to shreds. This humble home, little more than a stable, had become something of a haven to him. Here, he could be any simple peasant warming his family by means of productive gains. He could be tending to the needs of someone who'd chosen to live with him. A soft, willing woman, who'd let him into her heart, and her bed, for the pleasure of his company. Not for his coin.

In this fantasy, when he turned to her, joy and contentment sparkled in her eyes untainted by violence and loss. She would invite him to her. Seduce him with that husky voice until they joined each other in that alien place where passion and emotion entwined. A place he'd never known existed.

Until tonight.

Finn had never realized how entirely alone he was. Though he resided among other men of his kind, they never accepted him. Only a few Berserker bloodlines existed and they were all represented at the temple of Freya.

Yet no one claimed him as their issue, therefore he had no voice. He had no family with which to dine. No banner to display.

As a younger man he figured that if he'd outrun, outmatched, and outfought his brethren, they would clamor to add him to their ranks. Instead, he unwittingly set himself as the default champion, one who had to be overthrown by any means necessary by a Berserker seeking to prove himself.

Life until now had been an incessant battle, his only human contact consisting of the impact of combat or the arms of a woman he'd paid for pleasure.

And none of that mattered anymore.

Finn refocused on the lilting melody emanating from the direction of the bed behind him. Rhona did sound contented, despite the uncertainty with which she treated him before the child had awoken.

Just yesterday, he would have yearned for his ill-fated battle, hoping to take one of his opponents into the afterlife with him.

But what about the two delicate creatures on the bed? How could he ensure their survival? Why did he even feel like it was somehow his responsibility?

Because in another life, it would be. Were he anything but this, he would claim her as his own, and for once, he'd have a family with which to spend the Solstice holiday.

Chapter Eight

"The fire, it feels—" Rhona's thoughts collided with each other as Finn's head swiveled toward her from where he crouched, contemplating the blaze. "Incredible," she finished, lowering her eyes to the child latched at her breast.

She understood that if one dared to gaze at the sun, they were eventually struck blind. And yet, the urge often proved overwhelming, such was the alluring beauty of the golden radiance in the sky.

Finn's physical magnificence was equally awe inspiring, but likely held just as grave a risk.

A part of her still denied that anyone so flawless had wanted her. Touched her.

Been inside her.

Warmth that had nothing to do with the glow of the fire spread through her limbs and she smiled down into the sweet face of the babe. Tiny, feather-fine lashes rested on cheeks that needed to plump. His pulls on her breast dwindled to intermittent as he drifted into slumber, but she couldn't seem to put him down. Instead, she caressed his unruly patches of downy black hair and savored the bittersweet ache in her womb.

"I just can't believe someone would abandon such a precious bundle to the brutal winter," she murmured.

"How do you know he was left?"

"There's a convent to the south and east of here on Campbell land. It is well known that Christian women from all over Scotland go there and pay to give birth to unwanted children." Rhona shivered. "It is whispered that many of the children meet such a fate, if their parents cannot pay for other arrangements. A babe is left in the snow, as it is mostly painless to freeze to death."

Finn grunted and spat into the flames.

"'Tis what I think of the practice as well." She pulled the lad free and situated the furs around her to cover her nakedness. Leaning over to gingerly rearrange the makeshift cradle on the floor, she wondered what would become of the bairn. Would the barbarian take him back with him to the North? Did he expect her to care for him indefinitely? He must know that this was no place to bring up a small child.

She looked up again at Finn, who watched her with a new intensity. This time, a bleak desolation marred the sharp, strong angles of his face.

There it was. His flaw. An impenetrable casing of ice protecting a yawning abyss of pain. Somehow it shone for a moment through a chink in the frigid armor.

He unfolded to his full height, and even still, her insides trembled, and she had to clench her thighs together.

He was not of this world, certainly. Bestowed by an ancient Deity with a cruel and feral beauty meant to tempt and destroy. Firelight licked his skin, inviting her to do the same. It cast shadows into the deep grooves between his thick, corded muscles. It burnished his flesh and hair with such a pure gold that he seemed to glow with some kind of divine light.

He truly was an angel. Sent to consecrate her body and redeem her soul from the depths of her own personal hell.

Rhona's mouth flooded with moisture and she swallowed convulsively. A renewed rush of liquid desire drenched her loins.

Finn's nostrils flared and a growl escaped his clenched teeth, but he remained motionless, eyes filled with a primal need and something else that broke her heart.

Rhona lifted herself to her knees, dropping the furs behind her. She couldn't tell if it was the warmth from the flames or the heat in his possessive stare that singed her naked skin.

Maneuvering to the edge of the bed, she knelt before him, her eyes never wavering from the dangerous, emerald intensity of his gaze.

"Come to me," she beckoned. She knew what this moist, needy emptiness was now. And that only he could fill it.

He stepped to her, hands clenched into tight fists at his side.

As Rhona reached for the hastily strung laces of his trews, she vowed that though she'd promised herself to him for the night, this satisfaction belonged to her. She wanted to explore his body as he'd done with hers. To taste him. To watch and feel the effects of the pleasure she was about to give.

There was power in this. And she felt it coursing through her as she brushed the hard length of him through the soft animal skin.

A pained gasp escaped his lips and Rhona smiled, releasing the laces and unleashing his cock.

She'd almost forgotten how big it was. How intimidating it could seem, jutting from a wreath of dark bronze hair, and every bit as immense as the rest of him.

Casting a glance back up at his face, she captured her bottom lip between her teeth enjoying the thrill of anticipation that coursed through her.

"You don't have to," he breathed. "Rhona..."

She loved it when he said her name. She loved that when she wrapped her hand around the thick base of his shaft, he hissed and every muscle in his body went splendidly rigid.

And she loved the slew of harsh, foreign words that ripped from his throat as she enclosed the blunt tip in her mouth.

He tasted good. A mixture of salt and musk and something ultimately familiar. Something altogether her very own.

Rhona slowly worked her mouth past the ridge of his head and reached lower, opening her jaw wider to take in as much as would fit. She used the moisture suffusing her mouth to ease her way, leaving as much of it on his velvety flesh as she could when she drew back.

Finn jerked and groaned, but still didn't touch her.

The second time she used her hand to guide his length past her lips, inch by inch, sucking softly when she drew back.

He growled again. This time it sounded like a warning.

Rhona didn't hurry, exploring his shaft with a rhythmic hand as she used her moist tongue to find sensitive veins beneath the thin skin. Carefully covering her teeth with the fullness of her lips, she sucked him into her mouth and ran her tongue along the thin slit of his head that now welled with something slick and succulent.

A hand clamped behind her head, threading strong fingers through her unbound hair. A fist closed around the one stroking his cock, gripping with a gentle brutality as he fed her its length.

Rhona sucked it in greedily. Eyes locking with his, she used her free hand to brace against his hip. She set a rhythm of pulling him in deeply and sucking as she drew back. The many inches that her mouth could not take, she stroked with her fist, palmed within his bigger, stronger hand.

He panted like a wolf after taking down a fresh kill. He blessed her in his own language, then cursed her. He moaned a prayer to his Gods, and maybe a few of hers as well. His hand left hers to stroke her face, to touch her mouth where they joined. To cup her jaw.

His expressions quickly varied from heart-rending tenderness, to lusty desperation, to a demanding snarl and back again.

When she used her tongue to swirl around his head in rhythm to her strokes he moaned her name.

"Stop," he gasped.

Rhona knew what was coming and she increased her pace. She could feel it building. Feel him growing larger in her mouth. Feel the desperate pull of his muscles as his blood gathered to free him from the frenzy of his need.

"If you don't stop, I—" A raw sound tore from deep within his chest and emerged on a curse. His every muscle bulged and flexed before locking tight. His cock jerked twice before long streams of his release pulsed into her mouth.

Rhona opened to it, swallowing his pleasure. Using it to further ease his way.

He'd thrown his head back, the muscles of his neck and jaw obviously battling to keep in a cry of release. He was most beautiful this way. A sleek, lethal beast incapacitated by her lips, a prisoner of the pleasure she drained from him.

She didn't stop until his hand tightened in her hair and pulled her away from him.

Finn's shoulders slumped forward and he shook greatly as one last tremor ripped through his massive frame. Though the ecstasy had released its hold on his body, his manhood remained full and strong.

His firm grip on her hair held Rhona immobile on her knees. She licked his essence from her lips. Her limbs were weak and shook with arousal and need. Her womanhood ached and throbbed with a new intensity. She wanted to shamelessly rub against him like a cat in frantic heat.

Finn's eyes, at once feral and desperate with passion, began to warm and clear as he tracked the movements of her tongue.

"Gods, woman," he panted. Eyes never leaving her lips, he bent down to her, bringing their faces so close that they shared the same air. She rested her forehead against his, energy arcing between their bodies, as though small bits of pleasure leapt from his skin to land upon hers.

Her nose leaned against his and she closed her eyes. His lips were right there. So close. That angelic, broad, sinful mouth. The one that had pleasured her so methodically and entranced her so thoroughly would surely claim her now. Thank her for his pleasure with a tender kiss. She knew he wanted to. She could feel the desire emanating from him. All he needed to do was to close the gap between their open mouths and...

Rhona found herself gripped by his strong hands and suddenly facing the opposite direction, bent over on her hands and knees. Her eyes flew open and she gasped as Finn seized her hips from behind and swiftly buried himself to the root in her throbbing depths.

Pleasure immediately exploded from where they joined as she was stretched and invaded in this new and primitive way. He kept his thrusts slow and strong as she shivered and convulsed in agonizing ecstasy, covering her sobs with both hands as she supported her weight with her elbows.

His strokes increased in pressure and speed after the intensity of her climax had passed. Rhona was certain that it took all the strength she possessed not to collapse into a puddle of boneless satisfaction. But as he drilled into her body, the hard planes of his hips pounding against the yielding softness of her bottom, Rhona could feel another wondrous storm already brewing in her loins.

As his thrusts became more demanding, he bent over her

and brought his arm around her to delve his fingers into her cleft and brush against the bundle of sensation that nestled there. He plucked it with his fingers, thrumming the wet, engorged nub until another jolt of pleasure screamed through her with all the speed and strength of a lightning bolt.

She bucked against him, her traitorous body trying to escape the intensity of the pleasure that bordered on pain. And yet, she reveled in it. Knowing that it must end soon or she'd die of it. Her blood would cease to flow. Her heart would cease to beat. Her chest would cease to draw breath as the strength to do so would all be drained from her by this beast burying himself within her against and again.

Pressing her face against her mattress, she bit down, releasing her cries into the linens. She was dimly aware of his grip on her hip becoming painful and the desperate sound of his muffled groan against her back.

As the storm began to pass, she wondered if there would be anything left of either of them when dawn finally decided to break, heralding the end of their night together.

Chapter Nine

Finn squinted down at the babe wrapped so tightly in his fur-lined cloak and frowned. He hadn't exactly thought this through when he'd swaddled him thus. How was he going to slip away with it?

His eyes slid to Rhona, who curled tightly onto her side, hair covering her face as she breathed deeply in repose. A tight band of sorrow squeezed the air from his chest.

She could keep it. Along with the gold she would find inside. He wanted something to warm her. Perhaps, when she put it on she would remember him fondly.

With a careful, painful breath, Finn crouched to retrieve his weapons from each side of the slumbering child. The sword came free without a hitch, but the bundle shifted when he moved his axe, and a tiny squeak emerged.

Finn looked down into the clear blue of the child's open eyes and cursed.

The babe's breathing sped and he opened his wee toothless mouth to, no doubt, emit some godforsaken sound.

Snatching him up, Finn frantically begged the lad in a whisper to keep quiet. Short of smothering him to death with his hand, he couldn't for the life of him figure out what else to do.

Another plaintive squeak from the babe accompanied a strong kick of his legs. Inside his bindings, the child wriggled and fussed and Finn instantly set to freeing his limbs.

When his skinny arms were flailing about in the narrow slants of morning light, a sigh that could only be called appreciative lifted and fled the child's narrow chest.

Followed by a sneeze.

Wiping the offending moisture from his face, Finn grunted a warning at the babe.

Who in turn grunted back at him.

The sound was so absurd that Finn felt the corner of his mouth twitching. Walking with the boy over to the fireplace, he avoided the noisy chair to crouch at a safe distance from the heated coals.

If the lad was nearly naked, the cold morning air couldn't be healthy for him. Almost no insulation covered his frail bones. God's teeth, the child's arm had to be as thin as Finn's own thumb.

Finn leaned his face down to truly inspect the child while the babe seemed content to engage in a staring contest and flap his arms about like a deranged game hen. It was inconceivable that all of mankind started out so small. So weak and guileless. Dependent on the goodwill of others for survival.

Rhona had been right; it was nothing short of miraculous.

Finn's head jerked with the child's sharp tug on his hair and he grunted again. Obviously, the babe wasn't as weak as he looked.

Carefully extracting the strands from the child's unyielding grip, he found his pinky captured with the other hand.

Five perfect, tiny fingers barely spanned the width of his smallest one. He tugged on his hand trying to release it, uncomfortable with the warm feeling that settled in his chest. The babe tugged back and somehow Finn's finger ended up in the slimy, toothless mouth.

He frowned. The lad's grip was surprisingly strong. He would someday hold a sword with ease and skill.

But who would teach him to wield it?

Finn glanced up at the bed and froze. Rhona sat with the furs clutched to her chest, her hair curling wildly around her, and a disconcerting glitter of moisture in her eyes.

She blinked it away, lifting a hand and smoothing it over the unruly copper mass.

Finn liked her hair like that. It reminded him of the many times he'd taken her over the course of the night.

A slight pink blush crawled up her chest and settled in her cheeks. Perhaps she was remembering how she'd slung her leg over his waking body and ridden them both to oblivion only a few short hours ago. He'd watched the silver streaks of dawn break on her glorious breasts while she'd come for him.

His body hardened at the memory, and he looked down at the innocent boy in his lap who somehow owned a piece of his soul along with his finger.

Finn opened his mouth to tell her that he was leaving now. That she wouldn't see him again. That his Goddess had sent him to his doom and he must obediently oblige or be forever damned.

What came out was, "He needs a name."

"I agree." She sounded pleased, which brought Finn an absurd amount of joy. "Did you have one in mind?"

Finn looked up in time to see the shift she'd snatched from atop her trunk lower over her pale, naked body.

"No," he had to fight to keep the groan out of his voice. After witnessing that, how could he think of anything else?

The woman gingerly crawled off the bed as though using untried muscles and padded over to them, leaning down to caress the baby's cheek.

Finn could smell his own scent on her. He found that he hoped she didn't wash off his scent for a good long while. It marked her as his.

His blood heated and he bunched some of the fabric of her shift in his hands. "I want you again," he demanded.

She put a hand to her cheek, then her chest and refused to meet his eyes as she flushed.

"We can't," she informed him. "He's awake. It wouldn't be... I just couldn't."

Finn glared down at the child, who'd begun gnawing on his finger in earnest. It was the strangest sensation, but not unpleasant. He found himself wondering when a man started to grow teeth.

"I'll turn him like this," he suggested, facing the babe toward the door.

Rhona gifted him with the warmest, most blindingly beautiful smile he'd ever witnessed in his life. It reminded him of the sun peeking over the mountains at dawn. The sparkle of her eyes as vibrant and electric as his northern lights. "If you can free your grip from his, I'll be more than happy to oblige you."

Finn gave his hand a gentle tug, then stronger, dislodging his finger from the babe's mouth. A disturbing squeal pierced his sensitive ears and he plugged the mouth with his finger, effectively cutting it off.

"'Tis what I thought. You keep him busy," she ordered in that sweet, melodious voice, studying the angle that the light slanted into the room. "It might be too late for breakfast, but I'll make it, anyhow." With that, she disappeared through the tiny door and into the stables.

Finn knew this was his chance. He should place the babe on the mattress, leave coin on the hearth, and duck out. If he left for Castle Lachlan now, they'd be mounting his limbs on the battlements by the time she embarked for her own appointment.

Sighing, he looked down. He might have to cut off his own finger before the little one released it back to his keeping. Also, no one had ever cooked him breakfast before. At the temple, he wasn't allowed to eat with the men and therefore had to procure his own food.

Why not enjoy a last meal prepared by a beautiful woman?

"What about Hamish?" Rhona suggested, settling deeper into Finn's cloak.

She looked up in time to catch Finn's grimace. Lord, but he was so handsome.

"No. I suppose he doesn't really look like a Hamish." Chewing on her lip, she listened to the snow crunch beneath the weight of Finn's boots. Even though he carried her while she clutched the nameless child to her, his gait was sure and strong, as though she wasn't a burden in the slightest.

He'd taken one look at the holes in her stockings and shoes that she'd donned to wear to the castle and had scooped her into his arms.

Again.

Rhona had to admit she could get used to being carried around, especially since Finn seemed to rather enjoy doing so.

A sharp pain jabbed through her.

Then again, perhaps not. She had to stop planning like he was going to be around long enough for her to get used to anything. He could leave at any time. And take the child with him.

In fact, Rhona had expected to Finn to abandon her after breakfast. Luckily all six of her chickens had laid eggs that night, which she boiled over the coals and served with fresh goat's milk. He'd eaten slowly, as though savoring each bite, and watched her nurse. His gaze slid to the door again and again. And each minute, with a curious lump of dread in her throat, Rhona waited for him to stand and leave.

He never did.

"What do you think of something simple, like John?" she continued, desperately hoping to keep his attention with conversation.

He shook his head, glaring down a townsman who gawked at their passing. "Nothing too... biblical."

Rhona nodded and looked around. She knew they made an odd sight, a well-dressed foreign barbarian giant hauling a woman and child through the streets of town. But, for some reason, she found it difficult to care. She was no longer invisible. The scant number of people milling about their business though the market street stared for as long as they dared. Woman gaped with obvious envy. Men eyed Finn with open distrust, careful to give them a wide berth.

This teased a smile from Rhona and she surveyed her surroundings with uncharacteristic good humor, pushing her worries for the future from her mind to enjoy the moment.

The only open vendors in the square were for food and other goods that would be needed for the Solstice night's revelries. The sun had broken through the last night's storm and reflected brightly off of fresh, bright snow. Crisp, clean air tangled with the scents of baking bread, roasting meats, and mulling wine.

'Twas the jolliest of times in the Highlands. The olde commemoration of the Winter Solstice followed in a matter of days by the Christian Yuletide. Their traditions and celebrations wound together in pure Highland fashion until one drunken, boisterous feast bled into the next.

As they passed the market street, Castle Lachlan loomed ahead like a golden and grey stone beacon. Obviously one of the prosperous ornaments of the Highland moors and a forbidding fortress to anyone who would dare to attack.

Finn eyed it suspiciously, slowing his gait.

"Why don't you accompany me inside?" she invited, suddenly apprehensive to let him out of her site. If she did, he might just disappear into the winter's snow like an elusive fantasy. "Didn't you say you had business with the MacLauchlans?"

Finn shook his head, testing the wind with his nose. "Nay, I'll wait for you outside the gate and carry you home. I'll return... later."

Her shoulders fell, along with her mood.

"We'll stop by the damn cobbler's on the way back," he insisted. "I'm not leaving you to tromp about in the snow without boots."

So he was leaving her, then.

Rhona shook herself. Of *course* he was. She'd known that all along. What was she to him but a nursemaid for the boy and a pleasant night's dalliance? One he probably felt like he paid too much for. Within hours, he'd probably be out of her life for good. Just because he'd swept in with his feral, golden good looks and changed her world in one night, didn't mean she meant an equal amount to him.

What business did he have with the Laird and his brother? Was it some kind of dangerous Berserker business? Could the rumors be true?

Perhaps she'd been quite mistaken. Maybe his purpose had nothing at all to do with them, but was instead regarding one of their women. Rhona thought back to his intense reaction to the news that the MacLauchlan men had recently taken wives.

Did he love one of them? Did he mean to take her back?

A tight ball of jealousy and suspicion knotted low in her stomach.

Lord, but she was such a sentimental fool.

"You smell different," he noted. "Darker. What's wrong?"

Rhona tried to paste on a sunny smile for him, but she knew it was weak. "What about Iain? Do you like that name?"

Distracted, Finn tested the name in his own tongue, which sounded beautiful. "What does it mean?" he asked.

"A gift," she glanced down at the dear child, who blew tiny

bubbles in his sleep. "A treasured gift or a beloved gift, if I remember correctly."

"Iain is good." Finn sounded like he very much approved. Which was to say his voice varied in tone and inflection for once.

"Well then." She forced some cheer into her words. "I'm very fond of Iain. He's a good lad."

Finn looked down at the baby. "How can you tell?" he asked wryly. "He's never awake."

"That'll change soon enough," Rhona assured him, still trying to force a false brilliance into her voice. "Then you'll get to know him better."

Finn's jaw muscles clenched and jumped and he looked away from her, glaring at the gate of the castle.

When they approached, an armor clad man-at-arms looked at them askance before demanding they state their business. The only part of him not sheathed in silver armor was his eyes, so Rhona explained to the man's helm that Lady Evelyn was expecting her. The guard gestured to the gatehouse to lift the gate.

"And who's this?" the burly Scot demanded, his winged brows drawing into a tight frown as he looked up into Finn's cold, forbidding face.

"This is..." Rhona chewed her lip, unsure of how to present Finn. "This is my escort."

"He cannot enter. Least of all with his weapons. The Laird decreed that no man should be armed when the ladies are in residence."

As the gate lifted, it revealed an inner courtyard that was small and empty for such a sizeable castle. The entry doors stood open across the short, snowy span.

"May he conduct me to the eaves so my feet don't freeze?" She lifted the hem of her kirtle enough to show her unsuitable shoes.

The man laid a hand on his sword.

Finn seemed unconcerned, and Rhona could tell that his icy, implacable expression unsettled the armored Highlander.

"Make it quick," he ordered.

Finn strode across the courtyard with his long, sure strides and set her in front of the entry.

Rhona turned to face him, unsure of what to say. Would he indeed be there when she returned? He hadn't paid her yet, but she couldn't bring herself to ask for the money. He could easily take this opportunity to leave her. Should she hand Iain to him while she was inside? But then she might lose them both. In truth, he was the one who found the bairn, though she had no idea how he would keep him without a nurse.

Oh Gods, she wasn't going to cry. Not here.

"Finn, promise me you'll—"

"Berserker." A dark brogue broke through the shadows of the entry a promise of wrath in its depths. "Before I kill you, explain what you're doing in my castle.

Rhona jumped, her eyes widening as Finn drew his sword and axe. A green fire glowed in his eyes. Duty. Fanaticism. Perhaps a little bit of anticipation.

"Don't come in, Rhona," he ordered. His gaze roaming her face like it would be the last time, like he committed her to memory. "Not until it's done."

"Finn?"

He lunged through the doors, moving faster than she'd ever thought humanly possible.

Rhona didn't want to turn around. Didn't want to see what happened next, but couldn't seem to stop herself.

She whirled in time to see Finn leap through the air an impossible distance, both sword and axe lifted over his head. The speed at which he flew combined with his incomprehensible strength would surely decimate the dark-clad warrior who stood at the back of the dimly lit entry.

Rhona recognized the long black hair only partially pulled back from the Highlander's broad and brutal face.

Her lover was going to slaughter Roderick MacLauchlan.

With a speed to rival that of Finn's, the Laird's brother drew his great sword and side-stepped the axe, though he barely had time to parry the blade. The sound of metal meeting with such force echoed through the stone entryway and reverberated through the keep. Sparks from the blades showered the few tapestries and portraits decorating the hall.

Using Finn's momentum, Roderick pivoted and pushed Finn from his sword, following through with a swift kick to the back that sent Finn staggering.

"No," Rhona cried, clutching Iain to her chest. "Don't do this."

Roderick turned his chilling notice on her for only the space of a breath. Though Rhona couldn't seem to find one.

His eyes. They were that of a Demon. Of the Devil himself. As black and hellish as the starless, storm-swept night that had blown Finn to her door.

Rhona shrank back with a gasp, unable to believe what she was seeing.

The moment as all Finn needed. He turned his body and took a wild swing at Roderick's middle with his axe.

Roderick dodged, but the axe blade sliced through thick, ebony leather. It came away clean, though, claiming no blood. Lips pulled back into a vicious snarl, revealing teeth sharpened to an unnatural point, the Highlander lunged at Finn.

But the Northman was ready.

Their weapons met. Thrust free. And collided again. All of it happening with such impossible speed and agility that Rhona barely had time for her mind to process what her eyes had seen before the monolithic warriors produced another assault.

Their growls and cries could surely be heard throughout the hall, and Rhona was dimly aware of a commotion in the square behind her. But she paid it no heed. She was too frightened to even blink, afraid if she did she'd open her eyes to find someone dead at her feet.

Finn leapt back from a strong slash of Roderick's sword. It seemed to take all he had to keep up with the frightening, feral speed of the dark warrior. He collected himself, drawing his weapons back and preparing another strong, devastating, overhead two-handed attack.

As she watched the death arc of Finn's weapons, Rhona screamed as she was seized from behind by cold, iron-clad hands.

Chaos commandeered the moment.

Iain let out a screeching wail.

Frigid metal in the form of a dirk pressed against Rhona's throat, immobilizing her.

A second black warrior emerged from the shadows of the keep, his sword intent on running Finn through.

Roderick took the flat of his blade in his off-hand and lifted it to shield his head from the dual attack.

Their weapons caught on each other, effectively locking them together with their combined strength.

Blades bound between them, each man surged forward in an attempt to drive the other back. Neither gained any ground. Muscles bulged and growls erupted from the effort of the stalemate. Facing each other thus, they looked like conflicting, legendary Titans. One the color of a golden day, using the power and strength of the Sun as his influence. The other claiming the artifice and obfuscation of night to fuel his command.

The sight was breathtaking.

Finn drew his head back as though to ram it into Roderick's, but everything about the dark Highlander changed in the space of an instant and what he said next saved Finn from being skewered by the Laird of the castle.

"Father?"

Chapter Ten

At first, Finn didn't think that he'd heard the Gael Berserker correctly through the cacophony.

Had the man called him father? Was he daft?

Suddenly he wasn't glaring into the fathomless black eyes of the Berserker beast, but instead a clear, alarmingly familiar green gaze inspected him as though he were the rarest of oddities.

What did this mean?

Iain's angry wails and a frightened whimper from Rhona snapped his attention to the doorway.

Beneath the arch, the armored guard had her hair in his clutches, a dirk pressing against her delicate, exposed throat. She clutched the squalling baby to her and mouthed his name, her eyes wild with fear.

Finn lunged for the guard, knowing he could relieve the fucker of his head before he even processed the intention to move the dirk across Rhona's precious skin.

A different pair of strong hands cut Finn's action short and he found himself shoved back against the stone wall and imprisoned by a sword to his throat.

An older, fiercer copy of the man he'd just been fighting glowered at him from identical eyes. If not for his black hair almost shorn to the scalp, lending him a leaner, more vicious cast, Finn would have a hard time telling the Highlanders apart. A flare of shocked recognition shadowed the man's harsh features before they locked down into a promise of certain, lethal wrath.

"He unhands the woman or he dies," Finn promised, lunging forward to break the hold. His life meant nothing, but his innocent Rhona couldn't be harmed because of this.

He found himself divested of his weapons and his prison reinforced by the long-haired Berserker. "Connor, this is impossible," he remarked, never taking his eyes from Finn's face.

"I know." Connor's voice was hard as the ice caps over the fjords in winter. "Take those two to the dungeon," he ordered over his shoulder to the guard. "We'll deal with them later."

"Aye, Laird."

Rhona's pained gasp ripped at Finn as she was roughly shoved forward.

Finn growled and struggled with all his might, but the strength of the two mated Gael Berserkers held him fast.

"Of course they're not going to the dungeon," a feminine voice decreed. "Connor, really!"

All eyes focused to the grand stone staircase that flanked the entryway. At the top stood a stunning, raven-haired beauty with a bearing as regal as any queen. Beside her, a shorter, honey-colored woman with the largest doe eyes Finn had ever seen laid a hand to her obviously pregnant stomach.

"Roderick?" the latter's pretty face drew into a disappointed frown but held none of the amethyst fire snapping from the taller woman's eyes. "You're fighting in front of a baby?"

"Uh, he attacked me." The long-haired Berserker, obviously Roderick, had the sense to look ashamed, though he put more strength into his hold on Finn.

"Lindsay, get back to yer chambers and doona come out until I say it's safe," Connor ordered.

"My God," Lindsay remarked, picking up her skirts and descending the stairs, ignoring the command of her mate. "He looks just like—"

"Lindsay," the Laird warned with a fierce growl.

"We're collecting Evelyn's appointment, Connor." Finn watched, dumbstruck, as Lindsay and Evelyn crossed in front of the men, who remained locked together at a physical impasse, as though strolling through a country garden. "Then you gentlemen can return to your business. Though if you're going to insist on murdering each other, you'll take it to the courtyard. I'll not have you getting blood inside the house."

Approaching Rhona, she laid a hand on her arm, causing Finn to tense. "You are the nurse, Rhona McEwan, are you not?"

Having been released by the guard, Rhona nodded. "Aye, my lady," she answered in a trembling voice, barely audible over Iain's wails.

"Let me help you." Evelyn plucked an angry Iain out of Rhona's hands and bounced him against her considerable bosom.

The babe's cries began to subside.

"Goddammit, Lindsay, she brought this enemy into our home," the Laird boomed.

Evelyn cut in with a soft, reasonable tone. "Anyone can see that man is family." She gestured with her chin to a depiction of an imposing, golden-haired man mounted to the right of the entry. "I suggest you ask his purpose before you call him an enemy."

Finn found that he suddenly couldn't draw in a breath. In front of him, in this foreign castle, innumerable leagues from his homeland, was an exact likeness of himself. The similar white-gold hair wasn't as long as Finn's, and Gaelic war braids dangled from the temples. The garb was a sporran and tartan in the MacLauchlan green and blue, adorned with a chieftain's badge instead of his own leathers, seal skins, and furs.

But the face. Finn couldn't take his eyes from it. It was impossibly like his own. The same strong angles. The same sharp lines. Only the green eyes burned from the likeness, too bright with a cruel fire. Beside him, in memoriam, hung the likeness of a beautiful, dark-haired woman.

Evelyn's words had silenced everyone as they each studied the implausible resemblance.

Family?

Heart pounding in his ears, Finn stared at Roderick, then Connor, their faces close to his as they held him captive. The same strong angles. The same sharp lines.

The same green eyes filled with similar suspicions, doubts, and boundless questions.

"Holy Christ," Roderick whispered.

Connor let out a breath, his jaw clenching and working on a decision. "Where do ye hie from, Northman?"

"Kirk Eden-by-the-Sea," Finn answered honestly, seeing

no reason to do otherwise. "The temple of Freya."

"How old are ye?"

"Nine and fifty."

The women gasped.

"Nay," Lindsay argued. "Nay, you must mean nine and twenty."

Connor shook his head. "The years make sense, as I am two and sixty and Roderick is only four and fifty."

"Fifty and...Upon my word," Evelyn breathed, one hand leaving the baby to clutch at her belly. "I just assumed you were—well— younger. I never really thought to ask."

"Jamie, take the women to the hall," Roderick ordered, his concern for his mate obviously warring with his need to keep her safe should Finn take it in his mind to attack. "See that my wife rests and puts her feet up by the fire."

Finn's eyes sought Rhona. She stood ashen-faced, with her arms at her sides, hands fisted in her kirtle. Though her garb was certainly dowdy and threadbare, and her one unruly braid couldn't compete with the splendid coifs of the noble ladies, neither of them could hold a candle to her beauty.

A longing to be back in her cramped, cold stable, held into her soft body, gripped him with such ferocity it felt like one of the brothers had punched him in the gut. His soul felt as though it wanted to rip from his body and reach out to her. To touch her face and soothe the uncertainty lurking in the shadows of her eyes.

Family? What did that word mean to him? Was it blood? Was it duty?

Or love?

Breaking their eye contact, she cast her gaze to the floor and allowed the guard, Jamie, to shepherd her along with the other ladies to a large door at the side of the stairs.

Finn didn't take his eyes from her until she disappeared.

He was released once the heavy door closed behind Jamie, but his weapons were not returned.

Not that he expected them to be.

"Regardless of what happens here, I want your word she won't be harmed," he insisted. "She had nothing to do with this."

Connor nodded and crossed his arms over his chest while

Roderick stood at the ready, not willing to let his guard down just yet.

"I'll have yer name," the Laird demanded.

"Fionngall."

"A Gaelic name. Fionngall of what?"

Finn's face tightened as he fought to keep his impassivity. "I have no surname."

Connor nodded. Luckily for him, the Berserker Laird showed no sign of mocking judgment. No contempt for the bastard who stood before him.

Connor locked eyes with Roderick, who cryptically nodded. "Sixty years ago our father left the Highlands in search of the Temple of Freya." The Laird's face was grave as he imparted the tale. "He wanted to find out about his ancestors and force the other Berserkers at the temple to induct him into their ranks."

Finn stared at the floor, unable to meet eyes so like his own.

"He returned, three years later, furious that he'd been dubbed Fionnley the Black, and denied entrance to the temple because of his impure Gael blood."

"Fionnley?" The evidence mounted, but Finn dared not accept it.

"It means Fair-haired warrior," Roderick explained, his eyes flicking to Finn's own pale locks.

Finn's notice returned to the portrait, which was almost painful to look at. Connor and Roderick had their mother's dark coloring.

But not him.

"Where is he now?" he asked, emotion threatening to choke him.

"Our father was a violent man drunk on his own power," Roderick's voice turned dark and something froze within Finn. "In my twenty and fifth year, he killed our mother when he struck her too hard for displeasing him. Connor relieved him of his head at the same moment I ran him through with my sword."

"I was told a Berserker cannot harm his mate," Finn said.

"They canna," Connor answered. "It wasna the beast that harmed her, it was the man."

Finn nodded. Their actions mirrored what his own would have been. He was sorry for their mother. Sorry that their hands were forced to patricide.

Connor motioned toward the heavy door to the great hall. "That woman, she is under the protection of my clan. I can smell ye all over her. Has yer Berserker claimed her as his mate?"

Finn's chest tightened. "Nay." An emptiness opened up inside of him that he hadn't allowed himself to feel for many years. He didn't allow himself to hope for such things, especially not now.

"Then ye canna take her back to the temple with ye."

"She is *mine*," Finn roared, surprising even himself with the vehemence of his reaction. His blood simmered at the thought of being denied her. His beast brewed with possession and he grappled with his self-control.

Roderick's hand tightened on his sword, but Connor held a palm up to stop him.

"Why are you here, Fionngall?"

Finn closed his eyes, willing the blood pounding through him to settle. The unfairness of it all ate at him. The cruelty of the men to whom he'd devoted his entire being. Surely the Goddess wasn't so heartless.

"The elders of the temple have been watching you." Finn knew in his heart that from this moment his allegiances had shifted. Once the MacLauchlans knew what he was about to impart, his betrayal would be complete. Irrevocable. "Magnus the Eldest told me something had transpired that spurred the Goddess to call for your blood. I was chosen to spill it."

Finn noted the violent tension flowing through the brothers. He felt it, himself. "But, you see, they didn't send me to assassinate you. They knew you were mated, that your power is now more than mine. Than anyone's. And they told me nothing." Finn's voice hardened, his fists cracked before he realized he'd been clenching them.

"They sent you to be slaughtered by your own *brothers*." Connor said what he could not and spat on the earth at his feet.

Roderick's hand landed on Finn's shoulder, his gaze earnest. "They failed. None of us will die today."

Finn shook his head, his whole body trembling with rage. "No. Not today, as it is a holy day for us all. But you don't understand how much they want you dead. You and your entire household." He met the intense gaze of Connor, whose eyes sharpened with understanding.

"They'll not be far behind me," Finn warned. "If they sent me to fail, they'll come to kill not just us, but the women and small ones as well."

Chapter Eleven

"Here, I can take him." Rhona hovered wringing her hands as Lindsay helped Evelyn into a comfortable chaise situated by the roaring fire in the great hall.

"No, it's perfectly all right. I'm going to have to get used to carrying a little one about with me everywhere, and this wee darling hardly weighs as much as his blanket." Evelyn patted his bottom and smiled down at Iain who seemed contented to charm the noble lady with soft sighs and tiny sounds.

Rhona noted that the pregnant woman's accent was very proper English and she couldn't help but wonder where Roderick had found her.

"Sixty and two!" Lindsay exclaimed. "Did you know we were married to men in their dotage, Evelyn? My husband is old enough to be my father, nay, my *Grand*father!" She motioned to Jamie, who pulled another comfortable chair near to the fire for Rhona. His warning glare told her she was still being closely watched.

Evelyn just smiled. She struck Rhona as the sort that didn't ruffle easily. Her eyes had the wisdom of one who had seen much hardship, and Rhona felt a small and immediate kinship with the woman. "I can't believe Roderick and I have been mated for nigh on a year and never spoken of it," she shrugged. "It's incredible how you can learn something new all the time about your mate." Her brow wrinkled. "They spoke something of a longer life, but do you truly think we should live so long? That we'll look so young?"

"I bloody well hope so," Lindsay muttered. "I'll be nine kinds of cross if I end up gnarled and wrinkled and Connor still looks like a God of no more than five and thirty."

Evelyn chuckled at that.

Mated? How oddly they talked of marriage. Rhona sat where she was told, a cold sort of shock numbing her to her bones. Even the great hall fire, built as high as they stood, couldn't quell the chill. She could only worry that Finn might, at this moment, have his limbs torn from his body by the dark brutes these women were married to. He might have overwhelmed one, but the both of them were a force unto themselves.

Could all this be true? Was he some sort of long-lost Berserker kin? If so, why the violent altercation in the entry?

"Don't fash yourself about him, dear." Lindsay put a comforting hand on her arm. "They'll work it out."

"Yes," Evelyn agreed. "I know it's not his time to die."

Rhona wondered at Evelyn's odd comment, but nodded and tried to summon a smile. She hated that the Lady of the clan was touching her soiled dress. Though she'd brushed and brushed at the soot marring the bodice, she'd been unable to completely hide the stain.

Lindsay MacLauchlan's deep purple dress shimmered like a rare jewel against the faded grey of Rhona's sleeve.

"I thank you for your kindness, My Lady."

"Not at all." Lindsay reached beside her large chair into a basket of holly sprigs and held out a few along with two spools of ribbon, one red and one gold. "Do you mind helping me while we sit? I'm afraid I'm behind on decorations."

Rhona took the offerings, grateful for something to do with her hands. The ribbon was fine, finer than anything she had ever owned in her lifetime. Using the skill she'd garnered from her years of dressmaking, she began to wrap the holly sprigs, wondering where in the grand keep they were going to put them. The hall already sparkled with candles, runners, and lush, expensive garlands.

Evelyn rocked Iain, who strained to capture the wheat-colored tendrils framing her pleasant, round face. "Is he your child, then?" she asked. "Pardon me for asking but the midwife who recommended you led me to believe..."

"Finn brought the boy to me last night." Rhona saved her from the painful end of her sentence. "He saved the wee thing from a cold death, as he was abandoned to the snow."

"Oh, how sad! Poor little lamb," Evelyn cooed at the boy. "How could someone do such a thing?"

"Finn, is that your Berserker's name?" Lindsay's eyes sparkled with curiosity.

"He's not my—"

"He is *sinfully* handsome," the lady remarked with a conspiratorial wink.

"Lindsay!" Evelyn laughed.

"What? I'm happily mated. I'm not blind."

Mated. There was that word again.

"He did seem rather protective of you," Evelyn lifted a fair brow.

"*Intimately* so," Lindsay persisted.

Rhona felt the blood drain from her face. Was it that obvious? How could she tell these ladies that she'd never laid eyes on him until the night before? What if they knew she had coin awaiting her on her hearth because of what she'd allowed him to do to her body?

In truth, she'd done the same to him. And enjoyed every illicit, wicked act.

Rhona found she wasn't ashamed of the lust that she and Finn had shared. He'd showed her more tenderness in one night than she'd felt in the entirety of her life. He'd given more pleasure than he'd taken from her.

And she'd give everything to have him again.

Regardless of all that, she needed the trust of these women if she was to survive. She still counted on Evelyn's hiring her as a nurse.

She cleared her throat and focused very intently on the holly sprig in her lap. "Like I said, he brought me the boy to nurse last night. Finn merely... employed me."

"Oh, aye?" Lindsay's voice was bright with amusement. "How many times?"

Rhona stared, horrified as the two MacLauchlan women dissolved into peals of laughter. She hadn't forgotten that Jamie, the surly Highlander, still lurked somewhere behind her chair and her cheeks burned with a flame hotter than their impressive blaze.

"You're too wicked, Lindsay, you've dismayed poor Rhona." Evelyn cast her an apologetic glance.

"Do forgive me." Lindsay wiped a tear of mirth from the corner of her eye. "You'll find we hold very little sacred here. And don't let Evelyn's sweet manner fool you, she's just as wicked as I. Ask her how long she knew Roderick before she jumped into his bed."

"I didn't jump." Evelyn picked up a bobbin with her free hand and chucked it at her sister-in-law. "You'd have been ravaged just as quickly if you weren't such a stubborn shrew."

Their giggles echoed merrily off the stones of the great hall.

Rhona let her tense shoulders drop and her mouth relax into a self-conscious smile. A pang of envy for the affectionate companionship these women shared pierced her relief. They obviously held no judgment against her and she found herself more than passing curious as to how they became the wives of the two handsome, forbidding MacLauchlan brothers.

Iain wriggled and squawked and Evelyn gave him a few conciliatory bounces. His movements became more unsettled and his cries increasingly demanding.

Rhona gasped as her milk rushed forward.

"Pardon, but is there anywhere I can go to feed him?"

Evelyn sobered. "Of course. Of course." She wriggled to the edge of the chaise and Rhona rushed to help the woman stand and gathered Iain back into her arms. "Follow me, I'll show you to your chamber. I've been sitting all day and would like to walk a bit."

Rhona curtsied to Lindsay, who smiled and went back to concentrating on her holly project. She hurried after Evelyn who moved swiftly and efficiently for such a short and pregnant woman.

Jamie followed at a distance, ever watchful of his mistress.

"I'm sorry, did you say *my* chamber?" Rhona asked as they entered a hallway that stretched toward a spiral staircase.

"Well, you certainly can't walk back home, it's trying to storm again." Evelyn motioned to the cold draft that caused the torch flames to dance. "Unless we're keeping you from celebrating the Solstice with someone?"

Rhona thought of her empty, forlorn room at the stable house and shivered. Before Finn arrived, she'd planned on using the last of her wood for a Solstice fire. She'd contemplated slaughtering one of her chickens to roast, but then decided against the luxury. Until the stable master's rooster decided to fertilize a few of her eggs, she couldn't risk the loss.

Shaking her head at Evelyn, she held Iain closer to her. Where was Finn now? If he truly was a brother to the MacLauchlans, did that mean he would stay in StrathLachlan? Even if he did, it wouldn't at all mean that he would want her as a part of his life.

Why would he? Berserkers were some kind of preternatural warrior blessed by an ancient Goddess. They married women like Lindsay and Evelyn, sparkling jewels alight with laughter and happiness.

She followed Evelyn up the winding stairs, choking on her own insecurity.

"I'll have a hot bath drawn for you before the staff is dismissed to take their holiday meal in the great hall." Evelyn was saying. "It seems they'll have such a festive night, but we all decided we wanted something a little more cozy for our first year together as a family. So you'll join us in the private dining room."

Though she was behind Evelyn, Rhona could hear the smile in the woman's voice.

"I don't want to intrude on a family gathering."

"Nonsense, you can borrow one of my dresses for the feast. I'm afraid they're all too small for me now. Even this one is beginning to bind." She tugged at the bodice.

Stunned and humbled by her generosity, Rhona offered, "I can let them out for you. I've some skill with a needle."

"Bless you!" Evelyn huffed, reaching the top of the stairs. "I'd given up on being able to breathe until after Yuletide when Mrs. McConnell is available."

Evelyn led her down another warmly-lit hall with dark green runners and thick, high-arching chamber doors. Stopping in front of one, she put her hand on latch and paused, turning back to Rhona. Her whisky-colored gaze was gently earnest.

"All levity aside, your Berserker, Finn, did he lie with you last night?"

Rhona studied a break in the rushes on the floor. "Aye."

"Pardon my asking, but did he kiss you? On the lips, I

mean."

Why would the woman want to know that? Images of everything they'd done flashed through Rhona's mind. Over the course of the night, Finn had explored every bit of her body. With his hands and his mouth.

Except her lips.

She remembered his forehead against hers, their breath tangling in the stormy darkness. She'd wanted him to kiss her then, but he hadn't.

Why not?

"Never matter," Evelyn chirped with false brightness. "After you're done with the lad, come and search me out in the hall and we'll prepare for the feast." She opened the chamber door and gestured inside. Though Rhona didn't miss the pity in her eyes.

Finn leaned back from the table as the staff filled it from trays laden with smoked haddock, spit-roasted rosemary mutton, aromatic bread, honey-glazed and custard-filled pastries, and brandied bread pudding. His stomach rumbled in anticipation and he searched the doorway for any sign of Rhona and Iain.

They hadn't eaten since her mean breakfast, and some primitive instinct within him wanted to feed her from his hand. He yearned to watch her enjoy the luxury of the succulent dishes until her every hunger was satiated. He wanted to fill her gaunt cheeks with robust health and replace the shadows from beneath her eyes with lines born of laughter.

Though he'd spent the last few hours learning about his brothers, he needed to see her again.

Brothers.

Family.

He shook his head, still trying to test the tenuous, unfamiliar concept.

The MacLauchlans were obviously Highlanders first and Berserkers second. Their every thought and concern was for their mates, their clan, and their land. They'd told Finn of a journal in their possession belonging to a northern Berserker ancestor. This man had ridden as general to William the

Conqueror and taken the last hill in Ely, finally unifying the Isle of Britain under one rule. The name of the Berserker was unclear due to the age of the book, but Roderick was certain it began with a "B". When William turned his eye to Scotland, subduing the clans at England's border by means of terror and slaughter, the Berserker had defected to the Highlands, mating with a MacLauchlan chieftain's only daughter.

Roderick cited many strange and improbable myths contained in the tome. Tales of shape-shifting men and priestesses with untold power. Night-stalking demons, Fae acquaintances, and a war to end all wars.

Finn should have been listening with rapt attention. This was everything he'd wanted. A history. A bloodline. A fucking identity. But his thoughts kept wandering back to Rhona. The desolate look on her face when she'd been led away haunted him. Did she still want to see him? Was there a chance she'd taken the child and gone back home?

"They'll be along," Connor regarded him from beneath dark brows; sipping the fine stout ale they'd all been nursing over the course of the afternoon. "'Tis a woman's prerogative to keep her man waiting. Ye'll learn that in time. They take pointless hours trying to look pleasing to us, so it behooves a man to comment on her efforts, though they be unnecessary."

Roderick drank to that.

The table at which they sat was not long, but square, able to seat two large persons very comfortably on each side. Finn occupied one side, an empty chair to his left. Roderick sat on the side to his right and Connor across from him. A fire flanked the reclining, contented Laird, casting a warm glow over his boulder-wide shoulders.

How could he be so relaxed? Finn had discussed with him the probability of the wrath of the mighty Berserker temple wrought against his entire clan. It would be a massacre. An ocean of blood with no depth.

"The sea is too angry to bring any ships to my shore on this night, be they Berserker long-boats or not." Connor addressed his unspoken thoughts yet again. "I've assigned my fastest riders to dispatch after the storm and patrol the coast. We'll see them coming and we'll be ready. But tonight, I'm celebrating the Solstice with my mate and my family."

"How is it that you know my mind?" Finn asked.

Connor shrugged. "Since I mated I've found that the impressions in another's thoughts are often made known to me. 'Tis the power I was granted."

"And it's a pain in the arse most of the time." The warm affection in Lindsay's voice belied her words as she appeared from the shadows of the doorway. Dressed in a diaphanous crimson gown that flaunted the sleek lines of her body and accentuated the sheen of her raven hair, she floated into the room, dazzling her husband with a smile.

Connor set his tankard down so hard the liquid sloshed over its lip. His heavy chair scraped loudly as he stood. "Get thee over here, wife," he ordered, a banked fire igniting in his eyes.

She melted into his burly arms with a kiss that Finn thought shouldn't be displayed in mixed company. He watched the Laird devour his woman with a physical ache.

What could be contained within a kiss like that? What would it feel like?

"Where's Evelyn?" Roderick queried, casting an expectant glance at the doorway.

"Oh, she's just—"

"I'm here!" Evelyn sing-songed from the hall before she rushed around the corner in a swirl of golden skirts. She tugged reluctant Rhona behind her. "Sorry for the delay, but Rhona was kind enough to quickly alter my dress. I've grown bigger than I thought."

Indeed, soft billows of shimmering fabric flowed from beneath her breasts over the orb of her belly. Finn stood as Roderick hastened from his seat to wrap her in his arms and help her to the table, leaving Rhona standing alone, looking rather dazed.

Finn's heart stopped.

She'd been freshly bathed, her thick hair twisted into some kind of intricate braid around the crown of her head, but enough of it still curled down her back in ringlets that had not yet fully dried. A simple dress of soft green velvet adorned with black and silver ribbons hugged the curves of her body and fell to the floor from her generous hips. The same ribbons laced the bodice up each side, lifting her breasts. Finn's fingers itched to untie her wrapping like a Yuletide gift.

While he'd been staring, rendered speechless by the sight of her beauty, the other ladies had been seated next to their mates.

Rhona's anxious gaze flitted to the empty chair beside his and Finn scrambled to pull it out for her. Settling into it, she thanked him and the sound of her voice flooded his memory with images of what she hid beneath her dress.

Struggling to find composure, Finn took his seat, remembering Connor's sage words about women.

"You look..." He tried to conjure anything in her language or his that could aptly express her magnificence. Not being a man of many words, he failed miserably. She looked like a Goddess, like a forbidden temptation that any man would sell his soul to possess. She was sin and salvation wrapped in pretty ribbons. "You look very fine," he said lamely and scowled at his tankard.

But not before he missed the becoming blush creep above her bodice.

Obviously, he could only be master of his tongue when they were alone. When he had her naked he was a goddamned poet.

But then, last night, he'd had nothing to lose.

"Where's Iain?" he asked.

"I left him asleep." Rhona seemed pleased at his query.

"I see you men have become better acquainted," Evelyn observed with delight. "What have you been talking about?"

Finn thought it over, wondering how to answer. War, bloodshed, the past, the future. The fact that their very lives were in danger. He took a long sip from his tankard, hoping one of the other men would take the initiative.

"It sounded as though they were discussing their mating powers," Lindsay answered.

Finn choked on his stout and it burned into his sinuses before he forced it down.

"Pardon?" Rhona sounded scandalized.

Chuckles passed around the table until Lindsay continued. "No, nothing like that. When a Berserker is mated he is granted a rather magical ability, more powerful than any predilection he'd had before."

"Aye," Evelyn fondly caressed Roderick's forearm. "Roderick has a gift for healing, though he also can touch a person and create a wound. Often times a fatal one."

"Why didn't you touch me when I attacked you?" Finn asked before he could stop himself.

"I canna say," Roderick shrugged a wide shoulder. "Something stopped me."

Their eyes met, gratitude and meaning passing between them until Finn had to look away.

"Connor can understand the intentions of a person, or see the truth through their lies," Lindsay explained. "Other times, he can outright read their minds."

Rhona looked over at the Laird with wide eyes, and then glanced at Finn. "Can you do that, as well?" she asked, her face draining of color.

"Nay," Finn assured her, though he'd give his right eye to know what she was thinking now. "I'm not mated. None of us were allowed to be unless granted permission from the Temple Elders."

"How many of the Berserkers at your temple are mated?" Connor asked.

Finn shook his head. "Only one man in my recollection has ever been granted the privilege, he was an Elder and his Berserker killed the woman he chose. She was not his mate."

Beside him, Rhona gasped and he dared not turn to look at her.

"What sort of powers do they wield at the temple?" Connor prodded.

"Nothing like a touch of death or reading of minds," Finn assured them. "The elders wield curses and dark incantations. The rest of us can sometimes manipulate elements. Ignite and extinguish fires, summon and dispel mists and wind."

"You can do all that?" Rhona queried. "Is that what your power would be if you were... mated?" She breathed the word as though it sounded foreign to her.

"I hardly possess any ability. Maybe a small bit with fire, but I never much had a talent for anything of that sort. My value was always my strength and size. To this day I'm stronger than any Berserker at residence in the temple. Elder or otherwise. 'Tis probably the only reason I'm not dead."

"I believe it," Roderick nodded. "Even unmated, yer blows are mighty." He rubbed his sword arm and continued. "I encountered one of those dark curses when I was a youth. I bested a Berserker in combat once. He called himself Alrik the Blue. He shouted something at me as I was about to deal the killing blow and I lost my breath. Thought I was going to suffocate, but instead, I spent a decade without my ability to speak."

Finn smirked. "I'll admit I was not sorry to hear that Alrik would never return. Though his curse *was* meant to suffocate you to death, he didn't have the power to finish it."

"I didna mind being without my voice so much." Roderick nuzzled his wife. "Turns out I didna need it."

Evelyn leaned into her husband, but turned her attention to Finn. "Before you were sent here, did you know anything about your father?"

Taking a breath deep into his lungs, Finn conjured an image of his homeland, of the temple in which he'd dwelled for over half a century and felt... nothing. "I remember nothing of him," he admitted. "I'm told that my father was banished from the temple. He snatched a woman from the nearby village and kept her as his whore while he attempted many times to gain entry. That woman was my mother."

Connor grunted, his fist tightening on his tankard. "That sounds like something he would have done. I am sorry for your mother."

"And I for yours," Finn offered.

"Then how did you come to live at the temple if he was denied?" Roderick asked, reaching for some bread and tearing a piece for Evelyn. His action spurred those at the table to begin dishing their food, though Finn couldn't bring himself to.

"My mother dropped me at the gate of the temple when I was a small boy. She found a man who would take her but would not raise a bastard. Even a Berserker. The Elders at the temple pitied her and let her abandon me there."

"Did they take pity on you, as well?" Lindsay asked.

"*Nie*." Finn denied in his own language. "I was charged to keep the sled dogs for the first ten years. I was fed what the dogs were and not clothed at all. If I was lucky, the pack would let me sleep with them for warmth."

"One day, Magnus the Eldest and his favorite warrior Jorgen came down to the pit to request the dogs. Jorgen loved to beat me. It riled the dogs, and one of them bit him. When we saw the blood, Jorgen and I both went berserk. I was the only thing left alive in the pit when I came out of it. More beast than boy."

All movement ceased as they stared at him. Rhona's hand slipped into his beneath the table, and that one gesture nearly undid him.

"Magnus took me to the weapons trainer after that. I was clothed and taught to fight. He's used me to kill many men since that day. But I've always had to eat with the dogs."

"Why?" Rhona whispered.

"Because I had no ancestor to speak for me or offer me his table. No color to call my own."

"Color? I don't understand."

Finn turned to Rhona, noting that the green of the dress brought out that shade in her eyes. Funny, he'd thought them mostly blue the night before. "Eight Berserker lines are represented within the temple and they each declare a color of the sacred northern lights as their banner. Alrik was a Thorsen who claim the banner of blue. He was dubbed Alrik the Blue because he was the Elder of his line."

"Oh," she squeezed his hand. "I see."

Connor rubbed the dark shadow stubble on his chin. "And our Gael line was dubbed black because?"

"Black isn't a color, it's the absence of one. Therefore it is reserved to shame a lineage such as ours."

Roderick snorted. "Aye, but black is the shade of the night sky, and that is constant."

"It's also the shade of my wrath as I wipe out every Berserker that threatens my family." Connor spat on the stone floor, summoning a dark promise. "Any man foolhardy enough to storm my gates won't live long enough to see the MacLauchlans end his line and burn his banner."

Roderick added his vow to the stone and looked to Finn. "Yer Fionngall MacLauchlan now. Will ye take arms with us against those who would threaten our line?"

An emotion so complex and exhilarating swelled inside of Finn, he thought his chest would burst trying to contain it. He gripped Rhona's hand, as it was the only thing that kept him anchored to his body.

"Aye," he pledged. "I've no loyalty to them. Not anymore"

"I should say not." For the first time since he'd met her, Rhona's voice held a note of anger, a mirror of rage that he held in his own heart. "They deserve to die for their treatment of you, every last one of them."

Finn found her gaze and held it. Something burned between them that he couldn't define and it made him want to take her into his arms and lay claim to her mouth in the same way Connor and Roderick had their own mates. He was seconds away from doing it, in front of everyone.

"Enough talk of war and vengeance," Lindsay said gently. "On this, the darkest day of the year, we need to focus on the light returning. And give thanks for those we have in our lives that help us through the darkness."

"Well said, my love." Connor gave his wife a tender smile.

"Also, the food is getting cold." Evelyn lifted a platter and handed it to Finn, who took it and filled Rhona's plate, then his own.

As the family feasted together, Finn listened to the dialogue surrounding him, enjoying the novelty of eating at such a fine table for the first time in his long life. He didn't contribute much, if anything, to the conversation, though even Rhona added her husky laughter and a quip now and again.

Strains of cheery music from a pipe, fiddle, and drums drifted from the great hall. It danced with the crackle of the Solstice fire and harmonized his brothers' deep brogues with the lilting cadence of the women's voices.

Tall candles illuminated the love and affection glowing on the faces before him. He looked at the dress plaids the men had donned for the occasion then down at his own northern garb.

A plan formulated in his mind. He wasn't going to let either of these women live without their mates on his account. He wouldn't let the warriors of Freya wade into Strathlachan and leave nothing behind them but food for the buzzards. But if he was going to fight on the morrow, he'd do it wearing the MacLauchlan colors.

For they now belonged to him.

Chapter Twelve

Rhona laid Iain on her bed. He was drowsy and good-natured after feeding and a clean change, but fought the pull of sleep with the valiant heart of a warrior. She patted his belly and looked about her cozy chamber as he wriggled in his bindings and grabbed at her hand.

The casements, locked tight against the howling storm, were draped in wine-red, umber, and gold that matched the drapes on the largest framed bed she'd ever imagined. She ran her bare toes over the heavy furs that covered the rushes.

Lord, the MacLachlans walked on finer furs than she slept beneath, though in spite of their wealth she found them to be humble and generous.

It would be difficult to return to her stable after sleeping on such a lovely bed. Though it seemed that she'd be staying until after the danger had passed.

The thought of the cruel monsters with whom Finn had sheltered descending on their village terrified Rhona. It was a danger she'd never known existed. Wasn't there enough in this world to be frightened of? Was there no happiness for people like them? No peace?

The well-oiled hinges made no noise as the chamber door opened behind her, but Rhona knew Finn was there. She could sense his presence.

His need.

Her breath hitched as the door latched quietly closed.

"How is he?" Finn's breath teased her hair, but though he was so close, he didn't touch her.

"He's contented."

From behind her, he reached his long, muscled arm and

placed his hand over hers on Iain's stomach. This brought his hard body flush against her back.

Rhona held absolutely still, as though movement might frighten him away. His hand was so large, engulfing hers and nearly covering Iain's entire torso. The warmth radiating from it traveled up her arm and spilled into her chest.

Iain's large blue eyes locked behind her where Finn stood, his chubby face splitting into a toothless grin.

"Would that this was my son," Finn murmured in a low voice.

Tears stung Rhona's eyes and she had to blink them away.

"Back at the temple, I used to watch other Berserkers train their progeny. I always wanted to know what it was like, to have that kind of pride. To pass my knowledge on to another."

Rhona swallowed her heart as it tried to creep into her throat. "When you lived at the temple, was there ever a woman that you wanted to be... mated to? Someone you loved?"

"Every Berserker dreams of becoming mated. 'Tis the ultimate need." His low voice conveyed a yearning borne of many years. "But the only women I ever... met were prostitutes from Kirk Eden."

"Prostitutes." Her hand curled into a fist beneath his. "Like me."

"*Nay.*" He caught her wrist. "It's not like that with you. Never think that."

"But you didn't kiss me." She hated the bitterness in her voice. Couldn't she just be grateful for the time they'd shared? Why did she yearn for more of him? Why did she want to demand *all* of him? "You *wouldn't* kiss me. Is that because you had to pay?"

Finn cursed roughly and seized her shoulders, wrenching her around to face him. His chest heaved and his fingers bit into the flesh of her arms, but she barely felt it. The look on his provocative face was untamed and indescribable. Equal parts fear, resolution, and longing. His eyes burned with an emotion Rhona dared not name.

Without preamble, he crushed his lips to hers.

Hard, demanding, and ruthless, Finn's kiss was different than anything Rhona could have imagined or ever experienced. He instantly opened his mouth, forcing her lips to part.

His groan was one of a parched man falling into an oasis. His tongue was hot, wet silk inside her mouth, spearing and retreating in a rhythm that flooded Rhona's loins with passion.

She cherished the feel of his hard, unyielding body pressed against hers, his lethal hands cupping her face. Sensing a wild desperation in his kiss, she responded and submitted to him all at once, allowing him to plunder her mouth in any way he desired. He explored every dark, moist recess, nipped at the corners of her lips, and then plunged inside again.

An aching urgency rose within her and Rhona reached beneath his shirt, her fingers brushing the hard, roped flesh of his stomach.

To her surprise, Finn broke the kiss.

"'Tis done." He sounded rather dazed. "I am bound." Gazing down at her, a most peculiar look in his eyes, he tucked a ringlet back from her face. Then he firmly set her away from him, stooped and lifted Iain in his arms, turned, and carried the babe from the chamber, shutting the door soundly behind him.

Confused, Rhona sank to the bed on trembling legs, pressing her fingers to her swollen lips. They still tingled and pulsed from the strength of his kiss. Where had he gone? Did she displease him somehow? A terrifying thought jolted her. What if he'd merely come to say goodbye?

She wasn't sure how long she sat there, but when the door opened she jumped to her feet, surprised when Connor strode into her room.

"Laird?" she blinked.

His teeth glowed bright against the bronzed skin of his face as he flashed a devilish grin. "'Tis a family trait to clinch these things quickly," he winked.

Rhona was about to ask his meaning when Roderick entered carrying the thickest chains she'd ever seen. She could barely contain her shock.

Finn ducked in behind them, securing thick shackles around his wrists.

When he'd declared himself bound, she'd assumed he meant figuratively.

He'd abandoned his skins and furs for the green and blue of the MacLauchlan tartan.

And nothing else.

In fact, though a snowstorm surged outside the castle, each of the MacLauchlan brothers dressed likewise. No shirt or boots, merely a plaid wrapped about their muscular hides and secured over one shoulder. Rhona suppressed the urge to fan herself as a sheen of sweat bloomed beneath a dress that had become too tight. With all three in one small bedroom, she was surprised there was any room left for her as their pure masculinity consumed so much space.

"I suppose we could use that fixture there, it's bolted to the crossbeam and should create support if I slip." Roderick tossed a length of chain through a looped fixture as thick as her wrists. Finn gave him his back, locking both wrists behind him, causing his shoulders to bunch and his chest to bulge.

His eyes found hers while Roderick secured the chains to his shackles. A feral excitement burned within their depths, but they were also resolute.

"Don't let me harm her," he looked to Connor. "Even if you have to put me down."

"Aye," Connor nodded and drew a sharp, frightening dirk.

"I'm sorry, what exactly is going on?" Rhona eyed the knife with apprehension.

"Now that he's kissed ye, he has to introduce ye to his Berserker," Roderick explained.

"Doona worry," Connor smiled again, which seemed a little more dangerous now that he brandished a knife as long as her forearm. "This has to be done. We have to see if his Berserker wants ye, as well."

Rhona swallowed and took a step back. "What if he doesn't?"

"That's what we're here for, and the chains, of course." Roderick lashed them in a fashion that was blocked from her view by Finn's immense body and pulled tight.

Finn winced. And then nodded as though satisfied.

"And the both of us will be here to subdue him, so yer safe either way. It's up to ye to accept or reject him after that."

Rhona looked to Finn. Even with his hands bound behind him, he still looked formidable. Lethal. All but for the boyish vulnerability glimmering in his gaze.

"Of course I accept him," she blurted.

The men paused and three pairs of identical green eyes gaped at her.

"Of course I accept you." She went to Finn and pressed a tender kiss to his lips. "Your Goddess answered my prayers when she sent you to my door. If you'll have me, I am yours."

Finn pressed his forehead against hers. "No matter what happens here, you are mine and Iain is mine," he vowed. "We'll make it work."

"All right."

His lips took hers again in a searing kiss. She was his. He belonged to her. No matter what sort of creature lurked dangerously within him. They were bound together by need and, in time, by hope and love. Rhona's heart rejoiced.

"Neither of us procured our acceptance so easily." Connor muttered. "Ye'd better keep this lass, she's mighty rare."

Roderick chuckled and then grappled Finn into a secure hold from behind, looping his arm about Finn's thick neck. "Do it," he ordered.

"Tell me what I am to do," Rhona said.

Connor advanced on her with the knife. "He needs to see fresh blood. It is better if it's yer blood."

"Fresh blood?" Rhona hid her arms behind her and retreated another step.

"'Tis only fresh *living* blood that stirs the beast. He subsides once a battle is done or the quarry is dead."

The worry tightening Finn's features didn't help to allay her trepidation. "Wait. Won't that awaken your Berserkers? You'll both slaughter me."

Connor shook his head and stopped coming towards her. "Come lass, we wouldn't risk that. We're mated. We have control over the beast. He doesna come out without my say so."

"'Tis an unmated Berserker that is most dangerous to those he loves," Roderick supplied.

Rhona leaned against the bedpost for strength and lifted her gaze to Finn's. The hope she read on his features spurred her into action. Rolling back the fine billows of her sleeve, she lifted her forearm to Connor.

"Do what you must."

Gripping her wrist gently in his palm, Connor placed the

knife against the meat of her forearm.

A warning growl erupted from Finn and Rhona carefully studied his stark, brutal features. He tracked the movement of the blade, a storm already brewing in his eyes.

"A good sign," Roderick murmured.

When Connor applied the slightest pressure and broke the skin, Rhona winced, hoping with everything she had that he hadn't just condemned one or both of them to death.

The cut wasn't deep at all, more of a scratch, really. But when Connor took the knife away, blood welled above the pale skin.

Finn closed his eyes and his body jerked as if captured by an invisible force.

Connor stepped in front of Rhona, his every muscle readied for an attack.

When Finn's eyes opened, an abyss of shadows replaced the familiar green. If the shadows weren't moving in a most disconcerting fashion, Rhona would have thought his eyes had been plucked out.

He surged against Roderick's hold, aiming for Rhona, his already-straining muscles seeming to build on themselves until he was half again as large.

"Holy Christ, he's strong," Roderick's voice hissed from between gritted teeth as he struggled to restrain his brother. "I canna hold—"

A sharp crack sounded as Finn threw back his head and connected with Roderick's jaw. Rhona was shocked that the other Berserker still clung to him after such a blow, but he did, his own muscles bulging with the effort.

Roderick's pupils began to overtake his eyes, the black swirling about as he called his Berserker forward to help.

Connor rushed forward, securing the chains and hastening to wrap them again around Roderick's torso for extra leverage. "She's yer mate," Connor hissed. "Stop yer thrashing and we'll let ye have her."

Finn's teeth bared in an enraged snarl, uncovering sharp, dangerous teeth.

One heartbeat erupted into hundreds as Rhona heard the ominous sound of metal snapping. In three untraceable moves, Connor was sprawled on the floor and Roderick flew backward through the air, crashing against the stone wall next to the fireplace.

Finn honed in on her again, his lips pulling apart in a low growl. His demonic eyes pinned Rhona where she stood before he lunged at her.

There was no escape.

The air whooshed out of Rhona's lungs as Finn snatched her and vaulted the entire expanse of the bed. He landed and pinned her to his impossibly muscled body, roaring at Connor and Roderick who'd already gained their feet.

The stunned looks in both their eyes did nothing to dispel the unease surging through her. She half expected him to tear her limbs from her torso at any moment.

Connor's shoulders slumped in relief. "I'm sorry lass, we couldna have known the extent of his strength."

Roderick cracked his jaw, eyes returning to normal, and stooped to retrieve the broken chains from the floor. "We'll leave ye to it, then." He circled Finn with a wide berth and nudged his brother to the door on the opposite side of the bed from her.

"Wait," Rhona pleaded, eliciting a warning growl from the beast currently imprisoning her. "You're just going to leave me with him like this?"

"The danger is passed." Connor looked ashamed. "If he was going to kill ye, it'd be done. We couldna have stopped it."

"He's yers to do with as ye please," Roderick grinned, then grimaced and rubbed his jaw again.

"But I—"

The door clicked softly behind them, ominous in its finality.

Rhona gasped as she was roughly turned to face Finn. He consumed her with fathomless eyes and Rhona found herself absorbed by them. His impossible strength frightened her. She could feel it in the hands that gripped her shoulders. She could sense it in the muscles that vibrated with some kind of Herculean restraint.

The Berserker wanted her. His nostrils flared with quick, uneven breaths. His powerful body bunched and quivered in the firelight and Rhona could swear that the flames grew brighter. Her eyes lingered on his body. All that unmitigated power. All that primal, bestial masculinity belonged to her. Finn was pledged to her as she was to him.

And the Berserker meant to claim his mate.

The knowledge hit her a breath before the force of his raw passion unleashed with the primitive strength of a Highland tempest. It erupted against her, as a tidal wave against the rocks as he backed her against the wall, tossed her skirts up, and thrust his tartan above his hips.

One arm encircled her and lifted her entire body off the floor, pinning her against him and the wall. It seemed the stone would give before he would. The inevitability of what he was about to do caused a rush of desire so intense that she gasped.

He wedged himself between her legs with a possessive growl, his nostrils flaring and his black eyes churning. His arms reached beneath her knees, imprisoning them wide apart as he gripped her bottom, exposing her intimate flesh to him in a way that left her utterly vulnerable.

He claimed her mouth, his tongue thrusting deep as he drove inside her. The pleasure was excruciating and Rhona lost her haggard cry into his mouth. He gave her no time to adjust, withdrawing and plunging deeply once again. This was not the considerate, patient lover of the night before. This was the beast, and he denied himself nothing.

His need fueled her own and she used the wall to push her body back against him. He pulled his head back, breaking the contact of their mouths. He growled a warning at her and hitched her higher against the wall, pulling her legs impossibly wider and surging against her in long, relentless thrusts.

His face was brutal as he took her, but other things swirled in the miasma of his eyes. Passion, of course, but also awe, wonder, need, and a sort of worshipful desperation that brought tears to Rhona's eyes.

Release found her faster than she could have imagined. With no building ache, no straining to capture it, it claimed her body as swiftly and unexpectedly as he had. Her fingers clutched and scraped at his unyielding shoulders as she lifted her chin and screamed her liberation to the shadows thrown by the flames at the ceiling.

His roar engulfed hers as liquid warmth bathed her womb

in strong jets, and he tensed and trembled against her, his thrust becoming jerks of straining pleasure.

Rhona sagged against the strength of his arms as the pulses lessened and died away. She expected for her sweet Northlander to her return to her, his green eyes sated with pleasure as they'd been last night.

But as she returned to the moment, darkness still claimed the depths of his gaze and she knew the Berserker, so long deprived, wasn't finished with her.

Pulling them both from the wall, he withdrew from her and tossed her to her back on the bed. He dropped the tartan from his hips and rent her dress clean in half with one commanding tug.

Standing above her, he took a moment to take in her nakedness. The possessive gleam in his unnatural eyes thrilled and humbled her and she took a moment to appreciate the cords of muscle and ropes of strength that made up his form.

His cock stood full and gloriously erect from his powerful hips. It glistened with the aftermath of their joining and Rhona knew he meant to take her again.

Right now.

He climbed up her body with the grace of a predator, stopping to kiss the tender flesh of her knee or the thin skin in the crease of her thigh, and the quivering muscles above her navel.

A flash of other men pressing her into a mattress for their pleasure seized Rhona's thoughts and she flinched.

Finn froze, looking up from her body and meeting her eyes through the valley between her breasts. She thought he was growling at first, a low rumble suddenly emitting from somewhere deep within him.

His eyes were warmer somehow, devastatingly needy as they searched hers.

Rhona realized the sound was not a growl, it was something like a purr. A deep ticking vibration that thrummed his satisfaction through his whole massive frame.

His lips parted in a wicked smile, made all the more alarming by the serration of his teeth. But he held still, waiting for her to make up her mind.

Suddenly, the past melted away. The future didn't exist.

This moment belonged to them. To her. And she meant to have it. Anyone before had taken enough from her. They would not dominate this moment she meant to share with her Berserker.

Opening her legs beneath him, she reached for his body, which he stretched over her like some kind of great, primal cat. She wrapped her legs around him as he entered her with a slick, slow thrust. Lowering himself completely, he kissed her again. As though he couldn't get enough. His lips explored the corners of her mouth, her cheeks, her chin, her nose, her eyelids; all the while his hips pleasured her with movements she'd never imagined possible.

She called out his name to the Solstice moon as he thrust her over the edge again and again.

Finn MacLauchlan. Her mate.

Chapter Thirteen

Rhona awoke next to Iain and realized that Finn was gone.

Evelyn had brought the babe to her in the wee hours of the morning, apologizing profusely. But he'd been hungry and inconsolable. Rhona, in turn, had to apologize for the damage done to Evelyn's fine dress.

"'Tis nothing," Evelyn assured her. "A common occurrence in a Berserker keep. What we need is a seamstress here all the time." She left a smile and a warm glow in Rhona's heart. She could be needed here.

Wanted.

Finn had caressed Rhona's skin as she fed Iain, watching the process curiously and asking adorable, ignorant questions about babies and child bearing.

They'd laughed together as she gently teased him, enjoying the quiet winter morning and their warm bed. Then still exhausted from her vigorous night, she'd fallen back to sleep nestled in the love of her new family.

Rhona lay watching Iain slumber for a few precious minutes while her body finished deciding to wake up. He truly was a precious gift.

A few new muscles ached and she smiled, entertaining a powerful urge to lounge in bed and soak up the warmth of last night's memory.

But she wanted to find Finn. To start the first day of the rest of their lives together.

To kiss her mate again.

A soft knock interrupted her happy thoughts. She slipped on the nightdress Evelyn had lent her this morning and padded across the room, expecting a summons to breakfast.

A burly man stood at the other side of the door, dressed in a tunic and the MacLauchlan tartan, his russet hair tied back from a wide, austere face. Rhona recognized wary eyes the color of a dark lager beneath suspicious brows.

Jamie, the gate guard, held firewood under one oafish arm and a bundle beneath another. He scowled at her and motioned with his consignment.

"I'm sent to stoke yer morning fire and give ye garments to wear."

Rhona narrowed her eyes. "Aren't there chambermaids to handle those responsibilities?" She glanced down the dark, empty hall.

Jamie shrugged. "'Tis dangerous times. I'm the one they sent to take care of ye." He looked as happy about the prospect as she was. Which was to say not at all.

"Please be careful, the baby is still asleep." Rhona took a step back to grant him entrance and he stalked to the fireplace, setting the bundle of wood down like it had been a heavy weight.

Finn would have hefted the wood like it was a sliver with which to pick his teeth. As soon as the thought crossed her mind, she felt guilty. It was unfair to compare his strength to that of a Berserker.

She joined him at the fireplace, accepting the rolled white wrapper he offered her and turning her back to him to put it on. It was heavier than anything she'd owned and so warm she could have worn it outside.

As she slid her arms through the sleeves and belted it at the waist with a silk cord, a movement of shadow warned her a moment before darkness bloomed in front of her eyes. The pain exploded behind that, blinding her completely. She was dimly aware of being crudely hefted over Jamie's shoulders before she succumbed to oblivion.

"You must have a spy in the keep," Finn speculated as he strapped his axe to his hips over his tartan. He had to admit, he enjoyed the freedom and ingenuity of the Scots garb, though he'd have to get used to the draft.

The accessibility was an added bonus, he thought with a

secret smile as he remembered the frenzied passion of the night before. He'd left Rhona sleeping like an angel in a pillar of early morning light. The riders had returned at dawn. One Northern longboat had been spotted off the Firth of Clyde.

Now they prepared for war.

"A spy? Impossible," Connor decreed, picking a serrated pole axe from his impressively stocked armory. "Everyone employed here is a MacLauchlan. This is one of the oldest clans in the Highlands. The MacLauchlan line reaches back hundreds of years and my people are fiercely loyal. Besides, I think I'd be able to tell if anyone meant us harm." He tapped on his temple, signifying his gift.

"Maybe." Finn remained unconvinced, but didn't want to anger his brother. "But it was no Berserker who watched the goings on here and reported it to Magnus," he said carefully. "I was told it was someone close to you."

Connor flinched, his hand tightening around his weapon. "It makes sense," he said in a voice made of gravel and suspicion. "I just doona want to believe it."

"You have no idea who it could be?"

"We have many allies and many enemies," Roderick cut in, running an oilcloth over his blade. "But the clans surrounding our lands are friendly. We've even made peace with the new Laird of the MacKays and they've been our bitter enemies for years."

"How did you achieve that?"

A meaningful look passed between the brothers. "We killed his father and brother," Connor said with a smirk.

Finn's brows drew together. He was no Highlander, at least not yet, but slaughtering a man's family didn't exactly seem like a good way to go about making allies. "You'll have to tell me about that sometime."

His sensitive ears pricked to Iain's cries coming closer through the castle's labyrinth of halls. Lord but that boy did have a set of lungs. He was glad for it, though, as he thought Rhona must be bringing the babe to see him off. His heart lifted at the thought.

If he returned from this, they would begin their lives together as man and wife.

As MacLauchlans.

It was Lindsay's dark head that poked around the corner of the armory arch. She clutched Iain to her as though holding a child was rather foreign. "Have any of you seen Rhona?" she queried. "I went by her chambers to collect her and found this one on the bed crying his wee eyes out."

A frigid alarm, hard and icy as the glaciers that guarded the northern fjords, crept between Finn's shoulder blades.

"Did ye try the garderobe?" Roderick suggested.

"Or the kitchens?" Connor shrugged. "I've heard a woman gets mighty hungry when she's eating for two."

"I've hauled this angry darling everywhere. The armory is the last place I checked. I'd hoped she was here with you." She turned to Finn, who felt as though the ground had sucked him into its stony depths and he stood shorter and immobile with a paralyzing terror.

Roderick and Connor looked at him uneasily.

"It doesna seem like her to leave the babe unattended," Roderick murmured.

"Aye," Lindsay agreed. "Evelyn said that a half hour past she sent a maid up with wood for a fire, but Jamie insisted on carrying the wood for the girl. We should ask him if she was in the room then."

Jamie. Finn remembered the burly Highlanders' contemptuous treatment of Rhona. The dagger he'd held to her throat.

His gaze collided with Connor's.

"Nay," the Laird insisted. "Not Jamie. He's been with us for decades. I would have known."

"But have you been looking or listening for espionage?" Finn demanded.

The Laird clenched his jaw. "Nay. Things have been quiet here, and I have to be intending to use my ability for it to work."

Finn leapt forward, rushing around Lindsay, sprinting across the courtyard and eating up the distance to the chamber he'd shared with Rhona. He could hear the echo of his brothers' boots as they followed him through the keep. The door almost swung off its hinges as he burst inside, needlessly calling her name.

No fire crackled in the hearth, but a rough load of wood

rested on the stones, waiting to be used.

A scent permeated the room that shrank the size of Finn's heart by half.

Blood. Rhona's blood.

He tore through the room like a man possessed, looking for signs of a struggle or a stain that would tell him how hurt she was. He came up with nothing.

"Jamie has been in here." Connor's nostrils flared.

Rage crashed through Finn with the speed and power of a war hammer. He bellowed, hoping to release some of it before it consumed him.

His Berserker rattled about inside of him, calling for vengeance, for the kind of death that broke the sheath of one's soul so entirely, no one could recognize the remains.

Wordlessly, Connor and Roderick fell into step behind him as he stalked out the chamber door. He knew where Jamie had taken her.

They were going to war.

"My part is done." Rhona heard Jamie through the haze of pain thrumming through her temples and throbbing in her ears. It sounded like the ebb and flow of the ocean, but she couldn't be sure through the rough bandage surrounding her head. "Now ye'll rid our clan of the Berserker usurpers and instate me as Laird, like ye promised."

The sound of a boreal chuckle shivered up her spine and Rhona squeezed her eyes shut.

"Your first mistake was thinking we'd leave any of the clan that sheltered the Berserkers alive for you to rule. Who knows how many bastards are spread amongst you fertile Highlanders who breed like rats?"

A spear of panic bolted through her. If she'd thought Finn's voice was cold, she now understood it to be a summer beam of sunlight compared to the absolute chill in the Nordic accent of the man threatening Jamie.

She didn't want to hear what Jamie's second mistake was.

Apart from the pain in her head, Rhona's shoulders ached. Her arms, bound at the wrists, stretched behind her around a wide wooden pillar. While she'd been unconscious, she'd leaned into her bonds, putting undue pressure on her arms. They trembled now, whether from terror or weakness she couldn't be sure.

"We have no quarrel with yer kind," Jamie protested frantically. "You promised to return the clan back to a true MacLachlan, not some Nordic line that weaved in with a weak-willed chieftain's daughter."

"Your second mistake was believing we'd let a traitor like you live." The speaker obviously decided to ignore Jamie's pleas.

"Your clan has been blessed up until now to share the sacred blood of the Berserker, impure as it is. But now the blessing has run its course, and we're here to cleanse the Highlands."

Jamie made a sound of such desperation that Rhona couldn't help but open her eyes and lift her head to look at him.

"This is the kindness we pay you for your service to us. You won't have to watch us slaughter your clan."

The man who held Jamie by the throat with one hand was distinguished by his uncommonly red hair and beard. Streaked with silver, they both grew to his chest in thick strings, hiding his visage but for a pair of vacant eyes the color of sapphires.

When he crushed Jamie's windpipe with a paltry squeeze, Rhona whimpered as her kidnapper collapsed to the floor, dead.

She regretted her sound when the villain moved in a blur of grey robes until he towered over her.

Fear dispelled some of her disorientation and she recognized the briny smell of the coast and the crash of the sea. She was tied to the mast of a boat, surrounded by maybe five and twenty men dressed after the fashion Finn had been when he'd sought her out. Different colored tunics splashed the unnatural silver mist with vibrant hues. The obvious leader's grey robes stood out in contrast.

Rhona tasted the sea on her tongue when her mouth opened to allow deeper terrified breaths. But the floor beneath her didn't sway with the roll of the waves. They must be wedged onto the golden sand, though she couldn't see over the edge of the boat for the thick fog.

She was now a captive of the temple Berserkers, and a dread certainty washed over her. These monsters would show her no kindness. Not even the variety they'd bestowed upon the traitor, Jamie.

"So, Jamie spoke the truth. Fionngall the bastard isn't dead." He bent at the waist, taking a deep inhale. "You reek of him."

"He is my *mate*," Rhona declared, her anger for the man she was bound to overrode her self-preservation. "And he is no longer a bastard, but a MacLauchlan."

Rhona got the impression that she'd stunned every single one of the enormous men surrounding her. They shifted and looked to their leader.

"Lies!" he hissed. "The fact that he fucked you doesn't make him your mate, regardless of what he told you to lure you into his bed."

"He kissed me." Rhona defended. "His Berserker accepted me and now he and his mated brothers are more powerful than all of you." Trying to throw veracity into her threat, Rhona narrowed her eyes at the leader. Magnus his name was? "Even *you*."

"Mated?" A young dark-haired man in skins the color of barley grains before harvest stepped from the faction of silent, fearsome warriors. "You said the Goddess forbade us to mate before the elders did. That only the purest bloodlines would be blessed with mates."

"He lied to you," Rhona accused, hoping beyond all that some discord would buy her time.

"Be silent, whore!" Magnus drew a long, jagged knife and pressed it against her belly. "Do not stir my men with your poisonous tongue."

"Magnus doesn't speak for the Goddess. He never did."

Finn! Rhona's soul leapt with hope as the man who held her heart materialized from the mist like a fabled Fae warrior and stepped down from the rail of the longboat. Roderick and Connor flanked him, weapons in hand, like two gigantic dark demons guarding her avenging angel.

Though execution burned on the features of the Scotsmen, the chill in Finn's eyes rivaled that of Magnus's. Utterly stark and nigh on dead. He stood taller, larger than any man present and his impossibly strong body was revealed by the deep colors of the MacLauchlan tartan.

Rhona tried to meet his eyes, but he barely flicked a glance her direction before scanning his former kin, his dull green gaze landing on Magnus.

"Fucking Celtic women." Magnus's breath hit her face like an icy blast. "The bane of my very existence. What sort of magic do you possess between your legs that continually draws my brethren away from the control of the temple?"

The knifepoint nipped at soft flesh of her belly and Rhona gasped, more frightened at what the sight of her blood would do if the blade broke her skin than of being stabbed.

Magnus sighed and focused his chilling eyes on Finn, the dagger staying right where it was.

"Do you think she'll live through this? No matter which way it goes?" His beard parted in a smile. "Do you think you can reach me before I gut her?"

"Do you think I care?" At Finn's monotonous words, Rhona's head snapped as though he'd physically slapped her. What was he saying?

"She's your *mate*," Magnus sneered.

"She's a local whore who my Berserker happened to want." Finn waved in her direction as though doing so might erase her from the ship. "Mating with her granted me untold power and a foothold among my brothers who have accepted me into their clan. It was worth the risk of her life."

A roaring began to build in Rhona's ears. He had to be bluffing. What about what they'd shared the last few nights, or their bond with Iain? She couldn't have imagined the sincerity of his feelings. The depth of his tenderness.

Could she?

Needles of uncertainty pricked her skin as she searched his implacable granite face for any sign of emotion and found nothing but ice. Then she turned her desperate gaze on his brothers.

They both refused to look at her.

"But you came for her." Magnus's voice rose in time with his apprehension.

"I came to subdue a threat," Finn's hands twitched at his sides beside his weapons that were lashed over the

MacLauchlan tartan. "She has outlived her usefulness to me as I'll retain my powers after her death and be beholden to no one."

Rhona's insides curled upon themselves, shriveling into parched husks of sorrow. Though her mind told her Finn's painful words were disingenuous, a dark part of her doubted not only him, but her own discernment. Perhaps she'd been so desperate and lonely that she'd attributed emotion to him where there'd been none. A tear slipped down her cheek. What if he'd used her completely and cast her aside?

It had happened before.

A swift murmur crept through the infantry as restless men watched the scene with growing agitation. "Are you saying we could have searched for mates all this time?" One of them asked.

"You promised us easy plunder. You did not say the Gaels were mated," another growled.

The murmurs of descent became louder.

"I don't believe you do speak for the Goddess." The first dark-haired Berserker advanced on Magnus. "I'll not risk my hide to a mated Berserker for a charlatan and a liar."

Magnus' eyes caught and held Rhona's and what she read in them stopped her breath and slowed time to an absolute crawl.

"You will," Magnus vowed. "You'll have no choice."

He plunged the blade into her stomach, the bite of pain more intense than any other penetration she'd endured in the past. Rhona could feel it tearing through her insides and knew that there would be no surviving this time.

She didn't even cry out, so complete was her shock. Looking down, she watched with a detached fascination as a wreath of red bloomed at the front of her white robe when the dagger wrenched out.

A cry rose above the roaring in her ears. It was raw and tortured and low, shaking the timbers of the longboat with the depth of its strength.

Magnus's head rolled into her line of vision on the deck beneath her feet. His eyes were no longer blue, but the black of a Berserker as they stared sightlessly up at her.

Someone was yelling her name through a distant and

muted pandemonium.

Rhona looked up to note that she was now the only one left on the boat whose eyes held any color.

Or did they? Everything seemed to dim. Shadows crept into the periphery of her vision and she searched desperately for Finn. He was nowhere to be found in the chaos of fighting, raging Berserkers.

Her bonds were suddenly broken and strong arms caught her before she collapsed atop Magnus's headless body.

"I'm here, lass."

Rhona was disappointed to hear Roderick's strong brogue. She just wanted Finn's cool, deep voice to escort her into the afterlife.

And didn't that make her a fool?

"I'm dying," she informed him.

"I know," his voice sounded grave. "Doona succumb to the darkness. Hold on for me as long as ye can." He sliced through the torso of an approaching attacker as though he swatted at a fly before propping her against the pillar and assessing the damage to her stomach.

Rhona nodded and turned her head toward the bedlam at the stern of the ship. Finn was surrounded by maybe ten Berserkers. His white-gold hair became increasingly saturated with blood as he used his familiar sword and axe as though they were appendages. His fierce black eyes promised death before his weapons delivered upon the vow.

There was a beauty in this, she thought as she found Connor cutting a bloody swath through his own opponents. A particular grace and speed accompanied the awe-inspiring strength they possessed. They wrought destruction like a dance, choreographed in the moment and organic in its execution.

Rhona focused on the fading brilliant crimson of the blood Finn shed with precision and prejudice. An ominous cold seeped into her limbs, counteracting the warmth she could feel from Roderick's healing touch. She knew that when Finn's golden brilliance was overcome by shadow, there'd be no hope left for her.

She would die wanting him, and unwanted by him.

Chapter Fourteen

Finn should have reveled in the death he wrought. For the first time in his life, he channeled the epic amounts of strength and rage surging through him. He was aware. In control. Time was no longer an impediment to his movement. He flowed through it like water through a fisherman's net. Scarcely displaced, fluid, and inescapable to those caught in his wake. He melded with the beast inside him to create a creature of indescribable precision.

And both parts of him howled in agony.

Rhona. His mate. He could smell her blood. And so could every other frenzied Berserker on the longboat. She was still alive, and every instinct overtaking each man screamed to finish her.

He would kill anyone who tried.

Finn could feel the vibration of her vital life's energy dissipating as though a part of himself hemorrhaged onto the pitch floors of the ship. Drawing the enemy away from her precious body, he paid in blood and pain each time her still form drew his focus from the battle.

His axe imbedded in someone's throat.

I called her a whore.

He wrenched his sword from the sternum of one man and hacked at the torso of another.

I denied her in front of everyone.

A sharp bite of pain sliced his shoulder as a blade found purchase. He pivoted and relieved the sword arm from the man's body before likewise taking his head.

Rhona had to know he was trying to save her life by denying her importance to him. But the tear that had escaped her eye imprinted upon his memory with painful clarity.

What if she dies believing I did not want her?

That wasn't going to happen. If her soul left this world, he would break down the gates to Nèamh to find her. And if she wasn't there, he'd storm Valhalla, then Elysium, and finally Tir na nOg. He'd kill every mortal that defied their love. He'd defy any God or Goddess who blocked his path to her.

Just like he cut down these men who should have been his brethren.

If someone broke away from his horde of attackers, Connor blocked the path to Rhona's body and sent the raging assailant to the afterlife. Roderick knelt with her, his hands working healing magic and Finn ached to be beside her.

He barely dodged a hammer that would have shattered every one of his ribs. He kicked the familiar, dark-haired beserker over the side of the ship. Though the man let out a roar of outraged shock, he would likely survive the drop.

A torn part of Finn wept for every Berserker who fell before him.

We should have been more than this.

The Goddess had created them for a purpose. Berserkers roamed the northlands since before time had been recorded. The temple was ancient and sacred and what had Magnus morphed them into? A pack of unstoppable mercenaries with no particular divine objective. His own private army to wield and control as easily as any weapon.

Finn wanted to kill him again.

His hatred of Magnus fueled his fury, and after a few swift strikes of his sword, there was no one left standing to fight.

Flinging his bloodied weapons to the ground, Finn lurched in Rhona's direction, not recognizing the raw sound that filled the air as his own. He dropped to his knees beside her.

She was still. Too still. The shallow breaths she took barely lifted her chest. The red stain on her white robe glowed in Finn's vision, taunting him with a consuming impotence.

"Bring her back!" Finn growled, his Berserker lending a dual note to the demand.

"I'm trying," Roderick said gently. His eyes were grim and full of compassion as they met Finn's. "But there are limits to what I can do."

"No." Finn refused to accept it. "No. No. *No!*" He clutched at her robes, her body, dragging her limp form desperately against him as if the heat of his rage could warm limbs turned icy by the loss of blood.

His vision blurred and swam. His throat stung before closing as if to tell him he would not draw breath if she didn't. Which was acceptable to him. What would be the point?

"I'm sorry," he rasped, his voice harsh with unshed emotion and agonizing pain. "Forgive me, Rhona. I'm so sorry." He chanted his regret like a prayer, rocking her in his arms as she had rocked Iain. Hoping against fate and heaven that her soul remained to hear him.

"I'm sorry," Finn whispered for what had to be the thousandth time in two days. He'd stopped expecting a response from her pale, still form. He sat where he'd been since the battle, at her side. He ate little. Slept even less. Terrified that if he stepped away from her, her soul would disappear before he returned.

He grimaced again as the last words he'd spoken in front of her screamed at him in the silence. They were blasphemies. A desperate attempt to marginalize her importance in the eyes of his enemy.

Roderick had tried again and again to heal her, but she still hadn't awakened. Her wound had closed and the bleeding stopped, but no one knew the extent of irrevocable damage done on the inside.

The entire castle held its collective breath, waiting for Rhona's condition to take any kind of final turn.

Watching the steady rise and fall of her chest, Finn felt a desperate vibration in his own heart, and a ragged sob escaped when he opened his mouth.

He thought of the hellish battle on the longboat. The satisfaction of killing Magnus wiped away by his horror at failing to reach her before the knife had pierced her precious skin. Only a handful of Berserkers had survived the day, having been pitched off the boat in the heat of battle. They'd left when the tide came to claim the ship and were to spread the word that Finn, Connor, and Roderick were coming to the temple once winter passed.

The plan should have pleased Finn, but he hadn't spared it a second thought. What use was a future if Rhona didn't share it with him? A part of him had died the moment he'd seen her lashed to the ship. The rest of him would follow if she didn't recover.

"I won't survive losing you," he admitted. "I can't go back to being the cold-hearted man I was before. Not after I've had a taste of your warmth.

"I understand if you can't forgive me for what I said. But think of Iain." The babe was being looked after by a new mother who was called into the keep from the village. "He needs you. I can't raise him on my own. It'll be disastrous.

"'Tis Yuletide this morning." He stretched onto the bed beside her and stroked her cool cheek. "'Tis a time for family and gifts and miracles. I know that neither of us has had much in the way of any of that." He laced the fingers of a hand through hers. "Until now."

He swallowed, lifting a desperate prayer to any and every deity he'd ever heard of.

"You are my miracle, woman." He pressed a gentle kiss to her lips. "I love you. You own me body, heart, and soul. Even my Berserker. You owned him from the beginning."

A soft knock on the door interrupted his plea, and Evelyn's belly preceded her into the room. She made her slow way to the bedside and looked down at Rhona's pale face with a soft smile.

At the doorway, Roderick and Connor stood in silence, looking to Evelyn as though she held the answers to the mysteries of the heavens.

Lindsay wriggled in between the two brothers and stood in front of them, Iain tucked into her arms.

"I have 'the sight,' you know," Evelyn murmured. "But since I've been expecting, it's been dormant."

Finn didn't care. He wanted to be left alone with his mate. But he dared not disrespect the sweet woman in front of Roderick.

"She can hear you," Evelyn prodded. "This whole time she's been fighting to return to you, to tell you something. And now..."

Finn's heart clenched. "I would give anything to hear her voice again."

"Would you?" A whisper rasped from the bed.

Finn froze, half expecting his mind to have conjured her beloved voice out of sheer force of will.

"Because you still owe me two gold coins."

Her clear, brindled gaze met his when Finn pulled back in shock and she lifted her beautiful mouth in a weak smile.

Evelyn touched Rhona's arm very softy, and her mouth split into a wide, sunny grin. "That's what I came to tell you. I knew this morning that she would be back. That she was going to live. Also, that I'm having twins. A boy and a girl."

A choking sound came from the doorway and Connor reached over to soundly pound Roderick on the back.

Lindsay rushed to Evelyn and wrapped her in a warm and careful one-armed hug before reaching out laying Iain into Rhona's arms. "This is just too much wonderful news for one day," she exclaimed, her voice full of happiness and thick with emotion.

Finn hardly paid notice to any of it. He just stared down into Rhona's open eyes, his breath captured in the moment.

"Say something else," he demanded on a painful exhale. "I want to hear your voice."

"I love you, Fionngall MacLauchlan." And he knew she did because her luminous face shone with it. "And you're right. It would be disaster if you tried to raise poor Iain on your own." She looked down at the small, wispy-haired head with fond love.

"Aye." Finn laughed, not at her words but because of the foreign emotion sweeping through his body.

"You'll never have to," she promised, her soft, elegant hand cupping his cheek. "Because I'll always be at your side."

"We've all known loneliness and fear and desperation," Lindsay gave Evelyn's shoulders a fond squeeze and reached her hand out to Connor and Roderick, who joined them at the bedside. "But now we have our growing family to give us security and hope for a long and prosperous future."

Family.

Finn looked down at Iain and now understood that family didn't necessarily mean blood ties and duty. Its meaning was tied to this moment. Where love and support, hope and kinship flowed between people who pledged their devotion, nay, their very lives to each other. And did so because they *wanted* to.

Joy. Exaltation. Love. Finn was certain now that no word existed for this emotion. But it flowed between them along with the certainty that this would be the first winter holiday of many that they'd have together, with the family that now surrounded them, and the clan they now called their own.

What's next for the highlands?
Read on for a preview of
Released...

Chapter One

If she could muster the courage, she'd burn him alive.

Katriona MacKay floated across one of Dun Keep's bedchamber floors.

She'd wait until he was awake to deliver his portent of death.

For untold months she had haunted the ashes of the washhouse with her sisters, watching their mother's slow and painful recovery. Keeping soft and helpless vigil as the burns blistered, bled, infected, healed, and then turned to painful scars. They'd never left their mother's side, forced to watch helplessly as she miraculously recovered. During those months, their anger and despair had become hotter than the flames in which they'd met their end.

Katriona's lips twisted at the sight of Rory MacKay, youngest of the Chieftain's family. How dare he linger in his father's well-appointed keep, reaping the benefits of MacKay brutality while his clan starved and his crops wilted?

Shirtless beneath the MacKay tartan, *his* flesh glowed a healthy bronze, stretched taut over thick, rangy, well-fed muscle. While her mother's skin was now a shiny mass of webbed scars hanging off weak, hungry muscles and old, brittle bones.

His chamber was warm and dry with thick, new furs on the large bed and sturdy, dark wood furniture like the desk he currently occupied.

Katriona snarled as she approached him. The lazy bastard propped his head against a fist and the back of his chair, full lips slightly parted in deep repose. In his lax hand, a quill bled black ink onto a large ledger volume. The circles beneath his eyes were likely from drink rather than exhaustion. His ledger must be a work of fiction, and padded with unfair taxes of his people.

The physical differences between Rory and his older twin Angus were markedly vast. Rory outweighed Angus by a few stone, at least. Also, Rory's square jaw, bronze hair, and high cheekbones branded him a McCrimmon, like his mother. Whereas Angus, Laird of the MacKay clan and his son, Angus the younger, had long, cruel features, dirty red hair, and bad teeth.

Watching the firelight play across his strong face, Katriona knew that Rory had not been there with his twin the night she and her sisters died. She would have remembered his handsome face. Even so, she'd found his cursed blood with her magic and before this night was through, he'd be begging for his life.

She'd pierce his ears with her cry before she ripped his soul from his body and send it straight to hell.

Justice would be a sweet victory she could take to her mother, and perhaps then, she and her sisters could finally rest.

"My Laird!"

Katriona shrank into the shadows as a gangly teen with knobby legs sprouting from his kilt burst into the room. He waved a missive with a broken seal above his wild brown hair.

Rory leapt from his desk and drew his sword, pointing it at the boy's eye with unerring accuracy.

The lad skidded to a halt mere inches from the lethal point and both men stood for a moment, their chests heaving.

Rory lowered his sword and ran a hand over his face. "Forgive me, Baird, I must have drifted off."

"It's all right. Angus would have cut me for certain." The

boy tapped a finger to a scar stretching from his chin to his ear.

A muscle twitched in Rory's braw neck. "What brings ye?"

"This." Baird shoved the letter to him. "I canna read, but Lorne told me it was important. A messenger arrived with it not five minutes ago. He's waiting in the hall for yer response."

Rory took the paper, his dark brown eyes quickly scanning the missive. "Fucking Lowlanders." He crumpled the paper and tossed into the fire.

"What is it, Laird?" Baird's voice cracked on the question.

Rory glared into the flames, his fist clenching tight on his sword.

Katriona frowned. Twas the second time the boy had called Rory *Laird*. Yet he was merely the youngest son of the current Laird, Angus. Perhaps they bestowed upon him the honorary title while his brother and father were off terrorizing the Highlands?

"Laird Bruce said he wouldna make the journey until spring." Rory slid his sword back to its scabbard. "Tis only Candlemas."

Katriona found herself momentarily distracted by the play of torchlight and shadow across the bared muscles of his back.

"Bruce?" Baird squawked. "He's coming now?"

"According to the missive, he'll be here as soon as tomorrow."

"But isn't that good news? He'll bring yer betrothed, Lady Kathryn with him? Along with her dowry."

Rory's face darkened from exhausted to irate. "Aye. But look around ye lad, we're not ready to host one of the richest men in Scotland."

It didn't matter. Katriona's lips cracked into a wicked smile. After tonight, the Bruce and his poor daughter, Kathryn, would arrive in time to attend his funeral. And, if her sisters had any luck, they could mourn the deaths of all three MacKay nobles.

"I'll get Lorne to rouse the house, Laird, we'll work through the night to ready yer keep. We'll do whatever it takes."

Katriona's stomach twisted at the loyal veneration in the young lad's eyes. Didn't he understand the evil this man and his family wrought upon their clan?

"I thank ye, Baird." Rory's eyes gentled. "And tell yer

brother to give the messenger our Highland hospitality. I'll be down to help in a moment."

"Right away." Baird sprang for the door, but paused with his hand on the knob.

"There's—one other thing," he said with obvious reluctance.

"Aye?" Rory lifted his eyes to the ceiling as though praying for strength.

"Some of the men want to go after the washer woman. Everyone's saying she's a witch. That she killed her own girls in that fire and deserves to burn."

Don't you bloody dare. Katriona thought, her heart pounding as she fought a surge of her deadly magic. She couldn't kill the innocent. She had to wait for the boy to leave.

"Does 'everyone' happen to be Brenda and Ennis?" Rory asked.

Baird looked down. "They said they spied a blue light coming from her ruins. That she was heard talking with demons."

Katriona scoffed. She'd been talking with her murdered daughters. Those who dared any man to attack their home again.

Rory waved an absent hand at the boy. "Tell Lorne and the men to leave the woman be. She's survived a terrible accident and lost her entire family." He slammed the ledger closed, his wide shoulders dropping as though laden with a heavy weight. "'Tis enough to drive anyone a little mad."

"Yes, Laird." Baird dipped his head and quit the room, his footsteps fading down the hall.

A terrible *accident?*

Cold fury wound its way through Katriona's soul, weaving dark bonds of hatred with her magic.

A little *mad?*

Power vibrated in whatever matter that manifested into her miasma of blue and white until she threw the full force of her glow into the room. Behind that, she emitted a keen so shrill and horrid that Rory's hands flew to his ears.

She reveled in the shock and disbelief on his face.

"Stop!" he ordered. "What is the meaning of this?"

Rory gritted his teeth against the eerie, ear-shattering scream. He'd never heard anything of the like. It grated on the skin and soul in equal parts like every offensive sound in the land warred for supremacy. The scraping of metal against stone, the bagpipes played by a deaf man, and the scream of an angry bairn couldn't compete with such a noise.

"Ye've been cursed with a Banshee for yer crimes, Rory MacKay." Fractals of magic shattered her voice into many until it came at him from every corner of the room. "I am the harbinger of your death and the reaper of your soul."

Rory opened his eyes. Blinding blue and white light assaulted his vision but he forced himself to gaze upon it. Whether his eyes adjusted or the light abated, he couldn't tell, but a form appeared in its center. Dark robes whipping about it in a non-existent wind, the image drew closer, congealing into that of a terrifyingly beautiful woman.

A Banshee.

Her red hair tossed about her and blue glowed from enraged eyes. She floated toward him above the rushes. An unhurried specter intent on making his punishment as slow and painful as possible.

Could this be happening? Rory had not thought to be called into account for his crimes until death. On the heels of his incredulity, a feeling of bittersweet relief uncurled inside. Perhaps the cursed sword hanging over the head of his entire clan would vanish with his death.

"Why do you not bleed?" the terrible voices demanded. "My shriek should drive you to your knees and fracture your soul!"

Rory lowered his hands from his ears. He wondered the same thing. According to legend, he should be bleeding from all the orifices in his head before she reached in and ripped his soul from his flesh.

"Perhaps my soul is already broken, my lady," he murmured. "Ye canna wreak damage already wrought."

The glow intensified again as the shrill scream bombarded him. "You would do well to fear me, MacKay! The pain I will inflict is like nothing you've ever imagined and is no less than you deserve!"

The apparition shoved her ghostly face close to his.

Rory felt his eyes go wide. He knew this woman. Knew of her at least. The thick, long copper hair had lost its luster in this form. No sunlight to catch its sheen, only the blast of otherworldly white to overwhelm it. Penetrating, cat-like blue eyes lost any of their femininity, glowing with hard anger and deadly intent. And yet, her delicate face remained unmistakable.

"Katriona?" No. Not *her*.

The power of her magic snapped and arced between them with chilling force.

"*You* don't have the privilege of uttering my name," she screamed. "Not after what has been done."

Rory stood frozen in place, searching his memory for what sins could have called upon this curse. He'd tried, Goddamnit. He'd tried so bloody hard to stop the evil spreading through his clan. Pushed to the brink, he'd done one thing to stain his soul for eternity.

"Is this because of Angus?" he asked.

His heart petrified before her bitter laugh. "Why weren't you there that night, Rory?" Her arctic lips burned his ear as they brushed it. "Didn't you want your turn with Kylah? Didn't you want to hear our screams as the flesh melted from our bones?"

What madness was she spouting? "Nay! I didna want Kylah. I never even *looked* at your sister. It was Angus who loved—" Rory's heart finally began to race, a sick knowledge knotting in his belly. Suddenly he couldn't breathe.

Angus. What did you do?

"*Everyone* wanted Kylah."

Rory tried to track her movements but the very air around her transparent form snaked and twisted in wretched vibrations. Like bones rubbing against one another and flesh tearing. One moment she leaned and whispered darkly in his ear. The next she was behind him. Then on the ceiling, her joints twisted in unnatural angles as though holding to the stones.

"Angus made my mother watch as he took my sister's virginity and then threw her to his men. They'd spent themselves on her and had already lit the washhouse on fire by the time Kamdyn and I returned from the woods or we would have suffered the same fate."

Her every word drove a spike through his chest until through he might die from the pressure, alone.

"Instead, they doused the three of us in scotch and locked us all inside." In the space of a blink her face floated in front of his again, which meant her feet were at least a span off the floor. "They didn't touch my mother with liquor," she snarled. "She burned more slowly. And for every excruciating minute she suffered, you and your family shall endure an eternity."

Rory swallowed, the contents of his stomach crawling up the back of his throat. He wished his brother alive so he could tear him apart with his own hands. He hadn't the stones to do it before.

He would now.

His twin created this creature of vengeance. Banshees arose from a soul so tortured and wronged that the Fae took pity and gave them a chance to reap justice. Rory gazed into the woman's eyes, so alight with hatred, and despaired.

For a glimmering moment, he'd begun to hope for the future. He'd thought that, with enough sacrifice on his part, he could heal the wounds created by his father and brother. He could pull the MacKay clan from the dregs of their massive defeats and mend broken clan alliances.

He'd been a fool to hope. The very word should have been ripped from his vocabulary decades ago.

The weight on his shoulders finally buckled his strong knees and they hit the floor.

"Do it," he rasped. "Take yer vengeance."

The creature cried and a thousand nails rained down upon his exposed skull, but a blast of cold air was all that touched his skin.

"Get up," she snarled.

Rory shook his head, affixing his gaze on the glowing coals of the fire. "I'll not ask yer forgiveness. It isna deserved. I'll burn for the sins of the Lairds before me if it puts ye to rest."

"Get *up!*" she screamed. "You'll not take this moment from me! *I* burned. My sisters burned. My mother burned. But not you, Rory MacKay. You'll beg me for a lot more than forgiveness before I strip the flesh from your bones!"

Rory looked up at her, a determined calm settling over

him. "I've never begged for my life," he informed her. Though he'd had plenty of chances. "I'll not be going to now. Maybe I deserve this. Not only for what my brother did to ye, but also for what I did to him."

Katriona paused. "What did you do to him?" she demanded.

"I had him assassinated." There. He'd said it. His most evil act and darkest secret.

Some of the weight abated.

"No." The fear and pain conveyed in that one word caused him to wince. The wind died down to a breeze. "No, it can't be. Where is your father? Is he not away raiding?" Her voice almost sounded human.

Confused, Rory shook his head. "He was killed in the Battle of Harlaw by the Berserker, Roderick MacLauchlan." She'd died right before then, but if she lingered in this world, how did she not know this?

"Two dead?" she whispered, a frantic light pulsing from her. "But there are *three*. Three of us. Three MacKays. Three deaths to keen before we can rest.

"I'm sorry," Rory murmured, wishing that words existed to express the depth of his regret. "Mine is the only life I can offer ye."

Her scream rent the night as she rushed toward him. Searing cold infused his body as she grasped his shoulders and opened her mouth. He felt a tear. Not in a physical way, but like the fabric of his very essence was being unraveled. The pain paralyzed him in place.

But the relief still lingered inside him, and soon, she would have her revenge.

About the Author

Kerrigan Byrne's stories span the spectrum of romantic fiction from historical, to paranormal, to romantic suspense. She can always promise her reader one thing: memorable and sexy Celtic heroes who are guaranteed to heat your blood before they steal your heart.

Kerrigan lives at the base of the Rocky Mountains with her husband and his three lovely daughters. She's worked in Law Enforcement for the better part of a decade.

*Kerrigan donates a percentage of all book sales to www.womenforwomen.org to help the innocent survivors of global war and oppression.

To find other books by Kerrigan, visit her website at:
www.kerriganbyrne.com